ONE LAST CHANCE

Also by Kat Martin

The Silent Rose

The Dream

The Secret

Hot Rain

Deep Blue

Desert Heat

Midnight Sun

Against the Wild

Against the Sky

Against the Tide

Into the Fury

Into the Whirlwind

Into the Firestorm

Beyond Reason

Beyond Danger

Beyond Control

Pivot

The Last Goodnight

The Last Mile

KAT MARTIN

ONE LAST CHANCE

www.kensingtonbooks.com

This book is a work of fiction. Names, characters, businesses, organizations, places, events, and incidents either are the product of the author's imagination or are used fictitiously. Any resemblance to actual persons, living or dead, events, or locales is entirely coincidental.

To the extent that the image or images on the cover of this book depict a person or persons, such person or persons are merely models, and are not intended to portray any character or characters featured in the book.

KENSINGTON BOOKS are published by

Kensington Publishing Corp.
119 West 40th Street
New York, NY 10018

All Kensington titles, imprints, and distributed lines are available at special quantity discounts for bulk purchases for sales promotion, premiums, fund-raising, educational, or institutional use. Special book excerpts or customized printings can also be created to fit specific needs. For details, write or phone the office of the Kensington Special Sales Manager: Attn. Special Sales Department. Kensington Publishing Corp., 119 West 40th Street, New York, NY 10018. Phone: 1-800-221-2647.

Library of Congress Card Catalogue Number: 2022940955

The K with book logo Reg. U.S. Pat. & TM Off.

ISBN: 978-1-4967-3681-9

First Kensington Hardcover Edition: December 2022

ISBN: 978-1-4967-4074-8 (trade)
ISBN: 978-1-4967-3684-0 (ebook)

10 9 8 7 6 5 4 3 2 1

Printed in the United States of America

ONE LAST CHANCE

CHAPTER ONE

Denver, Colorado

"MAKE YOUR CHOICE, SERGEANT LOGAN. YOU CAN RESIGN FROM the army with an honorable discharge, or you can face a court martial—where, no doubt, you'll be sentenced to years in Leavenworth prison."

Edge stood at attention in front of Colonel Raymond Miles, seated behind his desk at Fort Campbell, Kentucky. The office, with only a few framed certificates on the walls, a handful of photos of the colonel with his men, and not a single picture of his family or friends, was as stark and unforgiving as the man behind the desk.

"What'll it be, soldier? If it weren't for your outstanding record and the silver star you earned, you'd already be under arrest." Miles shoved the papers across the desk and set a ballpoint pen on top of them.

Edge looked down at the papers, his jaw clenched so hard it hurt. Given the circumstances—and not a shred of proof that his allegations against a highly respected army major were true—he had no choice.

"Sign them and get on with your life," the colonel advised. "You won't get another chance."

Edge reached for the pen and scrolled his signature at the bottom of the page. Colonel Miles took the papers and stacked them neatly in front of him.

"A very wise decision. Perhaps you'll be able to redeem yourself in whatever course your future takes from here on out. Dismissed."

Shoulders squared, spine straight, Edge turned and walked out of the office. Everything inside him ached. His time as a Green Beret was over. The life he had dreamed of since childhood, the years of brutal training, the men in his unit he thought of as brothers—all of it crumbled and gone.

He felt devastated clear to his soul. He thought of the man who had destroyed his life, Major Bradley Markham, the traitor who had managed to escape justice.

A muscle flexed in his jaw. *At least for now.*

With a silent curse and a vow of vengeance, Edge Logan closed the door on his past and headed into an uncertain future.

"Hey, Edge, what's up, bro?" Frowning, Trace Elliott stood in front of him. Trace was one of his closest friends, a tall, dark-haired man with eyes a less intense shade of blue than Edge's own. "You look like you're ready to kill someone."

He and Trace both worked at Nighthawk Security, offering mostly personal protection, but they were also licensed PIs.

He straightened in the chair behind his oak roll-top desk. "Sorry. Bad memory." He hadn't realized his mind had been wandering, traveling down a dangerous road into the past.

"Yeah, I've got a few of those myself," Trace said.

The two of them had served together in the 75th Ranger Regiment, Fort Benning, Georgia, then in Afghanistan, before Edge had gone on to become a Green Beret. Though Edge had been raised on a ranch with his two older brothers, ranching was never his calling, not like the army.

Trace had been smart enough to know he wanted something more than a life as a soldier and had resigned after his last tour of duty.

Edge had been forced to quit.

One of these days, he vowed for the umpteenth time, *Major Bradley Markham will get the justice he deserves.*

In the meantime, Markham was insulated and protected by the United States Army, which had no idea the sort of criminal activities the man was involved in.

"It's almost seven," Trace said. "You want to get a beer or something?"

Edge scrubbed a hand over his face, feeling the roughness of his dark, late-afternoon beard. The day had been long, but satisfying, as he had managed to wrap up a fairly straightforward investigation into a guy who was abusing his ex-wife. Stephen Reeves was now sitting in a Denver jail cell.

"A beer sounds good," he said. "The Goat?"

"Yeah." The Fainting Goat was just down the block and around the corner, a pub in an old brick building with exposed beam ceilings and a rooftop patio. With the late September wind blowing up a gale, they wouldn't be sitting outside.

Edge's gaze traveled across the office to where a pretty brunette, another Nighthawk agent, sat at her desk talking on her cell phone. The office was done in masculine autumn tones, with pictures of wildlife on the walls, along with photos of celebrities the company had done business with over the years.

In Edge's book, there wasn't a movie star who could top Skye Delaney's natural beauty. Skye was the sister of Conner Delaney, the man who owned and operated the company. Like Edge and Trace, Skye and Conn were both former military.

She glanced up for a moment, and her sea-green eyes shifted across the room in his direction. Edge felt the contact like a blast of heat to his groin.

So far, he hadn't acted on his attraction to a woman he considered a friend. They'd been working together for a while now, often alongside Trace, most recently providing security for an expedition into Mexico led by Edge's brother, Gage.

Edge inwardly smiled.

Rising from his chair, he walked over to Skye's desk to invite her to join them, just as a friend, of course. At five-foot-five, she was ten inches shorter than his own six-three, with a sexy figure despite her slender, lean-muscled body.

With her smooth, slightly sun-bronzed skin and perfect features, the lady was drop-dead gorgeous. Being former army, she was disciplined and always in control. Her stiff-spined military posture, even her softly curling, mahogany-brown hair, pulled ruthlessly back in a ponytail at the nape of her neck, seemed to send a warning not to get too close.

More and more, it was a challenge Edge wanted to accept.

Unfortunately, since they worked together, it wasn't a good idea to pursue any sort of relationship, and he knew Skye didn't want that either.

As he approached her desk, he didn't mean to eavesdrop, but he couldn't miss the change in Skye's body language, her growing tension as the conversation continued.

"Are you sure this isn't something she'll eventually outgrow?"

Edge couldn't hear the reply, but Skye's shoulders tensed even more.

"I admit that doesn't sound good," she said. "I'll check into it for you, see what I can find out. How long has it been since you've heard from her?"

Skye's fingers tightened around the phone. "That definitely isn't good news. All right, then, I'll stop by in the morning around nine. Try not to worry, okay?" Skye ended the call and set the cell phone back down on her desk.

"Problem?" Edge asked.

"That was my stepmother. Margaret's afraid her daughter, my half-sister, Callie, is in trouble."

Callie was an only child from Skye's father's second marriage, Edge recalled. "What kind of trouble?" he asked.

"Margaret says Callie got interested in the teachings of a church out in Chaffee County. It's called the Children of the Sun and it's some kind of commune. Margaret says it's more a cult than a church, and she's afraid something bad might have happened to Callie. She hasn't heard from her in nearly two months."

"Callie's young, right?"

"Not quite twenty-one. She dropped out of college last year and took a job as a server in a café called the Hummingbird, down in the LoDo district, but she quit that, too. I guess she met this minister in the café, and he convinced her to visit for a few days to check out the compound where he preaches. A few days turned into a few weeks and now nearly two months."

"I think her mom has a right to be worried."

"Maybe. Callie's always been irresponsible. She and her mother don't get along very well, and ever since my dad died, she's been acting out."

"So what's your plan?" Edge asked.

"I want to talk to Margaret, see what information I can get, then I'm driving out to Blancha Springs. The compound is a few miles out of town."

"That's a helluva drive. At least three hours from the city, out in the middle of nowhere. If there's a problem, you might need backup. How about I go with you?"

Skye opened her mouth to say no. Clearly, she didn't want him going along. Edge had a hunch she felt the same attraction he did but was determined to ignore it.

"We're friends, Skye. Be smart. Let me go with you—at least until you know what you're facing."

Skye released a slow breath. "You could be right. If you're sure you have time, I'll meet you here at eight tomorrow morning, and we'll drive over to my stepmother's house. I'll know more after I talk to her."

"I'll be here. In the meantime, you want to go with Trace and me over to the Goat for a beer?"

Skye shook her head. A few strands of dark silky hair had managed to escape and slide tantalizingly across her cheek. Edge wanted to pull off the elastic band and run his fingers through the heavy mass, spread it out around that pretty face. His blood headed south. *Damn.*

"I'm afraid I'll have to pass," Skye said. "I've still got some work to do. Thanks anyway."

"Next time." Edge ignored a sliver of disappointment. Catching up with Trace, he grabbed his black leather jacket off the back of his chair, shrugged it on, and walked out of the office.

Today's late September weather was windy, the temperature cool, but the sky was clear, the high mountain peaks surrounding Denver tipped with the first light flutters of snow. Edge and Trace headed over to the Fainting Goat, which was already packed, and had a burger and a couple of beers; then Edge headed home.

His newly acquired tenth-floor apartment on Acoma Street gave him a view of the city and was only a little over a block from the office. A lady friend had helped him pick out furniture, a comfortable burgundy leather sofa and chairs, dark wood tables, dark red and black Indian-print barstools for the counter in front of the open galley kitchen, and a Pendleton wool blanket and pillows for his king-size bed. He liked that everything he needed was in walking distance.

Since he wasn't much of a TV watcher, he turned in early.

Tomorrow, preferring to drive his own car if they decided to make the trip out to Blancha Springs, he'd toss his go-bag, his M9 Beretta semiauto, and his .38 caliber ankle gun in the back of his tricked-out black Nissan 370z sports car. In the meantime, he could use a little sleep.

Unfortunately, anticipation of tomorrow's meeting with Skye kept him aroused half the night and awake far longer than he would have liked.

He woke up grumpy and hoped his day would improve.

CHAPTER TWO

SKYE PUSHED THROUGH THE DOOR OF NIGHTHAWK SECURITY AT seven o'clock the next morning. Not surprisingly, her brother, Conn, was already there. Conn ran the office with the same efficiency he had demonstrated as a major in the army. A tall, handsome man, he had thick brown hair and a solid, athletic build.

Conn was dedicated to his job, determined to make the company he had inherited from their father a success. Unfortunately, his long hours had recently cost him his fiancée. Her brother would have no trouble replacing Rebecca—Conn had always attracted good-looking women—but his heart was still battered, even if he refused to admit it.

Skye waved at him through his open office door as she crossed the room and sat down in the chair behind her roll-top oak desk. The earth tones of the office interior always felt comfortable to her, with deep brown leather sofas in the waiting area, a conference room, and an employee lounge.

Skye focused on the computer screen on her desk, opened up Google, and typed in "Children of the Sun."

The founder, a man named Daniel Henson, was forty-two years old, born in Cooperstown, New York. No siblings. His father, Reverend Winston Henson, was deceased; his mother, Aida, still lived in Cooperstown.

Skye continued her search, pulling up several photos of Daniel with his father. Both men were attractive, the father an older, silver-haired, distinguished-looking version of his sandy-haired son.

She pulled up a map of the commune location, saw photos of the gated front, then a picture of the church itself, which was more a chapel, with a steeple and arched double front doors. In the distance, a cluster of modest, duplex-style, wood-framed structures surrounded the church and rectory.

Skye dug around a while longer, but there wasn't much information or any photos, aside from Daniel's, of members of the group.

She glanced up as the front door opened and Edge walked into the office. He was tall and black-haired, with the most beautiful blue eyes Skye had ever seen. Her pulse took a leap at the sight of him. She hated the way her body responded, no matter how carefully she worked to tamp down any attraction she might feel. It was not easy to do with a man like Edge.

Former Green Beret, one of the most intelligent and competent men she had ever known, he was unshakably loyal to the people he cared about and fiercely protective. With his height and broad-shouldered, V-shaped warrior's body, Edge Logan was sex personified.

She thought of the security detail they had worked in Mexico. Along with Trace, the three of them had operated seamlessly together to protect Edge's brother, his partner, Abigail Holland, and the members of Gage's expedition.

The mission had been successful—that was for sure—earning Skye a share of the gold bullion that had been brought back to the States.

She couldn't stop a smile.

"You're in a good mood this morning," Edge said, his lips curving as he approached her desk. The muscles across her abdomen tightened. With his high cheekbones and long black lashes any woman would die for, the man was beyond handsome. But his name fit him. Edge was a hard, dark, dangerous man.

Her own smile slowly faded. There was a time she might have considered an affair with a man as attractive as Edge. After the disfiguring injury she had suffered in Afghanistan, there was no way she would even think about it now.

She looked up at him. "I'll be in a better mood if my stepmother tells us she's heard from her daughter." She rose from behind the desk. "My car's parked in back. You still want to go with me?"

He cocked his head toward the door. "My car's in front. Why don't I drive?"

She wasn't surprised. Edge was full alpha male and, as such, a control freak, but she was used to that, having served. She could press the issue, but she liked to pick her battles, and this one wasn't worth fighting. "All right, fine."

He waited for her to walk past him to the door, caught up with her, and pulled it open, held it as she walked outside.

"My stepmother lives in a house out in Aurora." Skye flicked him a glance tinged with challenge. "Maybe I should drive."

Edge grinned and surprised her by handing over the car keys. "Why not? You know where we're going."

Skye found herself grinning back. Edge had a way of making her smile, which she didn't do that often. She'd always wanted to drive his sexy black sports car. Sliding in behind the wheel, she adjusted the seat, cranked the engine, stepped on the gas, and shot away from the curb.

It took nearly thirty minutes to reach her stepmother's simple white-with-blue-trim house on East Warren, but as they zipped through traffic in the sports car, time seemed to fly. All the while, Edge quietly watched her.

He had never asked her out. Aside from including her in a drink with other people, he had never shown any sign he was interested in her. And yet there was no way to miss the heat in those amazing blue eyes. An answering heat settled low in her belly. As always, Skye ignored it.

They finally reached Margaret's house and got out of the car. Edge held his hand out for the keys, and she set them in his palm. "Cool car," she said.

"Glad you enjoyed the drive. 'Course my heart stopped beating at least three times on the way out here."

Her eyebrows went up. "Are you kidding me? I remember the way you drove in Mexico. Talk about heart-stopping."

Unrepentant, Edge grinned. "When in Rome . . . or, in that case, Mexico . . ."

Skye shook her head but couldn't hide an answering smile. The man could be charming when he wanted, which wasn't all that often. Edge was too serious by far. On the other hand, since she'd returned from Afghanistan, so was she.

A big shade tree cooled the front walk as they made their way up the steps to the front porch, where Skye knocked on the door.

Margaret Delaney, a tall, thin woman in her fifties with short blond hair, pulled it open. She had once been beautiful, but the years were catching up with her, forming lines around her mouth and beside her brown eyes. Skye thought the problems with her daughter were aging her even more.

"Thank you for coming." Margaret leaned over and hugged her. "Come on in."

Skye led Edge into a living room with hardwood floors and beige drapes at the windows. An overstuffed sofa and chairs sat in front of a red-brick fireplace with a white mantel. The house was modestly furnished, but extremely neat and clean.

Skye turned to her stepmother. "Margaret, this is Edge Logan. He works with me at Nighthawk."

Edge made a curt nod of his head. "Nice to meet you, Mrs. Delaney."

"It's just Margaret." She smiled at him, her narrow face flushing with color. Young or old, women couldn't resist Edge Logan. "You're also a detective?"

"On occasion. Mostly I work personal protection."

"So you're a bodyguard?"

"Depends on the situation."

"Edge was head of the security team I accompanied to Mexico," Skye said.

Margaret smiled. "Nice to meet you. Skye, would you and Edge like a cup of coffee?"

Skye nodded. "Coffee would be great, thanks."

"Cream and sugar?"

"Just black for both of us," Edge answered as they sat down on the sofa. They were former military. Black coffee was a no-brainer.

Skye didn't really need more caffeine. She'd had plenty that morning. But working as a private detective, she'd learned that letting a person do something useful helped put them at ease.

Margaret had been "the other woman" who had wrecked Skye's parents' marriage. Even after twenty years, she and Margaret weren't close. But aside from her dad, who had basically abandoned Connor and Skye, family was important to the Delaneys.

Margaret returned with three mugs on a tray she set down on the coffee table. Skye and Edge each picked up a mug.

"Why don't you tell us the circumstances that led to Callie's involvement with Reverend Henson," Skye suggested.

Margaret seated herself in the chair and took a sip of coffee. "I'm not really sure. I know Callie met him at the Hummingbird Café, where she was working. He was staying in Denver for some sort of church event. He came in for breakfast every day while he was in town, and apparently Callie was impressed."

Edge walked over and picked up a framed photo sitting on the mantel. "Is this a picture of Callie?"

Margaret nodded. "That was taken right before her high school graduation. She was so excited. Then two years later, her dad was killed, and Callie was devastated. She's never really gotten over it."

"Beautiful girl." Edge's blue gaze went to Skye. "She's blond, but aside from that, she looks a little like you."

Skye absorbed the backhanded compliment. It shouldn't have felt important, but somehow it did.

Her thoughts returned to Callie. After her dad married Margaret, his attention had focused on his new family. Skye and Conner slowly fell off his radar. Their mother eventually remarried and moved them to a new town, which brought Skye and Conn closer, but distanced them from their father even more.

Her dad's death in a car crash two years ago hadn't affected either her or Conn the way it had her younger half-sister.

"After Thomas died," Margaret continued, "Callie went to community college for a while, but her grades went from A's to D's, and eventually she dropped out. She went to work at the café, but after the first six months, I could tell she was getting bored. Then she met this man Henson. Callie quit her job, and now she's living off the grid in some church collective out in the middle of nowhere."

"Did she ever talk about Henson?" Skye asked. "Did she tell you anything about him?"

"She was in awe of him, that's for sure. I looked him up, and he's a very good-looking man. Too old for Callie, of course, but undeniably handsome. I'm afraid . . ."

"Of what?" Edge pressed when Margaret broke off.

"I'm afraid her interest in Reverend Henson is some sort of father fixation. Callie worshipped Thomas. I think she might see Henson as a kind of replacement."

Silence fell. Skye knew the devastating effect of losing a father—a divorce wasn't the same as dying, but it could be nearly as traumatic to a child.

"I assume you've tried to contact her," Edge said.

"Not after her last phone call. Callie mentioned they don't allow disciples to communicate with family. *Disciples.* That's what they're called. No communication, and that includes cell phones. At least not for the first six months. According to Callie, Henson says it interferes with their immersion into the spiritual world."

The words gave Skye a chill. She set her coffee mug down on the table and rose from the sofa. Edge followed.

"We're going to take a drive out to Blancha Springs and talk to Callie," Skye said. "We'll let you know what we find out."

Margaret walked them to the door. "I really appreciate this, dear. Callie's a good girl. Right now, she's just a little confused."

Perhaps more than a little, Skye thought.

She and Edge walked out to the car. Edge slid in behind the wheel, while Skye belted herself into the passenger seat.

"Well, what do you think?" Edge asked, reaching down to start the engine, which instantly purred to life.

"I don't know. Callie's over eighteen. She's an adult. She can do whatever she wishes. On the other hand, I don't like this idea that Henson is keeping her isolated from her family."

"Neither do I." Edge pulled away from the curb and headed for the interstate. "It's a three-hour drive out to Blancha Springs. If we stop for lunch, it'll be afternoon by the time we get there. I've got my go-bag in the trunk."

Skye's glance went to his across the console. "You think we'll need to stay overnight?"

"No idea. But I'd rather stay than have to drive back and forth."

"You're right. Stop at my place, and I'll grab my bag. We can head out from there."

He signaled to change lanes and hit the gas to pass a slow-moving vehicle. "Remember to bring your Glock."

"Seriously? The guy's a preacher."

Edge made no comment, just cast her a sideways glance.

"I get it. Always better to be prepared." It was Edge Logan's motto. She had learned that in Mexico. Until they knew what was going on, those were words to remember.

CHAPTER THREE

HAVING SKIPPED BREAKFAST, EDGE SUGGESTED THEY HIT A DRIVE-through in Denver for a quick snack, then eat a late lunch in Blancha Springs, where they might be able to find out a little about the group who called themselves the Children of the Sun.

Driving southwest out of Denver on US 285, they traveled along a road winding through grassy valleys dotted with ranches and farms and small rural communities. Rolling forested hills rose up along the sides of the valley and became distant peaks.

The sky was a clear cerulean blue, and there was only a light breeze moving over the land. It was drier and flatter as Edge drove closer to Blancha Springs, but there were plenty of pine-covered mountains surrounding the valley floor.

The San Isabel National Forest reached heights over 14,000 feet, and the route was scenic enough to hold Skye's attention, though she managed to keep an eye on his driving—the reason he chose not to go more than a few miles over the speed limit.

Edge smiled to think he still made the hundred-fifty-mile journey in a little over two hours.

"There isn't much here," Skye said, glancing around as they pulled into the tiny town at the intersection of 285 and Highway 50, the road leading up to the Monarch Mountain ski area.

"Salida is less than ten miles away. It's a popular tourist destination. Got restaurants, motels, whatever you can't find in Blancha

Springs." Edge slowed the sports car as he spotted a sign above a small café.

"I'm ready for lunch," he said. "That biscuit-and-egg wasn't much more than a placeholder. How about we stop over there at the Hungry Bear? Maybe someone will know something about Daniel Henson or the Children of the Sun."

"Good idea. Looks like a locals' eatery."

There were a couple of pickups and a big Dodge dually hitched to a horse trailer in the lot. Edge pulled in and parked beside the rig. He climbed out, and so did Skye, their shoes crunching on gravel as they crossed to the café.

A bell rang above the door, announcing their arrival. A sign read PLEASE SEAT YOURSELF, so Edge headed for the long Formica-topped counter that stretched across the room. Pink ruffled valances hung at the windows, and there was a scattering of tables and chairs.

Edge took a seat next to a beefy guy with a thick barrel chest. A stout, gray-haired woman with a ruddy complexion sat on the stool on the other side of Skye. The big guy next to him was wearing mechanic's overalls with the name MAX embroidered on the pocket.

"You look like a local," Edge said. "What's good to eat in here?"

Max wiped his mouth with a paper napkin. "Burgers are good. They got great chocolate milkshakes."

Edge smiled. "Just what I'm in the mood for. Thanks." He ordered a burger and shake, while Skye ordered a Caesar salad with chicken.

When the food arrived, Edge dug in. The burger was better than passable, or maybe he was just hungry. He turned to the guy beside him. "This is great. Thanks for suggesting it."

"Not many places to go around here, 'less you go on over to Salida."

"Actually, we're headed in the other direction. We're looking for a place not far from here, a church of some kind called the Children of the Sun. You ever heard of it?"

"Not many people around so, yeah, I've heard of it. Guy named

Daniel Henson runs it. Doesn't come to town very often. Not him nor any of the folks who live out there."

"So I guess they keep mostly to themselves."

Max nodded. "Seen a few of the women in town buyin' groceries. The young ones are a fine-lookin' bunch. Probably the reason he keeps 'em wearing those long ugly dresses, like they was Amish or something. Hell, maybe they are."

Vaguely unsettled, Edge went back to his burger.

Max consumed his meal and polished off the last of a massive pile of fries. "So what's your business out there?"

"A friend has a daughter who joined the group. She's worried about her. We told her we'd make sure the girl was okay."

Max nodded, dipped the last fry on his plate into a spot of ketchup. "Probably a good idea, considering the way Henson watchdogs everyone who lives there." He popped the fry into his mouth and waved the server over for his check.

"Thanks again for the suggestion," Edge said. "The burger wasn't half bad."

Max nodded. "Good luck with Henson." Rising from the stool, he headed out the door.

Edge glanced over at Skye, who was talking to the older, gray-haired lady beside her. He couldn't hear the conversation, but Skye was definitely frowning.

As soon as she finished her salad, Edge asked for the check and paid the bill. They left the café and set off for the car. A couple of kids were riding their bikes in circles around the gravel lot, spinning wheelies like Edge and his brothers used to do when they were kids out at the ranch.

He'd been raised on the Diamond Bar, a big cattle ranch three hours northwest of Denver, but even as a kid, he'd wanted a different future. By the time their parents were gone, Edge and Gage had both been happy to let Kade run the ranch, a place their oldest brother dearly loved.

As Edge settled in the car, he returned his attention to Skye. "You were talking to the woman next to you. Learn anything useful?"

"It was kind of a strange conversation." Skye clicked her seat belt in place. "Dora—that was her name—said no one knows much about the group. They're a secretive bunch, according to Dora. They only come to town for groceries, and the women never come without the men."

"The guy next to me said basically the same thing, though he didn't mention any men. Seemed more interested in the women, said the young ones were pretty."

"Like Callie," Skye said. "Dora told me she feels sorry for the women who live out there. Says the husbands completely dominate them. According to Henson, they're only following what's written in the Bible, that a man is supposed to be the head of the family, but Dora says from what she's heard, they carry it to the extreme."

"This is getting more and more interesting," Edge said as he drove out of the lot. "I can't wait to meet Daniel Henson."

From what he'd seen on Google Maps, the property was off the highway, several miles out of town down a poorly maintained dirt road. Once they approached the tall wrought-iron gate, Edge could see the roof of a building with a steeple on top just over a rise. He pulled to a stop in front of the gate, which was next to a hip-roofed beige stucco gatehouse.

A big, thick-chested man walked out of the narrow building and came outside the compound through a smaller gate on the side of the main entrance. Edge buzzed down his window as the guard approached.

"Can I help you?" He was in his mid-thirties, with short red hair and a full red beard. Dressed in a khaki shirt, jeans, and high-topped, rough-out leather boots, he wore a sidearm clipped to his belt. Edge was suddenly glad he had brought his own weapons. Not that he traveled far without them.

"We'd like to talk to Callie Delaney," Edge said. "She's one of the women who lives here."

The red-bearded man straightened. "You'll need to speak to Reverend Henson about that, but the reverend ain't here. You'll have to come back tomorrow."

Skye leaned across Edge to speak to the guard through the open window. Strands of her hair brushed his cheek, and the scent of roses drifted over him. His groin tightened.

"We've driven all the way from Denver," Skye said. "Maybe you could ask Callie to come to the gate and we could speak to her here."

"Not my call. Like I said, you need to talk to the reverend." He didn't say more, and Skye ducked back to her side of the car. Edge didn't miss her softly muttered curse.

"Are you sure Henson will be here tomorrow?" he asked.

"He'll be here."

"What time?"

"What's your name?" the gate guard asked.

"I'm Edge Logan, and she's Skye Delaney. Skye is Callie's sister."

"You want to speak to the reverend, you best come out around ten. He'll be getting ready for his daily sermon."

Skye leaned over Edge again and a soft breast brushed his arm. Her nipple instantly hardened, and arousal stirred beneath the fly of his jeans.

"Could you give Callie a message?" Skye asked. "Could you let her know her sister wants to see her?"

"Talk to the reverend," the guard said curtly, then turned and walked back through the gate, which clanked shut behind him.

Edge put the car in reverse, backed up and turned around, drove off down the dirt road toward town.

"Looks like we'll be coming back out here tomorrow," he said. "We better find a place to land for the night."

"We could . . . umm . . . drive back to Denver, then return tomorrow morning."

Thinking of the tight fit of his jeans, it was probably best if they did. "Your call."

Skye's gaze remained straight ahead. "Seems stupid to drive all that way. We might as well get a room." The minute the words were out of her mouth, a flush rose in her cheeks. "I mean two rooms."

Edge flicked her a sideways glance. "One room or two. Like I said—it's your call."

Skye's pretty sea-green eyes widened. Nervously, she toyed with her ponytail, tightening the band that held it in place.

"I brought my laptop," she said, pointedly ignoring his comment. "I can use the time to dig around, see if I can find out anything more about Henson or the group."

Edge tried to convince himself he wasn't disappointed. He had never made an outright advance to Skye, never even hinted that he was interested in her as a woman.

Now that he had, he wondered why he'd waited so long.

"Why don't you take a look at your phone, see if you can find a room—or two—somewhere in the area?"

Skye took out her cell and began tapping away. In minutes, she was scanning the short list of motels in the tiny town. "There's one called the Trails West Inn. Looking at the photos, the rooms are definitely basic, but it has several vacancies."

The red neon vacancy sign was lit when Edge drove up in front. He wasn't surprised. The motel was nothing more than a row of six rooms with a gravel parking lot in front. At least the white stucco building appeared to be newly painted, and the corridor looked clean.

They went into the office together, and Edge rang the bell on the front desk. A few minutes later, the desk clerk arrived, an older man in a white T-shirt, with a big beer belly and iron-gray hair.

"We need a couple of rooms," Edge said, wishing Skye would change her mind and ask him to spend the night. His imagination was already running wild with images of her naked, her sexy smile inviting him to join her in bed.

Inwardly, he sighed. *Not going to happen.*

He almost smiled. *At least not tonight.*

The gray-haired desk clerk handed over two room keys, and Edge handed one of them to Skye. "Why don't we work a while, then drive over to Salida for supper? They've got a lot more restaurants to choose from."

Skye looked up at him. "I've . . . umm . . . got a lot to do. I think I'll just stay here and work on my laptop. If you go out, maybe you can bring something back for me."

"Sure, no problem." Turning away, he walked her down the corridor, waited until she opened the door to her room, then headed for the room next door. It wasn't often a woman he was interested in had no interest in him. It was hard on his ego, that was for sure.

But as he shoved his key into the lock, he noticed that Skye still stood in the corridor watching him. Edge couldn't help hoping that in time he could change her mind.

CHAPTER FOUR

CALLIE LIFTED HER STRAW BONNET AND USED AN ELBOW TO WIPE away the perspiration on her forehead. Long blond hair stuck to the back of her neck. The day wasn't really hot, but she had been working in the garden for hours beneath a cloudless sky and relentless sun.

She took a better grip on the hoe to dig out a particularly determined weed and looked up to see her friend and roommate, Lila Ramirez, shovel in hand, as she walked toward her. Lila started digging in the spot right beside her.

"What is it?" Callie asked.

"Did you hear what happened to Molly?" Lila was Latina and beautiful, with long black hair and a voluptuous figure.

"What happened?"

"She and Harley got into an argument last night. I guess his shift ran late, and when he came in, he had been drinking. Molly didn't know where he got the liquor, but Harley can be really mean when he drinks. Molly said something he didn't like, and Harley started hitting her, beating her with his fists. When she tried to fight him, he pushed her down and he . . ."

Callie straightened. "And he what?"

"He forced her to have sex. After he left this morning, Molly went to see Daniel. Daniel sent Harley away for a few days to think things over."

"That's it? That's all Daniel did? Send Harley on vacation?"

"Daniel probably sent him to work someplace else."

"It's against the rules for a man to beat a woman with his fists. Is Molly okay?"

"I don't know. Florence told me. Molly isn't working today."

"Maybe we should check on her." Callie dropped the hoe and turned toward the gate, but Lila caught her arm.

"You need to stay out of it, Callie. If you interfere, Daniel will find some reason to punish you."

A chill crept over her skin though the day was warm. "He enjoys it," Callie said darkly. "He says it's for your own good, but he looks for reasons to discipline the women he finds attractive."

She looked up at the bell tower of the chapel in the distance, thinking of the rectory next door, where Daniel lived. "How could I not have seen the kind of man he is?"

"You are not the only one." Lila glanced around, worried one of the men would catch them talking. "Go back to work. We can talk later."

Wiping her sweaty palms on her long cotton skirt, Callie picked up the hoe and started hacking at the weeds with renewed fervor, seeing Daniel's handsome face in her mind. *Daniel.* The man she had once believed she loved.

There was a time she would have done anything for him, a time she had ached to see him, to kiss him, feel his hands on her body.

Not anymore.

Now, like most of the women, she did everything she could to stay off Daniel Henson's radar. But Callie had been one of his favorites, and there was always a chance he would send for her again.

She had to get out of this place she had once seen as a refuge, a sanctuary from the everyday problems of life. She refused to wait much longer.

After a quick breakfast at the Hungry Bear, Skye climbed into Edge's black Nissan for the drive out to the Children of the Sun compound.

Determined to see Callie with or without Henson's permission, she felt her adrenaline pumping, her heart beating a little too fast. She didn't realize she was clutching her leather shoulder bag in a death grip until she heard Edge's deep voice.

"Take it easy, okay? We're going to talk to her today—one way or another. We won't leave until we do. All right?"

She relaxed a little. Edge didn't make promises he didn't intend to keep. "All right. But Callie can be stubborn. She might not agree to see us."

"I guess we'll find out." The trip seemed longer today, the dirt road bumpier. Still, Edge managed to navigate the uneven roadbed and arrive ten minutes early.

The same red-haired, bearded, broad-shouldered guard came out from behind the fence to talk to them.

Edge rolled down his window. "We're here to see Callie Delaney—same as yesterday. You going to let us in?"

"I need to see some ID," the guard said.

They pulled out their driver's licenses instead of their PI badge wallets and showed them to the guard.

He read their information. "Denver, huh? You're a long way from home." He handed back the licenses.

"You gonna open the gate?" Edge pressed, irritation in his voice.

"You'll find Reverend Henson in the church. You can see the steeple from here." The guard sauntered back to the gatehouse. A motor groaned as the wrought-iron gate rolled slowly open. Edge drove through and continued down the dirt road toward the church. He parked in front, and they got out of the vehicle.

There were people around, both men and women, walking toward the church, the women in long printed dresses, the men in jeans and colored T-shirts. Skye could see a couple of pickup trucks moving around, hauling bales of hay and fence wire.

They climbed the wide front steps to the arched front doors and went into the chapel. Henson came out from behind the pulpit and strode toward them. In his long white robes, a glittering gold sun on the front, he was an impressive figure, a tall man with sandy brown hair and a handsome face.

Henson stopped directly in front of them. "You must be Mr.

Logan and Ms. Delaney. I'm Reverend Daniel Henson. It's a pleasure to meet you."

Henson offered a handshake both of them reluctantly accepted. After the rumors they'd heard in town and being turned away yesterday, Daniel wasn't one of their favorite people.

The reverend's gaze slipped over Skye's body, and she caught a hint of male interest. Edge must have noticed it, too. His shoulders went straighter, and hard lines appeared beside his mouth.

Henson smiled at Skye. "I understand you're Callie's sister. I appreciate your concern—admire it, even. Callie's lucky to have someone who cares about her enough to drive all the way out here."

"When can I see her?" Skye asked.

"Well, that's the unfortunate thing. We have a strict non-communication policy that applies to any new disciple. It isn't fair to the others to break the rules for Callie. I hope you understand."

"I'm sure you have rules, but Callie's mother is worried about her, and I promised to come down and make sure she's all right. I'm not leaving until I talk to her. Once that happens, we'll be on our way."

Henson sadly shook his head. "I'm sorry. Your sister is of legal age. She made the decision to come here of her own free will. She agreed to accept the conditions. In a few more months, she can call you—or you can call her. Until then, there's nothing I can do. Now I'll have to ask you to leave."

Skye's stomach tightened as her concern for her half-sister escalated. "Can I at least see her? That way I'll know nothing bad has happened to her. I can tell her mother I saw her and she was okay."

Henson looked over Skye's head and motioned to someone behind her. Skye turned to see the big red-haired man from the gate standing in the doorway, his arms crossed over his chest.

"If you're that determined," Henson said, "Dutch will drive you out to the vegetable garden where Callie and some of the other women are working. That is the best I can do."

Skye flicked a glance at Edge. His intense blue eyes looked fierce. She knew him well enough to understand he was holding onto his temper by a thread.

"All right," she said. "I guess that's better than nothing."

"Come with me," Dutch said. Turning, he started striding up the aisle toward the door, and Skye fell in behind him. Edge started after them, but Henson's sharp command stopped him.

"I'm afraid you'll have to wait for her here. Visitors are not allowed in that part of the compound. For Callie's sake, I'm making an exception."

"You're pushing your luck, Reverend."

Skye heard the tightness in Edge's voice and came back down the aisle. She rested a hand on his arm. "You don't need to worry. I won't be gone long. I'll be fine until I get back." A silent communication passed between them. She could handle herself—something Edge knew. She would get a look at another part of the compound. After they left, they would decide the best way to proceed.

Edge gave a single brief nod. "Go."

Skye followed Dutch out to a silver Dodge pickup. He opened the door, and she climbed up in the passenger seat. Dutch climbed in on the driver's side and started the engine. Pulling away from the church, he drove past the cottages that surrounded it.

The pickup rumbled over the uneven ground. "Have you been here long?" Skye asked as the truck jolted and swayed.

"About a year, I guess."

"So you like living out here?"

"I like it fine."

"Are you . . . umm . . . married?"

His glance sliced toward her. "I got a woman. All of us do. That's part of the deal."

Her breath hitched. "The deal? What deal is that?"

"Look, lady, I'm just supposed to drive you out to the vegetable patch." He pulled up in front of a fenced-in area and put the truck in park. "That's it, right there." He pointed toward a large, rectangular plot. Women in long cotton dresses worked the soil, some bent over pulling weeds, others using long-handled hoes to dig up the earth.

"What are they growing?" Skye asked as her gaze searched for Callie.

"Beats me. That's woman's work. I think they planted cabbage and carrots last month, some broccoli, maybe some brussels sprouts."

"Sounds like you're pretty self-sufficient out here."

"That's the idea."

Skye spotted Callie, and her gaze zeroed in. "There she is!" With her long blond hair and trim figure, Callie stood out among the other women. Skye cracked open her door and started to get out, but Dutch's big freckled hand wrapped around the top of her arm, stopping her.

"Stay in the truck." His grip felt like a band of steel, and determination darkened his eyes. "You've seen her. You can see she's just fine. Now sit back down and close the door."

Skye thought about forcing the issue, but everything inside her warned that if she made a scene, Callie would be the one to suffer.

"Of course." She slammed the truck door. "Whatever you say."

Edge was standing next to his car when Dutch drove up in front of the church. Skye climbed out before the pickup had come to a complete stop, walked over, and slid into the passenger seat.

She didn't say a word until they were outside the gate and headed back down the road toward town.

"I saw her," she finally said. "She was working in the garden, just like Henson said. I don't think she saw me. Dutch wouldn't let me get out of the truck."

"Something's not right," Edge said.

"No, it isn't." She turned to look at him. "We need to come back tonight."

Edge nodded. A muscle flexed in his jaw. "My thought exactly."

He flicked her a glance. "It's going to be interesting to see what Henson is hiding out there."

"You think that's it? He's doing something illegal?"

"Maybe. Could be he's just on a power trip—you know, like David Koresh or Jim Jones. Either way, it's not good for your sister."

"The real question is how do we get her out of there?"

"Yeah, and whether she'll come willingly." His electric blue eyes locked on her light green ones. "Doesn't really matter. One way or another, your sister is going home."

CHAPTER FIVE

BACK AT THE MOTEL, EDGE WORKED WITH SKYE ON HER LAPTOP FOR a while, pulling up a tax assessor's map showing the size of the parcel of land, three hundred acres, where the church was located. She sent the map to the office printer for a copy, then pulled up ownership information, which turned out to be a corporation with a Denver address.

As afternoon became evening, Edge returned to his own room to change clothes. Dressing head to foot in black clothes from his go-bag, he grabbed a black bill cap and tugged it on, then headed out of the room. When Skye pulled open her door, he saw that she was dressed in a similar way: in black stretch jeans and a black pullover sweater.

They were both professionals. Neither of them needed to be told what to wear when you were going on a night mission. They would be trespassing on someone's property. They had no idea what they would be facing when they got there. With luck, they could get in and out without being seen, but there were no guarantees.

"You ready?" Edge asked.

Skye nodded. She had pulled her dark hair into a high ponytail, then covered it with a black wool cap. Her Glock 19 rode in a holster clipped to her belt. Her tight-fitting clothes outlined her curves, and arousal slid through him.

Damn. He did not need this right now. Unfortunately, his body disagreed.

They headed out to the car. Edge carried some basic gear in a canvas bag in the small space that passed for a trunk in the Nissan: a backpack, black face paint, a pair of black leather gloves, a pair of Night Owl Nexgen night-vision binoculars, bolt cutters, a set of lock picks, and miscellaneous other items.

He wished he'd tossed in body armor for the two of them. The gate guard was carrying a semiauto. Good chance other men were, too. A drone fitted with a night-vision camera would have been useful.

"Tonight we'll just be collecting information," Edge said. "If we have to go in and physically bring Callie out, we'll need more equipment and a workable plan."

"You think we'll be able to talk to her tonight?"

"Depends on what we find when we get in there."

Edge drove the Nissan down the dirt road, turned right about a half mile from the gate onto a side road that he had spotted on their earlier drive. The road ran parallel to the southern boundary of the property. In a wide spot, he backed the car in for a speedy exit and killed the engine.

The night was mostly dark, with enough clouds to intermittently hide the moon. He'd bought a black car for a reason, and it was paying off tonight. Always better to be prepared.

Skye quietly closed her door and walked around to where Edge stood in front of the trunk. He pulled out the can of face paint and opened it.

"Hold still." Catching her chin, he ran a blackened finger down each of her cheeks and down her nose. Her skin felt soft beneath his touch and smooth as glass. A ripple of heat went through him. He wanted to peel off her dark clothes and admire the rest of her, run his hands all over her sweetly feminine body.

"My turn," Skye said. Taking the can out of his hand, she drew several black lines down his cheeks and across his forehead, then screwed the lid back on and tossed the can back in the canvas bag.

Edge took out the bolt cutters and stuffed them into the backpack, slid the straps of the pack over his shoulders, and quietly closed the trunk. They had checked their weapons and ammo before they'd left the motel. The trick was not having to use them.

Following the side road on foot, they reached the spot they had chosen on the map, made a 45-degree turn, and started across the open country in front of them toward the southern boundary of the compound.

The ground felt solid beneath Edge's feet, but there wasn't much cover, just a field full of dry meadow grass, and a few stubby trees and bushes. The mountains were close, but here in the valley, it was fairly flat.

"This way," Edge said quietly, spotting the shallow ravine he had seen on Google Earth that ran the same direction they were headed. Traversing the bottom, staying out of sight, they reached the point where the ravine came to an end. Above it, a chain-link fence marked the property line.

Edge pulled out the bolt cutters, found a spot in the fence hidden by a leafy bush, and cut a square hole big enough for them to crawl through. In seconds, they were inside, the fence back in place behind the shrub.

Grapevines covered several acres of the property, he saw. He had noticed a sign for a winery along the highway and wondered if Henson supplied the grapes.

They moved silently forward, skirting the vines running parallel to the fence line. Edge spotted a guard standing at the corner of the property where the south boundary intersected with the east and motioned for Skye to drop down out of sight.

Patrolling the east fence, a second guard walked up beside the first, and they began to chat, one of them laughing at something the other said. Both men carried AR-15s and had handguns clipped to their belts.

What the hell is Henson doing out here?

The guards eventually split up, each of them traversing the fence line back the way he had come. Edge motioned to Skye, and staying low, they skirted the vineyards and moved deeper into the compound, finally coming up on a pair of metal toolsheds near the vegetable patch. The sheds provided cover and a chance to get their bearings.

"The cottages aren't far from here," Skye said softly. "I wish I knew which one Callie is in."

"The lights are all off, the curtains closed. The women will all be sleeping. Nothing we can do tonight but recon the area and come back better prepared."

"We need a drone," Skye said.

Edge grinned. "Exactly. Let's take a look around, get as much intel as we can, and head back to the motel. We'll call Trace, have him bring everything we need."

Skye nodded.

Edge made a motion with his hand, telling Skye to go left while he went right, then flashed all ten fingers, indicating a ten-minute timeline in which to survey the area, circle around and meet up back where they'd started.

As he watched Skye slip into the darkness, the muscles tightened across his shoulders. He knew how capable she was—they'd faced some tough conditions in Mexico. Still, he didn't like sending her out by herself with an unknown number of hostiles and so little intel.

He reminded himself to trust her, let her do what she was trained for; he took a deep breath and set off to see what he could learn.

As he moved through the darkness, he spotted two more men, both of them armed. There were two big metal Quonset buildings off to one side and another some distance away. He pulled the night-vision binoculars out of his pack and brought them into focus, saw what appeared to be two men guarding the building farthest away and had to figure they were both armed.

He wasn't ready to risk exposure to find out what was inside the structure. Tonight he was more interested in getting a layout of the compound.

Careful to stay out of sight, he pressed as far ahead as he dared, then began making his way back to the rendezvous point. He had almost reached his destination when a shadowy figure appeared in the darkness.

The outline of a slender shape and long flowing skirt said it was a woman. Carrying a small satchel, she crouched low to the ground and continued making her way toward the fence. Edge moved silently up behind her, easing closer, until he was just inches away. When she rose, he clamped a hand over her mouth and dragged her back against him.

"Take it easy—I'm not going to hurt you." He could feel her trembling, her terror so intense it turned every muscle in her body to stone. "I don't work for Henson," he said, low and soft. "I'm just here to help someone."

A little sound escaped her throat. She was taller than average and reed-thin. When the clouds parted for a moment, he saw that she had lustrous black hair cut in a shoulder-length bob around a heart-shaped face with very nice features and pale blue eyes. There was a bruise on her cheek and one on her chin.

"I have a woman with me," Edge said to reassure her. "She'll be here any minute. You don't have to be afraid."

Some of the stiffness went out of her spine.

"If you promise not to scream, I'll take my hand away."

She nodded, and Edge moved his hand a few inches from her mouth. He noticed her bottom lip was puffy. "What are you doing out here?" he asked softly, easing his hold on her a little. "Are you meeting someone?"

She shook her head.

"Are you trying to escape? If you are, I can help you."

Tears spilled onto her cheeks. "If they catch us, they'll kill us."

Edge's jaw hardened. "They can try."

Just then Skye appeared. "What's going on?"

The woman's knees went weak as she realized he had been telling her the truth.

His hold tightened to keep her upright. "Everything's okay," he said softly, setting her back on her feet. "This is Skye."

"Hello. What's your name?" Skye asked.

"Molly." She fiercely clutched her satchel.

"It's about time for the guards to make their rounds," Edge warned. "As soon as they're gone, we'll leave." He looked at Skye. "Molly's going with us."

Skye took one look at Molly's battered face and immediately understood. She grabbed the woman's hand and gave it a reassuring squeeze. "Just do what Edge tells you and you'll be okay."

Edge pulled his Beretta, and they eased back behind the metal sheds to wait. The guards moved along the fences, meeting at the corner, talking for what seemed hours but was less than five minutes, then started back the way they had come.

"Let's go." Edge motioned for Skye to lead the way. Molly fell in behind her, and Edge followed, weapon in hand. As they made their way silently back toward the hole in the chain-link fence, he wondered how Molly had planned to get out of the compound.

They reached the opening behind the bush, and in minutes, they were on the other side, the fence back in place behind them. Skye dropped down into the ravine, and Molly followed. As Edge fell in behind them, he noticed the uneven rhythm of Skye's footsteps as she made her way over the rough ground toward the car.

He knew she had been wounded in Afghanistan, knew her left leg had been injured badly enough to end her military service and send her home, but he had rarely noticed any physical impairment.

As soon as they got back to the motel, he'd take a look, make sure she was all right.

It didn't take long to reach the car. With no back seat, Skye and Molly both crammed into the passenger seat for the ride back to the motel. Not for the first time, he vowed to buy a second vehicle, one more practical for his job.

"You all right?" he asked Skye as the car bumped over the dirt road. "I noticed you favoring your leg."

"I stepped wrong, is all. No big deal."

"I'll take a look when we get back."

Her head snapped toward him. "I told you, I'm fine."

Edge didn't argue. No use upsetting her. Didn't mean he wasn't going to check her leg as soon as they got back to the motel.

As they were started down the road for the uncomfortable ride into town, Edge focused his attention on the other woman. "Molly, are you hurt or injured in any way?"

Molly shook her head. "I'm . . . I'm all right. Thank you for letting me come with you." She tipped her head back against the seat. "I can't believe I got away."

"How were you planning to get through the fence?" Skye asked.

"I dug a hole under the wire where a shrub would hide what I was doing. I had to be careful not to get caught, so it took me a while. Eventually I had a depression big enough to crawl through." She bit her lip and glanced away.

Skye touched her hand. "It's okay. We're almost back to the motel. We can talk about it there."

After long minutes of riding in the cramped conditions, they arrived at the motel, and all of them went into Skye's room.

Molly took a deep breath and glanced around as if she couldn't quite believe she was free. "I was so afraid they would catch me." She wiped a tear from her cheek. "Once you're in there, you can't get out. But I-I couldn't stand to spend another day with the animal who calls himself my husband."

Edge's glance went to Skye's face. She was thinking of her half-sister, terrified of what might be happening to her.

"Do you know a girl named Callie Delaney?" Edge asked.

"We only use first names, but I know Callie. She seems like a nice girl."

"She's my half-sister," Skye said. "We came here to talk to her, make sure she's okay. Her mother is worried about her. So am I."

"She's only been with the church a few months," Molly said. "Callie still lives with the unmarried women, but that won't last much longer." When she wiped away another tear, Skye plucked a Kleenex out of the box on the dresser and handed it over. Molly smiled her thanks and blew her nose.

"Why not?" Edge asked.

"By now or very soon, Henson will have a man chosen for her. He'll give her a few days to get used to the idea, then he'll marry them in front of the whole congregation. She won't have any choice."

Skye made a sound in her throat, disgust or worry, he wasn't quite sure.

Edge clamped down on a rush of anger. "Callie won't have to worry about marrying one of Henson's goons. We're getting her the hell out of there."

Molly started crying.

CHAPTER SIX

OUTSIDE THE WINDOW, RED NEON LETTERS FLASHED VACANCY BELOW the sign for the Trails West Inn. Skye sat on the side of the bed with Molly. Her leg was aching, but she hadn't done any real damage. She should have been wearing her neoprene stabilizing brace. Most of the time, she didn't need it, but on a mission like this, she usually took precautions. She should have put the damn thing on.

Sitting on the bed, Molly fidgeted nervously. "I-I have to leave. By tomorrow they're . . . they're going to know I'm missing. Harley's gone tonight. He's off doing something for Daniel. He's one of Daniel's most trusted men. With Harley gone, I figured this was my best chance. I thank God you came along when you did."

Edge sat in the chair next to a small, round Formica-topped table, watching Molly. Skye recognized the grim look on his face, the cold fury he had locked away.

"Harley is your husband?" Skye asked.

Molly nodded. "But I didn't choose him, Daniel did." The longer Molly talked, the darker Edge's expression became.

"You're safe with us, Molly," he said. "Tomorrow we'll take you away from here."

Molly's eyes filled. Skye felt a sting of sympathy behind her own eyelids.

"Talk to us, Molly," Skye urged. "Tell us what happened. Start at the beginning."

Molly gripped her hands together in her lap and took a steadying breath. Her face had a little more color now, but her lips occasionally trembled.

"I met Daniel Henson at a church picnic in Denver. Both my parents had recently died when their car hit a patch of ice and slid off the road. I was still in shock, still grieving. I had no brothers or sisters, no family, not many friends. I was always shy, worse after my parents died. Daniel took me to lunch and told me about this place where people like me—people left alone in the world—could help each other. He suggested I go out there with him and meet some of the others in the group, so I did."

"What happened when you got there?" Skye asked.

"It seemed like an interesting place, one that sits in a lovely valley surrounded by mountains. They had some horses and a few head of cattle. They raised goats and pigs and grew their own vegetables. There was even a vineyard."

She looked down at the hands in her lap, then back at Skye. "It was kind of old-fashioned, you know, with all the women in long dresses. Everyone I met that day seemed happy. When Daniel invited me to move into one of the duplex cottages with three other unmarried women, I thought it might be a way for me to get out of my old life and start a new one."

"So the people you talked to were happy?" Edge asked.

"The ones I met at first were all new to the program. They'd only been there a few days, so they had no idea what they were in for."

"What about the others?" Skye asked.

"Some of the women who live there like it. A few even have children. They don't mind taking orders. They like the idea of being taken care of and not having to make any decisions."

"But you weren't that way," Skye guessed.

"No. For people like me, it isn't so good."

"Go on," Edge prodded when Molly fell silent.

"I'd only been there a few days when Daniel took me aside to discuss the rules. That's when I started to worry. There were rules for everything. And there was punishment if you broke the rules."

Edge sat up straighter. "What kind of punishment?"

Molly's cheeks flushed. "Corporal punishment. You know, spare the rod and spoil the child? But it only applied to the women. Either Daniel administered the punishment or the husbands did. They couldn't use their fists, but they had other ways of hurting us. And you couldn't deny a man his husbandly rights. Daniel said that came from the Bible. But I don't think we were ever really married."

"Why not?" Edge asked.

"Because sometimes the men went elsewhere and never came back, and that seemed to be okay."

"How many women live there?" Edge asked.

"Right now, twelve women and fourteen men, plus Daniel. Two of the men don't have wives yet, but eventually they will."

"So once you're inside, you can't leave," Skye said.

Molly nodded. "You saw the guards. If you tried to escape, you were punished or . . ." Molly swallowed and glanced away.

"Or what, Molly?" Edge prodded.

A tear rolled down her cheek. "I had a friend named Sarah. We met those first few days. Sarah was unhappy almost from the start. Then Daniel married her to a guy named Webb Rankin, and things got worse. Sarah tried to make Webb happy, but he expected absolute obedience. Sarah was outspoken, not used to being treated that way. She went to Daniel and told him she wanted to leave, but Daniel reminded her that she had taken a vow. He said she had pledged to obey her husband until death parted them." Molly's lips trembled. She covered her mouth with her hand.

Skye moved closer on the side of the bed and put an arm around her shoulders. "It's okay. You're safe now."

"I just . . . I just want to get away from this terrible place."

"What happened to Sarah?" Edge asked, the words more demand than question.

Molly's pale eyes swung to his face. She took a shaky breath. "I think Daniel meant the words as a warning." Tears welled. "Sarah should have listened. She should have . . ." She whimpered and glanced away.

"It's all right," Edge said more softly. "Take your time."

Molly swallowed. "One night Sarah tried to escape. She had it all planned out. I wanted to go with her, but I was . . . I was afraid. At the last minute, I decided to go after her, make her see reason. I tried to catch up, but I was too late. I saw wh-what they did to her. I hid in the bushes and watched them beat her to death."

Molly pressed her lips together. "My husband, Harley . . . he was one of them. I saw them bury her body behind the toolsheds near the vegetable garden." Molly started sobbing. Skye pulled her into her arms, and Molly cried against her shoulder.

Edge got up and walked out of the motel room.

By the time Skye saw Edge a little before dawn the next morning, his iron control was back in place.

"How's your leg?" were the first words out of his mouth.

"It's fine. I just stepped on it wrong." They sat down on a wooden bench in the corridor outside her room. Molly was inside, still asleep.

"I should have looked at it last night," Edge said. "Let's go to my room, and I'll check, make sure nothing's broken."

The thought of Edge looking at her withered and burn-scarred limb made her stomach draw into a knot. The IED that had exploded beneath her Humvee had rained fire down on top of her, searing her flesh from mid-thigh all the way to her ankle.

"I'm okay, really," she said. "It's only a little sore this morning."

Edge cast her a disbelieving glance. "It'll only take a minute, and I'll feel better knowing you didn't do any real damage."

Skye glanced away, afraid he would see the truth in her eyes. She never let her injury get in the way of her job. Normally, she didn't care what people thought. But this was Edge. Everything was different with him.

She squared her shoulders. "I'd know if something were wrong," she said tartly. "Please, let's just focus on what we need to do."

She didn't know what Edge read in her face, but he backed off and nodded.

"All right, fine." Mercifully, he changed the subject. "One thing we know for sure. Henson has to be stopped. We need to bring the sheriff in on this."

"We can't," Skye said. "After you left, Molly told me the sheriff knows what's going on out there, but he says the women are adults—they can do whatever they want."

"We need to call him, get him over here to talk to her. If Sarah was murdered, Molly can lead the sheriff to the body."

"I think that's going to be a problem."

"Did you ask her if Henson's doing something illegal out there—aside from kidnapping and murder?"

"I asked. She says something is going on, but she doesn't know what."

"Whatever it is, I'm guessing the men are on Henson's payroll and providing them a woman is part of the bargain."

"Good chance. Most of the women seem to be orphans of some kind, either alone in the world or estranged from their families. A couple of them were living in homeless shelters when Daniel found them. The problem is the sheriff may be on the payroll, too."

Edge fell silent. Skye could read the worry in his amazing blue eyes. He always felt responsible for the people around him. He'd do anything in his power to protect them.

Though he was unbelievably handsome, her attraction to him ran deeper than the beauty of his face. She liked the man he was inside. She respected him as a fellow soldier, a Green Beret, one of the country's most elite.

Her gaze met his, and desire slipped through her, a feeling that had been growing since their trip together to Mexico. As they sat next to each other on the wooden bench, Edge's hard thigh pressed against hers, and a sliver of heat curled low in her belly. She tried to shift away, but the bench wasn't long enough.

She forced herself to focus, to continue the conversation where they had left off. "Molly says most of Henson's men carry weapons. She says they're extremely dangerous, especially Harley. He's a big man, I gather, and tough. Former military. All of the men like the control they have over their wives."

"Why don't you go check on her?" Edge suggested. "When you talk to her, get a description of Harley. As soon as she's up and dressed, I'm calling the sheriff. Once he finds out about the murder, he'll have to step up and do his job."

But what if Molly was right and the sheriff was involved? Skye opened the door to her room and heard the shower running. Last night, the woman had been completely exhausted, both mentally and physically drained.

And terrified Henson would come for her. Skye had assured her again and again that they wouldn't let anyone hurt her, but the sooner they left Blancha Springs, the safer Molly would be.

While Skye waited for Molly to finish her shower and get dressed, she pulled out her cell phone and dialed her stepmother's number. Margaret answered on the second ring.

"Skye! Thank God you called. I've been worried sick. Did you talk to Callie?"

"Not yet, Margaret, but I've seen her. We know she's in the compound, and we're going to get her out."

"Maybe she won't want to leave. You know how stubborn Callie can be. What if she refuses to go with you?"

It was possible, but Skye couldn't imagine her headstrong half-sister following Henson's rules. Or obeying a demanding husband.

"I have a feeling getting Callie to leave won't be a problem. We just have to figure out the best way to handle it."

"Are you sure she's all right?"

"Until we talk to her, there's no way to be absolutely certain, but we're setting a plan in motion. Be patient, Margaret. We'll get her out as soon as we can make the arrangements."

Margaret's relieved breath whispered over the phone. "That's very good news. I can't thank you enough, Skye."

The shower went off in the bathroom.

"I need to go. I'll keep you posted." Skye ended the call, and a few minutes later, the bathroom door swung open, and Molly walked out. She was taller than Skye and probably a year or two younger than Skye's newly turned thirty.

Wearing the ankle-length printed blue cotton skirt she'd had on last night with a clean blue knit sweater, Molly had brushed her straight black hair so it curled under above her shoulders. It gleamed like a raven's wing.

"I have to go, Skye," she said. "Breakfast is at seven. When I don't show up, Daniel will send someone to check on me. As soon as he figures out I'm gone, he'll come after me."

Molly went over to the satchel she had been carrying last night and dug around in the bottom. "I only have forty dollars. That's how much I had the day I arrived. It won't go far." She looked up at Skye. "Do you think you could loan me enough money to catch a bus, maybe enough to last a few days?"

Skye lightly squeezed the young woman's arm. "We aren't going to abandon you, Molly. We're going to take you somewhere safe and help you get back on your feet. But you're going to have to talk to the sheriff."

Molly's head jerked up. "No. The sheriff is a friend of Daniel's. I won't do it. I-I can't."

A light knock sounded at the door. "It's me," Edge said.

Skye walked over to let him in. No matter how much time she spent with him, the first sight of his gorgeous face and brilliant blue eyes was always a jolt.

"Sheriff Akins is on the way," he said.

"Oh, my God!" Molly grabbed her satchel and ran for the door.

Edge stepped in front of her. "Take it easy. We're not going to let anyone hurt you. You really need to trust us."

Molly was trembling. "Please . . . this . . . this is my chance. If they find me, they'll make me go back—or worse."

"Talking to the sheriff is your best chance of staying safe," Edge said. "You need to tell him about Sarah and what it's like out there for you and the other women."

Molly shook her head. "You don't understand."

"Then make me understand."

She released a shaky breath. "Henson gives money to the town, he helps local businesses, donates to the Blancha Springs church and the school. The town needs the money. He might even be paying the sheriff."

She looked ready to bolt any second. Her fear was contagious, and Skye found herself on the other side of the argument.

"You don't have to run," she said. "I'll take you somewhere safe." Skye flicked a challenging glance at Edge, whose mouth looked hard, but she was doing this with or without his permission. "Maybe in time, you'll change your mind."

Molly's pale blue eyes filled. "Where can we go? Daniel knows people. I need to be somewhere far away."

"Denver," Edge said, giving in, at least for the moment. "You'll be safe in Denver."

Skye cast him a look of gratitude. "Molly can stay at my place until all this gets sorted and she can get back on her feet."

"Henson won't look for you there," Edge said. "If he does, he'll be damned sorry." A faint smile curved his lips. "Skye will kick his ass."

The words broke the tension, and Molly relaxed. She smiled. "Okay, that sounds good. But what about Callie?"

"I'll work on the problem while Skye drives you to Denver."

"If we get on the road," Skye said, "I can be back this afternoon."

"Better idea. I'll call Trace and ask him to meet you halfway. He can bring the gear we need and take Molly to Denver while you come back here."

"Trace is a close friend," Skye said to Molly. "We work together at a place called Nighthawk Security. We're private investigators. My brother owns the company. You can trust Trace to keep you safe."

Edge made the call, then walked them outside and handed Skye the car keys. "Trace and I are trading cars," Edge said. "My trunk's not big enough to hold the gear we need."

And they'd need room for Callie when they brought her out.

Skye looked at Edge and grinned. "I'll bet Trace jumped at the chance to drive your car."

"Let's just say he wasn't hard to convince."

As soon as Molly was settled in the passenger seat and the car door closed, giving Skye privacy, she turned to Edge.

"You're still thinking about talking to the sheriff, aren't you? You said he was on his way."

"I won't mention Molly or Sarah. Henson already knows our names. He knows we want to see Callie. Talking to the sheriff about what's going on out there is a reasonable thing to do."

It did sound reasonable.

"You think it will do any good?"

"I don't know, but at least it'll give me some idea of what we're up against."

"I wish you'd wait for me to get back."

He gave her a sexy smile, and her stomach contracted. The man's masculinity was lethal.

"Sounds like you're worried about me," Edge teased. "I like the thought of that."

She didn't know what to say. More and more, Edge had been hinting at moving beyond their relationship as friends. Part of her wanted to—desperately. Another part couldn't imagine letting down her guard and taking that kind of risk.

Not only was her disfigured leg enough to send him running, but Edge was a chick magnet. He never stayed with a woman for long. Skye hadn't been with a man since she'd been wounded—except for her disastrous attempt at making love with her ex-fiancé.

"Of course, I'm worried about you," she said mildly. "I'm your backup. If something goes wrong, you might need me."

Edge glanced away. *Surely he wasn't disappointed.* They were friends; of course he mattered to her. He had no idea how much.

"I'll see you back here in about three hours," she said, striding around to the driver's side of the sports car. "Try not to do anything too dangerous while I'm gone."

Edge just smiled. “I’ll do my best.”

Looking in the rearview mirror, she could see him standing outside the motel as she pulled out of the parking lot. A few miles down 285, she passed a white-and-blue sheriff’s SUV driving toward the motel. A little sound of distress came from Molly’s throat, but she made no comment.

Skye just kept driving.

CHAPTER SEVEN

FROM HIS SEAT ON THE BENCH IN THE CORRIDOR OUTSIDE HIS MOTEL room, Edge watched the sheriff's vehicle approaching. The wheels ground to a halt in the gravel parking lot, and the engine went dead.

The man who stepped out of the SUV was younger than Edge had expected, late thirties, maybe forty. Sheriff Matt Akins had very short blond hair and blue eyes. His black uniform was perfectly fitted, his shoes freshly shined.

"You're Logan?" the sheriff asked as he approached.

"Edge Logan. Thanks for coming, Sheriff."

"You called about Daniel Henson's congregation, Children of the Sun. Did you have some kind of problem out there?"

"You might say that." Edge flipped out his badge wallet, displaying his PI license. "My client is a woman whose daughter is living out there. She's concerned for her child's welfare, as any mother would be."

"So what's the problem?"

"Henson won't let her speak to her mother. No phone calls in or out. Her sister came to see her, but she wasn't allowed to talk to her. Her mother hasn't heard from the girl in over two months."

"Henson has a lot of rules. One of them is no communication with the outside for the first six months. The women have to agree to that before they're accepted into the group."

"I realize that. Do you have any idea what's going on out there, Sheriff?"

"Blancha Springs is a long way from nowhere. We get a lot of reclusive individuals out here. The solitude they find is part of what attracts them. As far as I know, all the women are adults. They have the free will to do whatever they want."

"What if they want to leave?" Edge asked.

"Henson's group has been there a couple of years now. New members sign up. Maybe some of the original members have left—I don't know. It's none of my business unless they're involved in something illegal."

"Are they?"

"Do you have evidence of wrongdoing, Mr. Logan? Or are you fishing to see what you can find out? Maybe you just want to justify the money you're getting paid."

Edge ignored the insult. Alienating the sheriff was not a good idea, not when he needed the man's help. "I'm trying to check on the welfare of a young woman not yet of legal drinking age. I was hoping you could help me with that."

"I'm afraid not. As I understand it, all the women are over eighteen. Your client's daughter signed an agreement—that's the way it works out there. I'm sure if she wanted to leave—"

"That's the problem, Sheriff. Once a woman is in there—like it or not—she's forced to stay."

Akins frowned, his pale eyebrows drawing together. "Are you telling me Henson keeps those women out there prisoners?"

"Not all of them. Some of them are perfectly happy with the arrangement. Others don't have a choice."

"But you don't have any proof."

"If you talk to some of them, maybe you'll be able to get some proof." He could see Akins didn't like where this was headed, but he finally bowed to reason.

"All right, fine. I'll go out there and talk to your friend's sister. What's her name?"

Edge knew better than to mention Callie. The consequences could be brutal.

"How about we just go out there and ask around?" Edge suggested. "See what some of them have to say?"

The sheriff looked him over, his straight posture, the square set of his shoulders, the way he was standing, as if he were relaxed but at the same time ready for anything that might happen. Which he was.

"What are you . . . former military?"

"That's right."

"Army?"

"5th Special Forces."

The sheriff said nothing, but a muscle tightened in his cheek. "Henson does a lot for this town. You better know what you're talking about." He went over and opened the passenger door of the SUV. "Get in."

The drive out the highway didn't take long—cars had a way of moving aside when a sheriff's vehicle came up behind them. Soon they were rolling over the dirt road toward the wrought-iron gate at the entrance to the Children of the Sun compound.

The gate guard didn't bother to approach them, just picked up his radio to inform Henson that he was about to have guests, then pressed the button to open the gate.

The sheriff drove through and continued on to the small white church. The attached building, behind and off to one side, was about the same size, with white lace curtains at the windows, clearly the reverend's personal quarters.

The morning's service was just ending, women in long dresses or skirts streaming out, accompanied by a handful of men.

They got out of the car, and the sheriff approached one of the women. "I'm Sheriff Matt Akins. I'd like to ask you a few questions."

The woman's round face went pale. She was in her early thirties, a little overweight, but attractive. "What kind of questions?"

"I'll be frank. This gentleman believes some of you women are being held out here against your will. What's your name?"

"Mary. I'm Mary Demarco."

"If you could get into my patrol car right now, Mary, and I were to drive you away from this place, would you go?"

Mary's eyes darted away. She swallowed. "I have two children. Their father is here." She seemed nervous, but maybe it was just that she was speaking to law enforcement.

"So this is where you wish to live?" the sheriff asked, to clarify.

Mary looked torn. Edge thought if it weren't for her children, she would have climbed into the patrol car.

"My life is here, Sheriff."

Akins nodded. "Thank you for talking to us, Mary."

The woman turned, walked away, and didn't look back.

The sheriff's attention went to Edge. "You feeling any better?"

"I told you some of the women here were happy." Edge tipped his head toward a young woman leaving the church after the others were all gone. "Let's talk to her." She was dark-haired and pretty, but her long hair was mussed, and her cheeks were flushed. She looked as if she'd been crying.

As she fled down the wide front steps, the sheriff crossed over to block her way. "Excuse me, Ms., I'm Sheriff Akins. You look upset. Is something wrong?"

Her head jerked up and her eyes widened. "No . . . no, of course not. I was just . . . the service was very moving today."

"What's your name?"

"Dolores."

"Last name?"

"Delgado." She was black-haired, probably Latina, petite, and pretty.

"There's been some question, Ms. Delgado, as to whether the women who live here are free to leave, if that is their wish. If you decided to leave, what would happen?"

Dolores glanced back at the church. Her spine subtly straightened. "It takes a while to accept the way of life here. There are requirements, things we need to learn. Once we do, everything gets easier."

Edge caught her eye. "That sounds like something the reverend would say. What was going on in there, Dolores? I hear there are punishments if you break the rules. Were you being punished for something?"

Her face reddened. Her spine went even straighter. "I deserved it. I knew it was wrong. I shouldn't have done it. I-I have to go." Lifting her skirts, Dolores hurried away.

Edge turned to the sheriff. "Are you beginning to get the idea that something isn't right out here?"

Akins shook his head. "Everyone has a right to live the way they choose. Unless you have proof these women are being mistreated, there's nothing I can do."

Edge glanced up to see Reverend Henson descending the wide front steps and walking toward them, his long white robes floating around him with every step. A gold cross on a chain around his neck flickered in the sunlight. With his sandy hair and perfectly symmetrical features, he had the subtle good looks that usually appealed to women.

"Sheriff Akins." Henson smiled. "I heard you'd come to pay us a visit. And I see Mr. Logan is with you. I assume this pertains to our sister Callie."

"Mr. Logan wanted to see for himself that the women living here are doing so of their own free will. We spoke to several. Hopefully his concerns have been laid to rest."

The reverend fixed his gaze on Edge. His eyes were a warm golden brown, but a shard of anger burned in their depths. Edge wondered if the sheriff could see it.

"Are your concerns resolved, Mr. Logan?" the reverend asked. "Or do I need to bring half a dozen more women forward to convince you?"

More women who would say whatever Henson wanted them to. From what he'd heard from Dolores Delgado, the threat was understood. "I think I've seen enough."

The sheriff spoke to Henson. "I'm sorry for the inconvenience, Reverend."

Henson's smile looked forced. "I'm sure you are. I'm sorry you felt you had to make the trip out here to see for yourself."

There was a note of disapproval, perhaps even warning in the reverend's words. Akins's frown said he'd noticed.

Henson turned and walked back the way he had come, the sun gleaming on his thick, sandy hair as if the heavens themselves were bestowing their blessing.

Edge didn't buy it for a moment.

Henson had almost reached the top step when he was approached by one of his men, big, broad-shouldered, in a red-check flannel shirt. They conversed for several seconds, and the man shook his head. One of Henson's hands fisted. He said something and spun to continue up the steps.

Edge figured maybe the man had been ordered to search for Molly Lockhart and failed to find her. If so, Henson was bound to be in a temper.

Edge and Sheriff Akins climbed back into the SUV, and Akins drove through the gate toward town.

"I guess the reverend wasn't too pleased to see you," Edge said as the vehicle rolled over the bumpy dirt road.

"I have a job to do, same as he does. I'm sure he understands."

"Or maybe he doesn't. Maybe he'll pull his support the next time you run for office."

Akins frowned as if the thought had never occurred to him. Maybe he wasn't on Henson's payroll after all. If so, perhaps once the sheriff got his head out of his ass and saw what was happening in the compound, he'd be willing to do his job.

So far, Edge hadn't mentioned the murder Molly had witnessed. Until he had some kind of proof, it would only make matters worse. For now, getting Callie Delaney out of the compound and away from Henson was his top priority. He needed more information in order to make that happen.

Edge couldn't wait for Skye to get back with the drone.

CHAPTER EIGHT

"THERE'S SOMETHING I HAVEN'T TOLD YOU."

As the Nissan rolled toward Denver, Skye looked across the center console to the young woman in the passenger seat. Molly Lockhart was her maiden name, she'd revealed. She would no longer answer to Mrs. Harley Purcell.

From Molly's description of the man, Skye didn't blame her. Six-foot-three, barrel-chested, with dark brown hair and a long scraggly, pointed beard, he had a tat of a snake on the back of his hand and a coiled snake on his shoulder.

He's mean and he's tough. Those were Molly's words. At least he'd be easy to recognize.

Skye cast her a sideways glance. "What haven't you told me?"

Molly bit her lip, then took a deep breath. "Before Reverend Henson marries us to the man he has chosen, he . . . umm . . ." Molly made a sound in her throat. "He initiates us into the sisterhood."

Unease slipped through her. "What do you mean *initiates*? What does he do?"

Molly gripped her hands together in her lap, her nervousness clear. "The first week a new disciple is there, Daniel is very solicitous. He has private meetings with the woman. He talks to her about the wonderful life she can have as a sister in the church. He invites her for dinner at his home."

"*Dinner?* That's how he initiates a new member?"

Molly glanced over. "Daniel can be extremely charming. Most of the women come to the church because of him. He flatters them, makes promises to them, and then he . . . he seduces them."

Skye's stomach clenched.

"Daniel explains that joining with him is the only way for them to feel a kinship with the other women, part of a sisterhood. They're all Daniel's wives in the eyes of God. In a few weeks, sometimes a month or a little longer, they'll go to the man who will take Daniel's place as their earthly husband."

"I can't believe you thought this was okay. You were all right with the idea of being Daniel's temporary wife?"

"Yes. No." A shudder passed through her. "I don't know. At the time . . . the way Daniel explained everything . . . it didn't seem wrong."

"It seems like a way for Daniel Henson to provide himself with an endless stream of young, pretty women. Who the hell does he think he is?"

Molly's eyes welled. She jerked a Kleenex out of her satchel and dabbed her eyes. "I hate him."

Skye's gaze swung across the console. "Are you sure you hate him, Molly? Or are you still in love with him?"

Molly started sobbing.

Skye eased the sports car over to the side of the road and turned off the engine. She reached down and took hold of Molly's hand. "Whatever your feelings are for Daniel, none of this is your fault. He took advantage of a vulnerable young woman. That's apparently what he does. He targets women who need help of some kind, then offers it to them. In the end, the only person he's helping is himself."

Molly wiped away the wetness on her cheeks. "Thank you for saying that. In my heart, I know it's true. I feel like such a fool."

"It'll take some time, but eventually, that'll change. You're going to get a fresh start, and once you do, you'll be able to step back and see things more clearly."

Molly glanced away.

Skye started the engine and pulled back onto the road. They had almost reached Jefferson Depot, a meeting spot that was close to the halfway point between Blancha Springs and Denver. There was a burger and ice cream stand called the Hungry Moose Caboose where people could stop and buy food.

Skye pulled into the parking lot to wait for Trace, whose drive, with city traffic and collecting the gear Edge wanted, would take longer. They ordered a burger and a shake and sat at a wire-mesh table outside to eat. The air was chilly, but the sky was azure blue, and the sun was shining, warming them through their clothes.

Trace pulled into the parking lot not long after they'd finished their meals. Skye dumped her trash, Molly did the same, and they walked over to his black GMC Yukon.

Tall, dark-haired, and handsome, Trace climbed out of the SUV and started toward them. He was charming and kind, with a wonderful smile. He was also a very dangerous man when the need arose. Most women felt an instant attraction to Trace. Molly shrank away from him. Even her physical stature seemed to shrink.

Extremely perceptive, Trace noticed Molly's reluctance and didn't move too fast or too close, treating her as he would a frightened child.

"Molly, this is Trace Elliott," Skye said. "He's a very good friend and someone you can trust."

Trace smiled. "It's nice to meet you, Molly."

"You, as well, Trace," she said, but the words didn't sound sincere. Molly didn't trust men—not anymore. And Trace was definitely all man.

"I'll be driving you back to Skye's apartment," he said. "We can stop on the way if there's anything you need."

"The fridge is stocked," Skye said. "At least you'll have plenty to eat." She had given Molly enough cash for some new clothes, shoes, makeup, or whatever feminine products she needed.

"I'll be fine."

Trace handed Skye the keys to the Yukon, and she handed him Edge's car keys. Trace opened the passenger door to the Nissan and waited for Molly to settle inside. She gasped when he leaned across to fasten her seat belt.

"It's okay, sweetheart. I'm harmless." He smiled. "Skye can attest to that."

When it came to women, Trace was anything but harmless. But he was always up front with them and never took advantage, and he would defend a woman with his life if it came to it. Knowing at least a little of Molly's situation, he would be especially gentle with her.

Skye thought of Edge. She had never been interested in Trace as anything more than a friend, but her attraction to Edge grew stronger every day.

Like Trace, Edge had been raised to treat a woman with respect and defend her with everything he had. He was also honest with the women he dated—and there were legions of them.

He wasn't looking for anything permanent. He promised a good time while it lasted, but that was all. Though that kind of relationship had never appealed to Skye before, she had actually begun to give it some thought.

Maybe a quick fling with Edge would end her infatuation and she could get her mind back on work. If it weren't for her hideous leg, she might actually do it.

Her insides tightened as she remembered the terrible night two weeks after she had gotten out of the hospital and returned to Denver. Her fiancé had invited her to supper in his apartment.

Skye had been nervous, afraid of how Brian would react when they made love and he had to deal with her burn-scarred leg. She would never forget the repulsion on her fiancé's handsome face. When he was unable to get an erection, he had simply left the bed, left the room, gone into his study, and closed the door. Skye had dressed and fled the apartment. She had returned his engagement ring the next day.

Brian hadn't objected.

The thought of seeing that same look of repulsion—or, worse yet, pity—on Edge Logan's face was enough to put an end to any thought of having sex with him.

Forcing her attention back to the moment, Skye spoke to Molly through the rolled-down window of the Nissan. "I'll call you, keep you up to date on what's happening. Think about talking to the police. I know you're scared, but there are women in there who need your help."

Molly made no reply.

Trace walked up to Skye. "I'll get Molly settled and come back as soon as you've got the intel and you're ready to go in."

Skye nodded. It would be a snatch-and-grab operation. Both Edge and Trace had done a number of those missions during their time in the army. But they needed more information first.

Trace turned the sports car around, pulled out of the parking lot, and drove back up the road the way he had come. Skye adjusted the seat on the Yukon and started the engine.

She was anxious to talk to Edge, figure a way to get Callie out of the compound. She thought of the woman who had been murdered, thought of Callie, and a shadow of foreboding slipped down her spine.

CHAPTER NINE

DANIEL HENSON PACED THE FLOOR OF HIS STUDY, HIS LONG WHITE robes flaring out at every turn. He wanted to get into a pair of jeans and a long-sleeved Henley, but he had a problem to handle first.

He looked up at the sound of a light rap on the door. "Enter."

The door opened, and Callie Delaney walked into the room. With her smooth complexion, long blond hair, and big blue eyes, she was the perfect complement to his fair good looks. Her slender, feminine curves made his body stir to life beneath his robe.

After their first month together, he had considered installing her as his permanent mate, granting her his name, but she was simply too headstrong, too set in her ways. Today was no exception.

Irritation tightened his features. "Close the door behind you and come over here, Callie."

Callie closed the door. Crossing the room, she stopped in front of him. She was nervous. He could tell by the way she shifted from one foot to the other. *Good.*

"You know why I called you here?"

"I-I'm not sure."

"I think you are. I think you know exactly why you're here. It's my understanding you managed to get hold of Nathan Porter's cell phone. Is that correct?"

Callie wet her pretty pink lips, and beneath his robe, his arousal strengthened. He had wanted her since the first time he had seen her in that greasy café in Denver. Apparently that hadn't changed.

"I . . . borrowed it. I was going to call my mother. I didn't want her to worry. Nathan stopped me before I had time to make the call."

"We have rules, Callie. They're in place for a reason."

Callie clenched her jaw. She said nothing, but he could read the willfulness in her face. And the hint of fear. She knew the consequences. There was no getting around them.

"Go over to the closet and bring me my cane."

Callie didn't move.

"You heard me. You can't think I'm going to allow you to blatantly disobey the rules and not be punished. You should know better than that by now."

He thought of the last time he had called her into his study. She had skipped daily instruction two days in a row. He remembered the feel of the cane in his hand as he applied stroke after stroke. Then he had taken her—two times. His mouth dried, and his body hardened.

"The sooner you obey me, the sooner this will be over. Now fetch me the cane."

Her stubborn little chin went up. "No. I'm not doing it. I'm not going to let you beat me again, Daniel. I'm not a child. I'm a grown woman."

"Then you are mature enough to obey the rules you agreed to when you first arrived."

"Your rules only apply when you want them to."

His hand slammed down on the edge of his desk. "That is quite enough! Get me my cane, and let us be done with this."

The little witch just shook her head. "I won't do it. I'm tired of this place and all your stupid rules. I want to leave. I want you to have one of your evil minions drive me back to Denver."

Fury coursed through every artery and vein in his body. He

forced a calmness into his voice that was far from the way he felt. "You can't believe that is actually going to happen. You realize I can call a couple of my *minions,* as you refer to them, and they will hold you down while I administer the discipline you deserve."

Her pretty face went pale.

"But we've had such an enjoyable time together, I'm not going to do that."

Callie wisely said nothing. "Instead, since it's become clear you will no longer obey my commands, it's time I hand you over to someone who will make certain that you obey his."

He flashed her a cold, ruthless smile. He refused to put up with any woman's disobedience, even Callie's. "On Sunday, you will be married to Klaus Mahler."

Callie sucked in a breath. Mahler was a big German with a tough reputation among the other men. He was young, smart, and utterly ruthless. He wouldn't hesitate to bring Callie in line.

Mahler was German, but Daniel was an equal opportunity employer. The men who worked for him were diverse: Hispanic, Asian, African American. All he required was unquestioning loyalty, a vow of silence, and a willingness to do whatever they were told. For that, he paid more than they could ever think of earning anywhere else.

"Please, Daniel . . ." Callie pleaded. "I just want . . . I just want to go home."

"Day after tomorrow is Sunday," Daniel continued, ignoring the tears in her eyes that only angered him more. "Klaus is in need of a wife, and I believe he will know exactly how to handle one as disobedient as you."

"No . . ." she said, shaking her head and backing away.

"If you don't calm down and behave yourself, Callie, I'm going to call him right now."

Callie trembled but didn't move.

"That's better. There was a time I thought the two of us might have a future together. That time is long past. From now on, you will service another earthly master—God help you. Now get out of my sight—and prepare yourself to accept your new husband on Sunday."

Callie turned and ran out of the room.

CHAPTER TEN

As soon as Skye got back to the motel that afternoon, Edge took the wheel of Trace's big black Yukon, and they headed for the compound. He had a spot in mind to set up the drone, but they needed to scout the area, make sure it was a place they could fly the drone without being discovered.

"We need to pinpoint Callie's location," Edge said as he parked the SUV behind a low hill farther down the dirt road they had traveled before. "We need to know which house she's staying in and how many other women are in there with her."

"From what Molly said, there are only two unmarried women in the compound. They're probably staying together."

Edge nodded. "The afternoon's pretty well shot. We're going to need at least another day to chart Callie's routine: what time she gets up, what she does, and when she does it."

"Same for the men," Skye said. "We need to study their daily movements and time the guard rotations."

"There might be a better way than going in at night," Edge said. "I didn't notice as many guards in the daytime, but the risk of being seen is higher."

"What about the drone? How can we be sure they won't spot it?"

"Have you seen it?"

Skye shook her head. "It's still in the box in the back." She was wearing dark blue stretch jeans, low-heeled boots, and a dark green turtleneck sweater. Skye had a firm, lean body, but there were plenty of curves, all in exactly the right places.

He remembered seeing her in a wet T-shirt during a rainstorm in Mexico. The memory of her breasts, as round and delectable as a pair of ripe peaches, was seared into his brain.

When he opened the back of the SUV and Skye bent over to open the box holding the drone, his blood went south, and his mind went straight to the gutter. A woman's breasts were his weakness. But Skye's taut, round behind was pure temptation.

She had pulled her thick dark hair into a no-nonsense ponytail at the nape of her neck, but sunlight set off ruby glints here and there, and his mind conjured images of how the silky strands would look spread over his pillow. He wanted to peel off those snug jeans and take her right there in the back of the SUV.

Edge silently cursed. Bedding Skye Delaney was becoming an obsession. Even worse, there was nothing he could do about it. Skye was his partner, his friend. She wasn't the kind of woman you seduced, then just walked away from.

He took a deep breath and focused on the drone. "It's a real beauty," he said as Skye opened the box. "State of the art, that's for sure."

She ran a hand over the mini-drone, and he felt it as if she'd stroked him. The ridge beneath the zipper of his black jeans went harder.

"Where did you get it?" she asked.

Edge shook his head. "You don't want to know." He still had friends in the army, brothers in arms. They helped each other any way they could. Edge stayed in touch and was always there if they needed him. In return, they kept him posted on the whereabouts of a certain Special Forces Major Bradley Markham.

Edge might not be a soldier anymore, but he still intended to rain justice down on the man who had very nearly destroyed him.

Next to the drone, a long canvas bag held a brand new MK22 sniper rifle, two extra handguns, and a Mossburg Thunder Ranch twelve-gauge shotgun. Three tactical vests lay next to the bag, one small enough to fit Skye. If all went well, Trace would be joining them when they went into the compound tomorrow night. Trace had been an Army Ranger sniper. Edge hoped they wouldn't need his skills, but it was better to be prepared.

Edge carefully took the drone out of the box. It was on loan from a friend, a captain he'd taken a bullet for in Afghanistan. Pure reflex, as far as Edge was concerned, but he had saved Rick Emory's life. The bullet wound Edge had taken had been relatively minor, just another scar to add to a growing list.

Still, the captain considered it a lifelong debt, and a simple request to borrow an army drone wasn't much of a problem.

Even this very special drone, which fit in the palm of his hand.

The FLIR Black Hornet PRS (Personal Reconnaissance System) was only 6.6 inches long. Its flight time was just twenty-five minutes, but the way Edge intended to use it, much of that time it would be sitting, not flying, transmitting images of a particular area of the compound. It could stay out long enough to get the job done.

Edge couldn't wait to get the sweet little Hornet into the air.

"Wow," Skye said. "I've never seen anything like it." Her excitement matched his. Skye was so damned feminine and pretty, sometimes he had to remind himself she was US Army, same as he was. Or had been.

"Only weighs thirty-three grams," he said. "Got a mile-and-a-quarter range, transmits color images at speeds up to eleven miles an hour, and it's damn near silent. They finally got the Hornet down to a price the army could afford, so it just got approved for personal use. This one adapts for night vision."

Skye smiled. "Perfect for what we need."

Edge grinned. "Yeah."

They set up to work out of the back of the SUV. Edge assembled the drone, while Skye linked it to her laptop so they could watch the images on her computer screen.

The drone took off for the half-mile flight to the compound. Edge sent it in at high altitude, circled the perimeter, noting the guards prowling the fence along each side of the property, then eased down to a lower elevation.

He set the drone down on the roof of a big metal building that turned out to be a livestock barn. From the roof, the drone could watch the women in the vegetable garden. Others worked inside the barn cleaning the stalls, while some were outside with the cows, pigs, and sheep in the pens.

The drone zipped quickly by the windows of what appeared to be a commissary, confirming it was the place the group ate during the workday and probably fed the men who worked nights. Edge sent the drone toward the second large metal building, a heavy equipment shed, landing it on the roof to give them a bird's-eye view of the people moving around outside.

"It's Callie!" Skye said, spotting her sister as she left the vegetable patch and started across the compound with two other women. It was five o'clock, probably the end of the workday. Callie and one of the women, with a curvy figure, long black hair, and a very pretty face, disappeared into one of the white, wood-frame cottages while a thirty something redhead went into the unit next door.

The drone zipped down off the roof and flew just above the windows of the house, giving them a view inside. Callie walked into the bedroom, which was modestly furnished with two twin beds, a dresser, and a pair of nightstands. She sank down on the bed, wiping her eyes.

Skye gripped Edge's shoulder. "She looks like she's crying."

His jaw felt tight. "Christ knows what they've done to her."

"Edge, we've got to get her out of there."

He just shook his head. "We aren't ready yet. We'll watch the place tonight and come back again tomorrow, be ready to go in with Trace tomorrow night. We go in unprepared, we could wind up getting your sister killed."

Skye's attention returned to the screen. The drone was back on the roof of the building, the camera reporting movements in and around the compound. "You're right. I'm sorry."

"Hey, if it were one of my brothers, I'd feel the same way." He remembered being forced to hold his position in Mexico while his brother had nearly drowned.

Skye managed a smile that showed the same worry he was feeling. "Callie and I have never been close, but she's still my sister. Thinking of her being abused in there . . . it's just . . . it's hard to handle."

"You need to do what you've been trained to do—put your emotions aside and focus." The way she was gazing up at him, Edge couldn't resist leaning down and brushing a soft kiss over her lips. "And that is exactly what you'll do."

It occurred to him that he trusted Skye every bit as much as any of the men who had served with him in the army. Unfortunately, in Skye's case, his body wanted more from her than just a reliable partner.

Skye blinked up at him, and color rose beneath the sculpted bones in her cheeks. He wanted to kiss her again, just sink in and take and take and take. One brief touch wasn't nearly enough.

"Let's see what the men are doing," he said mildly, as if his whole body hadn't just caught fire.

Occasionally changing the drone batteries, they watched the compound from its rooftop perch for what was left of the afternoon. There were men moving around, walking alone or in pairs, a number of them carrying sidearms. Others drove pickup trucks, hauling hay or supplies, or delivering foodstuffs to the commissary.

The third metal building sat a hundred yards away from the rest of the compound. Edge itched to see what was going on inside.

"How much flight time do we have left?" Skye asked.

"Not enough." Working the controls, he sent the drone soaring upward off the roof, high enough not to be spotted, then set the machine on a path that would return it to the back of the SUV where it had been launched.

Dusk had begun to fall, a curtain of gray hovering above the fading yellow horizon. By the time the drone had landed, the last battery was dead, but once they got back to the motel, the batteries could be fully recharged with a USB cable.

"You still got any of those sandwiches you picked up at the café this morning?" he asked, though he would rather have a far different hunger satisfied.

The stolen kiss, the touch of his mouth over those full pink lips, had only made his desire for her deepen. He took the last sandwich, roast beef, offered her a bite she declined, and they headed back to the motel.

As the SUV rattled over a string of potholes in the dusty dirt road, he polished off the sandwich, but one look at Skye and his hunger returned. Either he needed to find another woman to take care of his needs or convince Skye to invite him into her bed.

Maybe he should call one of his Denver lady friends, women who enjoyed an occasional bout of no-strings sex. The sad truth was the idea of sleeping with another woman left a bad taste in his mouth.

Skye was the woman he wanted. He wished to hell he knew if there was any chance she also wanted him.

CHAPTER ELEVEN

THEY SPENT MOST OF THE NEXT DAY DOING RECON, COLLECTING THE rest of the intel they needed. Skye checked her digital wristwatch. It was late afternoon. Trace would be arriving at dusk. They would meet at the motel, go over the details, the timing, Plan A, Plan B, and Plan C, if the whole thing turned into what Edge called "a giant clusterfuck."

"We've got what we need," Skye said, watching as Edge frowned and paced back and forth behind the SUV, clearly not satisfied with the information the drone had provided so far. "What is it? What are we not doing that you still want to do?"

Edge stopped pacing, his intense blue eyes locking on her face. The impact made her breath catch.

"I want to know what's in that third building," he said.

Skye fought to control her feminine response and the uptick of her pulse. She tried not to think about how capable he looked, how utterly masculine and completely in control.

"We talked about this," she said. "We decided it was too risky. The building sits too far out in the open. We need to get Callie out of there. If the men spot the drone, they'll come after us, and we won't be able to get it done. We've already pushed our luck as far as we dare."

Edge still didn't look convinced. "Callie's our priority, no question, but she's not the only woman who needs help. If what

Henson is doing in that building is illegal, it'll force the sheriff to take action. That's the only way we're going to be able to help the others."

Skye said nothing. Unless they hired an army of mercenaries to go against Henson's heavily armed men, the only way they could free the other women who wanted to leave was with the help of law enforcement.

"We'll get Callie to testify," Skye argued. "She can tell the authorities what's going on and force them to do their jobs."

"The way Molly did?"

Molly had refused. Maybe Callie would, too.

"Callie might not even know what they're doing in that building," Edge said. "Molly didn't know."

Resigned, Skye blew out a breath. "All right. We go in tonight and get Callie out, but while we're there, we find a way to see what's going on in the third metal building."

"Or we do it right now. I've got one battery left. I can circle the drone around behind, take a quick look inside, and get out without being spotted."

She would rather wait until Callie was safe. But if they waited till dark and used the night vision on the drone, the hard-to-decipher pale green images might not give them enough intel to figure out what was actually happening.

Skye reluctantly nodded. "Okay, let's do it."

Edge flashed one of his devastating smiles, a blaze of even white teeth. With his olive complexion, amazing blue eyes, and neatly trimmed, shiny black hair, the man was as perfect as one of his smiles. To say nothing of his broad-shouldered, narrow-hipped, perfectly sculpted body.

Skye's heart squeezed. She'd once been as proud of her body as Edge must be of his. Not anymore.

"All right, let's get this done." Edge changed the drone battery and sent it off on one last flight, circling low along the hills outside the fence, then swooping in and silently flying along the eaves of the third building.

A FedEx delivery truck idled in front of two big metal doors that had been slid open. The drone darted in through the opening. Edge sent it up to the curved ceiling, out of the line of sight, then began to slowly circle around inside.

"Holy mother," he said, his attention glued to the laptop screen positioned in the back of the SUV beneath the open cargo bay door.

"It's some kind of laboratory," Skye said. Long stainless-steel tables stretched from one end of the big open room to the other, three of them, running parallel about six feet apart. There were huge stainless-steel cooking pots, big glass beakers, all sorts of thick copper tubing.

High windows, in a row along both sides, were open for ventilation, the air stirred by three big fans perched high on the walls.

"It's a frigging meth lab," Edge said as two of the men, both dressed in white hazmat suits, began loading the white-and-blue box truck. "And it's not just some amateur operation. These guys are in it big-time."

Skye's pulse speeded. "So that isn't a real FedEx truck."

"Not by a long shot."

Skye thought of Callie and felt a jolt of fear. Meth labs were extremely volatile and dangerous, the chemicals themselves incredibly toxic. The drone camera picked up stacks of what looked like plastic-wrapped bricks and a pile of fat green cellophane tubes, all of them undoubtedly packed with white powder.

"That looks like a lot of product," Skye said.

"Which equals a lot of money. I read somewhere that two hundred pounds of methamphetamine is worth over a million dollars."

Skye forced herself to focus on the computer screen. "It's made out of pseudoephedrine, right? I thought buying the drug in any quantity was banned a few years back."

Edge nodded. "That's right. It was banned in the US back in '05. Which means Henson's got a source, probably someplace out of the country."

"Mexico?"

"Maybe. But the cartels mostly make their own synthetic drugs."

"So somewhere else."

"That's right."

Skye's thoughts returned to her sister. "What about Callie? Should we call the police?"

Edge's blue eyes lasered in on her face. "The situation is different now. All of the women are clearly in danger, but we aren't equipped to get all of them out tonight. If we bring in the authorities, it'll take time for them to set up a raid, and the more armed men, the higher the risk to your sister. Your family, your call."

Skye's decision was already made. "Everything's set. We're ready to go in and bring Callie out. Tomorrow we can go to the sheriff."

"Good choice. Once Callie's safe, we blow the whistle on Henson and his illegal money machine."

Relief filtered through her. Taking action now was the best way to ensure Callie's safety.

Edge called the drone back, and they waited for its arrival. "The way it looks, the men are in charge in there. Good chance none of the women are involved. From a legal standpoint, the less Callie knows about what's going on, the better. The cops are going to bring these guys down hard. Better if Callie's as far from the situation as possible."

The drone arrived, and Edge stored it in the back of the SUV; then they belted themselves in for the trip back to town. When they arrived, Edge's snazzy black sports car crouched like a sexy panther in front of the motel.

Trace was there.

Skye should have felt relieved.

Instead, all she could think of was the danger they would be facing in the Children of the Sun compound later that night.

Edge unlocked his motel room door to find Trace Elliott lounging on one of the twin beds. Long legs crossed at the ankles, hands behind his head, Trace leaned back against the headboard.

Edge chuckled. "So I'm betting you didn't get a key from the manager."

Trace just shrugged. "Not exactly Fort Knox." He was wearing a black Molon Labe T-shirt with a Spartan helmet on the front. *Molon Labe.* The Greeks' response to the Persians who wanted them to surrender their arms. *Come and take them.* As a former Ranger, Trace always enjoyed a good fight.

Edge just smiled. The room at the Trails West Inn had the bare necessities, nothing more. Two twin beds with a nightstand in between and a scarred wooden dresser that had seen better days. The tiny bathroom cramped his style, but in his past life, he would have considered it first class.

Edge set the drone down on the dresser. "How's Molly? You get her settled?"

Trace sat up on the side of the bed. "We stopped at Walmart to pick up some clothes and a few other items. Molly's had a rough time of it. I'm glad Skye's helping her."

"So I take it you liked her."

Trace smiled. "She's kind of sweet, you know? Kind of shy, but once you get her talking, you can tell she's smart."

"Pretty, too," Edge said, just to see what Trace would say.

"Yeah. Off limits, though. That guy she was with did a real number on her."

"Harley Purcell. It's going to take some time for her to get back on her feet and her head on straight, especially when it comes to men."

"Maybe we'll get lucky and run into the rat bastard tonight, dish out a little payback."

"Be a whole lot better if we just get in and out without stirring up a hornet's nest. You get that, right?"

A knot formed in Trace's jaw. "I get it. Don't worry, I'll do my job."

Edge nodded. "I know you will." He trusted Trace the way he trusted Skye. The three of them made an exceptionally effective team.

"Another problem's come up," Edge said. "Turns out Henson

is running a drug operation out there. Guy's cooking meth, and in no small quantity."

"Jeezus. Molly didn't mention it."

"I don't think she knew. Suspected maybe, but the women know better than to ask questions."

"Or what?" Trace asked, the muscles tightening beneath his snug black T-shirt. "Their husbands beat them?"

"Looks that way. These are big, tough men, Trace. From what I gather, their women do pretty much what they're told."

Trace swore foully.

"Molly saw a woman who tried to escape beaten to death right in front of her," Edge continued. "They buried her body out near the vegetable garden."

"Molly told me. I held her while she cried." And clearly Molly's story had affected him. Trace was a pushover when it came to a damsel in distress.

"So far, Molly's too frightened to cooperate with the law. I'm hoping Callie will be willing to speak up. Soon as we get her out of there, I'll talk to Sheriff Akins about the alleged murder and Henson's drug operation. I'm just hoping Akins isn't on Henson's payroll."

A knock sounded at the door. "That'll be Skye." Edge walked over and opened the door. He didn't like the hunger that burned through his blood when Skye's soft breast brushed his arm as she walked into the room.

"Molly said to thank you for helping her," Trace said.

Skye smiled. "We're hoping once she feels safe, she'll help us in return."

"She's scared to death that guy she married will come after her."

"If they were ever actually married," Skye said.

"Either way, Purcell may figure she belongs to him. If she was my woman, I wouldn't want to let her go."

Edge felt his eyebrows climbing. Trace rarely got involved with a woman. He was a confirmed bachelor. Or at least he had been.

"With luck, Purcell will be spending his days in jail." Edge checked the Black Predator combat watch on his wrist. "It's still early. Let's head over to the café and get something to eat. We'll come back and work through the plan, catch a little shut-eye, then head out to the compound."

"Sounds good." Trace unwound his tall frame and stood up. They were both six-three, Trace a few pounds heavier. They were big men, physically fit and well trained. Skye could hold her own, but considering what they could be facing tonight, Edge was glad to have Trace along.

Edge opened the motel room door. He didn't glance at Skye as she walked past him out of the room. He needed his entire focus to be on the mission. It was what he had been trained to do.

But once their mission was complete and they were back in Denver, his objective was going to change. Skye Delaney was going to become his focus. His attraction to her was a problem he intended to solve, and like everything he did in life, he wouldn't quit until he had achieved his goal.

In the meantime, his complete concentration had to be on his team and their objective. He wanted Callie Delaney out from under Henson's control, home and safe. A simple snatch and grab should do it, in and out without firing a shot.

That was Plan A.

Plan B was the fail-safe. If unexpected problems arose, they'd do what was necessary to protect their charge and get out of the compound. Plan C would be implemented if all their planning went south. Then they would figure things out on the fly, do their best to get everyone out alive, and get the hell out of Dodge.

Edge's mouth tightened in grim anticipation as he closed the door to the motel room.

CHAPTER TWELVE

"You can't do it, Callie. It's too dangerous." Her roommate and best friend, Lila Ramirez, rose from where she'd been sitting on the edge of the twin bed. "We still don't know what happened to Molly. And what about Sarah?" It was after lights out, the simple lamp on the nightstand turned off in the bedroom they shared.

"You have heard the rumors," Lila continued. "People say she is dead." Lila had met Raul Ramirez at a local nightclub, a man as handsome as she was pretty. Three months later, they were married. When Raul took a job with Daniel, she had excitedly followed him to Blancha Springs.

A month ago, Raul had been killed in a car accident, or at least that was the story. Devastated, Lila wanted to leave, but Daniel refused. After a period of mourning, he said, he would find her a suitable replacement, and she would be happy again.

Callie believed the replacement would be Daniel himself. Then, in time, he would marry Lila to another of his men.

"Maybe you're wrong," Callie argued. "Maybe Molly and Sarah both got out and are living like normal people somewhere far away from this terrible place."

"The chances of you escaping are very slim, Callie, and you know it. What if Klaus finds out? He is expecting to be married tomorrow. What do you think he will do to you if you get caught running away?"

Callie shoved a long cotton skirt and flowered blouse into the big quilted purse one of the women had given her as a welcome gift. "In that case, I'd better not get caught."

Lila walked toward her. Only thin rays of moonlight sliding out between intermittent clouds lit the darkness outside the bedroom. "Callie, please. Why don't you wait until we go into town? Maybe there you will find a chance to escape."

"And in the meantime, I'm supposed to submit to that bastard Mahler? The man is a pig. Have you seen the way he eats? He disgusts me. And those hard, cold eyes? The way he leers at a woman makes me sick to my stomach."

She paced toward the wall and whirled back to her friend, sending her long skirt billowing around her ankles. "I have to go tonight, Lila. I'd rather be dead than marry Klaus and stay in this place."

Lila fell silent, knowing she would soon be in the same situation. Callie wondered if Raul had really died or if Daniel had just sent the man off to work somewhere else so that he could have Lila.

It wouldn't surprise her. Nothing Daniel Henson did surprised her. Not anymore.

She hitched the strap of the quilted bag over her shoulder.

"Even if you reach the fence," Lila said, "how will you get out?"

"I know where Molly dug the hole. I'll take my time, watch for the guards, and stay out of sight. I'll go out the same way she did."

Lila clamped a hand on a generous hip. "*If* she got out, you mean. If they did not kill her."

Callie made no reply, just leaned over and hugged her friend. "If I make it, I'll find a way to help you get out, too." Lila had no family. No one but Callie. "You and the rest of the women who want to leave . . . I won't just abandon you. I promise you I'll be back."

Lila hugged her. "I will pray for you, my dear friend. God bless you and good luck."

"You, too." Callie walked out of the bedroom.

* * *

Skye rode with Trace, who parked the Yukon in a secluded spot the drone had discovered less than a quarter mile from the fence line, an easy extraction point after they'd completed their mission.

Edge parked the Nissan farther away from the compound on the dirt road they had used before, a secondary vehicle in case things turned to worms and they needed another way out.

With luck, the hole they'd cut in the fence hadn't been found. While he and Skye accessed the compound, Trace would be covering them from a position on the hillside. The MK22 sniper rifle had an effective firing range of 1,600 yards, far more than they needed, and Trace was a crack shot.

Edge hoped it wouldn't come to that, but they were up against seasoned men, some undoubtedly former military. Others looked like gangbangers, ex-cons, or hardened street fighters. They were armed, and they were dangerous.

He rendezvoused with Skye and Trace at the Yukon, where they put on their tactical vests, grease-painted their faces, and tested their comms, the earbuds each of them were wearing.

"Any questions before we go in?" Edge asked, strapping his Ka-Bar knife to his thigh.

Trace and Skye both shook their heads. They were professionals. The plan was burned into their brains.

All of them were dressed head-to-foot in black, including knit caps and tactical vests, and armed to the teeth—Edge with his Beretta and an S&W .45, Skye with her Glock and a Browning .40 cal., Trace with the MK22 and his Nighthawk nine mil.

"All right, you know what to do," Edge said. "Let's get this done."

Carrying the assembled rifle, Trace split off and headed up the hill. Edge gave him time to reach the spot on the GPS where he would set up his sniper hide; then Edge and Skye started across the mostly open terrain toward the fence.

Moving through the dry grass from shrub to shrub, tree to tree, they reached the shallow ravine they had used before and followed it as far as they could.

Edge checked his watch and motioned to Skye, who sank down in the grass beside him. Using his night-vision binoculars, he scanned the compound.

The guards appeared right on schedule for their rendezvous at the corner where the fence lines met. They pulled out bottles of water and drank. None of them smoked, he had noticed, probably on Henson's orders. One of them laughed at something the other man said, then they turned and began their long trek back the way they'd come.

Edge motioned Skye forward. Keeping low as he moved through the grass, he reached the fence, lifted away the cut-out portion hidden behind the shrub, and ducked inside. Skye followed. Trace would be watching their progress through his Nightforce 7-35x scope, a thought that gave Edge the warm-and-fuzzies.

At least they wouldn't be completely on their own.

Moving quietly, they penetrated farther into the compound, heading for Callie's cottage. Edge said a silent prayer the girl would be glad to see her sister, willing and ready to leave. If not, things could go south in a hurry.

They reached the toolsheds next to the vegetable garden, and Edge marked the spot on his GPS as a place for the sheriff to look for Sarah's body. He noticed Skye's gaze running over the ground near the sheds. Her eyes came to his, and a flash of something moved between them.

Resolve, he thought. Determination that justice be done.

They made their way farther in, passing the Quonset-style barn where the horses were stabled. Edge spotted a big man in camos off to his right, motioned to Skye, and both of them eased back into the shadows.

As soon as the guy disappeared around the back of the building, they started toward the second barn, where the heavy equipment was stored. *Right on schedule so far.* Everything was going smoothly. *Too smoothly,* Edge thought, tension building as he waited for the unexpected turn that seemed to come with every mission.

Then the still night air erupted with a woman's high-pitched scream.

Skye's heart jerked.

"Go . . ." At Edge's soft command, she regained her focus, but her insides were shaking. Keeping low, she eased through the darkness toward the heavy equipment barn and flattened herself against the cold steel wall. The sound of a struggle and a flash of movement caught her eye. The clouds parted for a moment, and she saw a woman fighting with two big men. Long blond hair gleamed in the moonlight before the clouds knitted together and darkness returned.

Callie!

One of the men was a tall, thick-chested, heavily bearded blond man who looked like a Viking. The other had shoulder-length black hair and a patch over one eye. Skye glanced around for Edge but didn't see him. He was circling, moving into position on the other side of the men.

The one-eyed man grinned up at the bearded giant. "Looks like you bride is on de run, Klaus." His accent was Spanish. He looked like he ate nails for breakfast.

The Viking's mouth curved in a brutal smile in the middle of his beard. "You're right, Vasquez. Guess I'll have to start the honeymoon early." He squeezed Callie's upper arm so hard she winced. "Right, sweetheart?"

Callie struggled uselessly. "Get away from me!"

The blond man jerked her hard against him. "You want to fight me? Save it till I'm inside you. I'll enjoy the ride even more."

Callie didn't back down. "I won't marry you, Klaus. You hear me? I'd rather sleep with a pig than you!" Klaus slapped her so hard she went down in a heap at his feet.

Skye's hand tightened around the grip of her pistol, but she didn't move. Not yet. Not until Edge was in position. Her heart thrummed as she waited to hear his voice through the earbuds.

Vasquez laughed. "You gonna have your hands full with that one, *ese.*"

Klaus hauled Callie to her feet. "Yeah, and I'm gonna enjoy every minute."

"Let me go!"

Klaus shook her. "Henson's marrying us tomorrow, but I'm not waiting that long." Klaus started dragging her off toward the animal barn. "You were Daniel's whore. Now you're gonna be mine."

Callie whimpered and fought to get free, but Klaus just kept going, half carrying, half dragging her across the dirt. He had almost reached the barn door when Skye heard Edge's command through her earbud.

"Now." Edge moved, and so did Skye. Klaus took one more step before Edge appeared, the barrel of his Beretta pressed into the flesh beneath the Viking's chin. "Let her go."

Vasquez started to move. "Stay right where you are." Legs braced apart, Skye held the Glock two-handed, the muzzle pointing straight at the one-eyed man's heart.

Vasquez froze.

"I said let her go," Edge repeated, shoving the gun barrel deeper into Klaus's flesh.

Klaus released his hold, and Callie stumbled out of his reach.

"Hands in the air," Edge commanded softly. Very softly. They didn't need a swarm of armed men pouring out of their houses. "Get down on your knees."

"You, too," Skye said to Vasquez, her Glock held steady. Fury burned in the man's single black eye as he complied.

A few feet away, Edge was disarming the blond giant, tossing his weapons into the shrubs well out of reach. Skye did the same to the man on his knees in front of her.

She looked over at her sister. "You ready to leave, Callie?" Her sister's head came up, recognizing for the first time the woman beneath the tactical vest and black face paint. Callie made a sound in her throat and ran toward her, stopping a few feet away at the sight of the gun in Skye's hands.

"Start walking," Edge said to the Viking, forcing him to move toward the barn.

"I'll kill you," Klaus said. "Whoever you are, you're a dead man." His ice-blue eyes swung to Skye. "Both of you are dead."

Edge shoved him hard, and Klaus stumbled forward.

"You're mine, Callie," the giant said, looking back over his shoulder. "Wherever you go, I'll find you and make you pay."

Edge cuffed Klaus on the back of the head with the barrel of his pistol. "If you want to live, you'll shut your mouth and do what I tell you."

Callie hurried ahead to open the barn door, and Edge shoved Klaus inside. Skye followed with Vasquez. In minutes, they had both men gagged, their wrists and ankles secured with plastic zip ties.

Skye leaned over and hugged her sister. "Everything's going to be all right, Callie. We're getting you out of here."

Callie hugged her back, blue eyes full of tears. "Thank you for coming. I can't believe you're really here."

"Later," Edge said flatly, motioning them toward the door at the rear of the barn.

They were outside and moving fast toward the hole in the fence, Callie stumbling, Skye holding onto her, keeping her upright, Edge behind, protecting against threats from the rear.

They'd almost made it to the fence when one of the guards stepped out of the shadows right in front of Callie, the barrel of his big semiauto just inches from Callie's heart.

"You move and I shoot her." He was dark-skinned and thick-chested, his face pockmarked and cruel.

Callie made a sound in her throat and started to tremble. Skye didn't doubt the man would pull the trigger. The grim pleasure on his face said he was enjoying himself.

"Drop your weapon," he demanded.

Skye's heart pounded, and her fingers felt numb. She forced herself not to search for Edge or the second guard as she set her Glock on the ground in front of her. She caught the flash of Edge's blade, though he had ducked out of sight into the shadows.

Before Skye could stop her, Callie exploded into action, shoving aside the barrel of the pistol, then hurling herself toward the grim-faced guard. Trusting Trace to have the man in his sites, Skye shoved Callie out of the way, and both of them hit the ground. Trace fired, and blood erupted on the front of the pock-marked man's chest as he crumpled into the dirt.

Skye spotted the second guard just as Edge stepped out of the shadows. His knife flashed as he pressed it against the man's throat. "Drop your weapon."

The guard, tall and hard-muscled, with a scar bisecting one black eyebrow, made no move to comply.

Edge's blade carved a thin line across the man's throat. "I said: Drop your weapon."

CHAPTER THIRTEEN

THE GUN FELL TO THE GROUND WITH A CLATTER. "HENSON WILL SEE you dead for this."

With Skye back on her feet, her Glock zeroed in on the guard with the scarred eyebrow, Edge slid his knife back into the scabbard on his thigh. In seconds, they had the guy zip-tied, hand and foot, and solidly gagged. Edge dragged him behind the metal toolshed near the garden.

He glanced at Skye. "Go."

Glock in hand, Skye urged Callie forward, and Edge fell in behind them. Someone must have heard something because an alarm roared to life, crackling through the air as if there were an escape from Folsom State Prison.

As Skye and Callie ducked through the hole in the fence, half-dressed men carrying pistols and AR-15s streamed out of their houses. With the guards down, the men had no idea which way to run and scattered like roaches around the compound.

The confusion gave them a few extra seconds, not much more.

Edge followed Skye through the fence, then took a position in the ravine to provide cover for her and Callie as they made their way back to the Yukon.

On the hill, Trace fired a series of covering shots into the compound. Edge fired several rounds and moved. Trace changed position, fired more shots, then shifted again, each time moving closer to the Yukon.

By the time Edge arrived, Skye was already behind the wheel, the engine running, Callie in the front passenger seat. Trace had backed the SUV in, so they were ready to roll, just waiting for the rest of the team.

"Get Callie out of here," Edge said to Skye through the open window. "Head for Denver. I'll wait for Trace, and we'll meet you there."

"No way!" Callie leaned toward him across the console. "I need to talk to the sheriff. I have friends in there. I promised I'd help. If we leave, there's no way to tell what Henson might do."

"We don't know if we can trust the sheriff."

"We have to try," Callie argued. "I'm not going back until I talk to him."

Edge glanced around. Time was running out. He could still hear distant gunshots. "Fine," he said. "We'll meet back at the motel. Give us ten minutes. If we aren't back, forget the sheriff and head for the city."

Skye's sea-green eyes slid over his face, her worry clear. She didn't want to leave him. Maybe it meant something. Maybe it was just a soldier's honor—no man left behind.

"Get going," he said.

Skye gunned the Yukon, and the SUV shot off down the dirt road. Edge moved toward the place designated as a secondary rendezvous point. He sent out a call through his earbuds, but got no reply. Time passed, turned into minutes. He could hear men's voices as they searched the area, fanning out and moving closer.

He made several more attempts to raise Trace but got no response. He checked his black tactical watch. He'd give Trace another two minutes, then head out in search of him. Worry dripped acid into his stomach. Where was Trace? Had he been wounded? A few seconds later, he heard the hoot of an owl, soft but distinctive.

Edge breathed a sigh of relief as his friend rose up out of the shadows, sniper rifle in hand.

Neither of them spoke, just moved off together into the darkness, heading for their secondary vehicle, the Nissan, a low-slung, welcome black shadow awaiting their arrival.

Trace found a place for his weapon, and they both slid into their seats. Easing quietly down the narrow dirt track with the lights off, Edge picked up a little more speed, stretching the distance between him and their pursuers.

"About that guard . . ." Trace said, his features grim in the faint light coming from the gauges on the dash.

"You kill him?" Edge flicked him a sideways glance as they reached the wider dirt road that led away from the compound to the highway. He made the turn and pressed the accelerator.

"Not unless the shot scared him to death," Trace said. "Upper chest wound. Should be survivable. I came damn close, though. I would have taken the kill shot if Skye's sister hadn't engaged with the bastard the way she did. Damned brave thing to do."

"Or stupid." Behind him, several pin-dots of light appeared in the distance, but no way was he letting them catch up. "Could have gotten herself killed."

"She took the risk, changed the odds, and gave me another option. I figured it would cause less trouble if I just wounded the a-hole and ended the threat."

The road was rough and bumpy, tough on the low-slung sports car. Behind him, the pin-dots of light in the distance held steady but made no visible gains.

"Shoot anyone else?"

"No." Trace's mouth tightened. "Not that they didn't deserve it."

Edge grunted. "That's for sure." The car fishtailed a little as he took a flat curve, and the lights behind him disappeared. Edge turned on his headlights and pushed the car faster, leaving Henson's men in the dust. Literally.

If he didn't get back to the motel in time, Skye would head for Denver. Or maybe not.

Edge pressed harder on the gas.

At the Trails West Inn, Skye and Callie loaded the rest of their clothes and gear into the back of the Yukon; then Skye moved it around to the back of the motel out of sight.

She checked her digital wristwatch. Time was up, but Edge and Trace hadn't returned. Fear for them soured her stomach.

She glanced over at Callie, whose skirts swirled around her ankles as she paced the motel room. They needed to leave. Henson's men could arrive any second. She needed to get Callie back to Denver, where she would be safe.

Skye walked over to the window. She didn't want to leave, not until the rest of the team was safe. Not until Edge was safe.

She turned back to Callie. "We've waited long enough. Henson's goons could show up any minute. Get in the car."

Callie shook her head, shifting her long blond hair across her shoulders. The pale strands were covered with dirt and leaves, her long skirt dusty and torn.

"You hid the car," she said. "There's no way for them to know we're here. I'm not leaving till I talk to the sheriff." She walked over to the phone on the nightstand. "I'm calling him right now."

"What if Akins is on Henson's payroll? If he is, you could wind up back in the compound. Or both of us could end up in jail on some bogus charge. We'll go back to Denver. I know police there we can trust."

Callie's eyes filled but her chin remained stubborn. "I'm calling him. I promised my friend. You can go back to Denver. I have to stay."

Skye hadn't told Callie about Molly or Sarah. There would be time for that once they were safe.

A car pulled into the parking lot. Skye ran to the window and saw Edge and Trace climbing out of the Nissan. Relief hit her hard. She opened the door and let them in.

"I see you two followed orders," Edge drawled as Trace walked in behind him. "Not that I really expected you to." His lips curved in a mixture of amusement and frustration, but she could tell he was glad she was still there.

"Callie's determined to talk to the sheriff," Skye said.

Edge nodded. "I called him. He's meeting us here."

Skye glanced toward the window. "What about Henson's men?"

"They cut out before we got to town, turned around and headed back the way they came."

Callie trembled as she sank down on the bed.

"It's all right, Callie," Edge said. "You're safe. Your sister's here, and we won't let anything happen to you." He turned. "By the way, I'm Edge, and this is Trace. He's the guy who was up on the hill."

Trace made a brief nod of his head. "Good to meet you, Callie. Nice work out there."

Callie managed to smile, though her face was pale, her bottom lip cut and swollen, dried blood in the corner of her mouth. "Thank you both for your help."

Lights filled the windows of the motel room, and Edge walked over to take a look.

"Sheriff's here. Let's hope he's in the mood to hear one helluva story."

Akins's blond hair looked mussed, as if he had just rolled out of bed—which at this late hour, he undoubtedly had. Faint circles appeared beneath his light blue eyes.

It took an hour to relay the happenings at the Children of the Sun compound and answer questions about Daniel Henson, including the news that Henson was cooking meth.

"You should have let the police handle it," the sheriff grumbled, clearly unhappy with their interference. "You could be facing all sorts of charges."

"Henson was holding Callie against her will," Edge said. "That's kidnapping. Callie wanted out. We helped her get out. Any casualties suffered are on them."

The sheriff eyed him darkly. Akins knew about the attack on Callie but not about Trace and the man he had shot. Edge didn't figure Daniel Henson would be pressing charges anytime soon.

"You're absolutely sure Henson's manufacturing synthetic drugs out there?" the sheriff pressed.

"We've got drone footage showing the interior of the lab," Edge said. "It's a big one. The guy is making millions, and the longer you wait to go in, the better the chances he'll rabbit."

Akins pulled out his cell phone and started making calls. It would take time to put together a tactical team to raid the compound.

"What about the women?" Skye asked, worried about what might happen to them. "Is there a chance you could get them out first? Callie says none of the women are involved with the drug operation. Henson doesn't allow them to go near the lab, and what Henson says is law."

"I'll have to take that up with the DEA. Their commander will be arriving first thing this morning."

Edge hoped it wouldn't be too late. On the other hand, Henson might not realize they knew about the lab. The women didn't seem to know, so Callie wouldn't be considered a threat. And Edge and Skye had made it clear they wanted Callie out of there. With so much drug money at stake, Henson might wait to see how things played out.

There was a chance the DEA would catch Daniel Henson with his pants around his ankles and bust the entire operation. But that was Akins's business.

"There's one more thing," Skye said to the sheriff. "There's a young woman. Her name was Sarah. A witness came forward who says Sarah was murdered when they caught her trying to escape. The witness gave us the location where the body is buried."

Callie made a sound in her throat. Skye had told her about Sarah and that Molly had witnessed the murder, but the pain was still fresh.

"What's the woman's last name?" Akins asked.

"She was married to one of Henson's men," Skye said. "A man named Webb Rankin. She used his last name. That's all we know."

The sheriff's blue eyes narrowed. "I want to speak to the witness."

"That's not going to happen," Edge said. "The woman escaped the compound. She's no longer in the area."

Akins fell silent. Edge could almost see his mind working.

"I only have five deputies for the entire county. That's not enough to tackle this thing head-on. Not if what you're telling me is the truth."

"It's the truth, all right. Henson's got a small army out there. The longer you wait, the better the chance he'll get away. By now he could be on his way to Mexico."

"The DEA is due to arrive in the next several hours. Until then, there's nothing I can do."

Edge didn't argue because the sheriff was right. Even if Akins deputized the three of them, they wouldn't have enough manpower to go against Henson's soldiers. Not without casualties, some of which were bound to be women.

Morning couldn't come soon enough for Edge.

CHAPTER FOURTEEN

IT TOOK THREE HOURS FOR THE DEA TO SET UP OPERATIONS FOR A raid on the Children of the Sun. Skye, Edge, Trace, and Callie had given their statements and answered questions at least a dozen times. They were free to go, but they all refused to leave.

"My best friend is in that compound," Callie had said. "Until I know Lila is safe, I'm not going anywhere. I promised I'd find a way to help her and the others. I have to make sure they're okay."

Skye understood. She felt much the same way. In truth, she was beginning to see her half-sister in a whole new light. Callie had made some mistakes, but she was strong, determined, and loyal. And she was brave in the face of danger. They were qualities Skye admired.

Since the DEA had arrived early that morning, they had been going over their strategies and plans. Supervisory Special Agent Derrick Cross was running the show, a lean, broad-shouldered man with neatly trimmed brown hair, a cookie-cutter version of a federal agent, who, for the most part, seemed to know what he was doing.

Edge had given Agent Cross access to the drone footage revealing the laboratory inside the third metal building. In exchange, no charges would be filed against the three people who had illegally entered the compound to rescue an alleged kidnap victim.

But Cross refused to let Edge, Skye, or anyone else accompany his agents during the raid. Instead, Skye stood next to Edge outside the perimeter, Callie and Trace not far away.

They had arrived in the Yukon and parked out of sight behind a row of black government vehicles. Low hills blocked the view of the front gate, but it wasn't far away. The entire area had been cordoned off, no traffic allowed on the road in either direction. Agents in black tactical gear had been dispersed around the entire perimeter of the compound.

With the possibility of a hostage situation, a DEA crisis negotiator assigned to SSA Cross's team waited tensely in a big black van, ready to make contact with the Reverend Daniel Henson. The hope was that he would give himself up peacefully, along with his men.

Skye glanced over at Edge, her tension escalating with every second that passed.

"I don't like it," Edge said, checking his watch for the umpteenth time. "Too many unknowns." His gaze went to the low hills blocking their view of the compound. "Something should have happened by now."

"Cross seems competent," Skye said, mostly to make herself feel better. "If they rush things, people could end up getting killed."

Callie's head came up. "You think that's what's going to happen?" She had finally stopped pacing and now hovered nervously next to Trace in front of his black SUV.

"They'll focus on the meth lab," Trace answered. "But they can't ignore the possibility that some of Henson's men are holed up in the church or the cottages."

"They'll do whatever it takes to secure the location," Edge said.

Skye reached over and caught Callie's hand. "You need to stay positive."

"Stay positive," Edge repeated. "But be prepared if things don't go the way they're planned."

Callie didn't say more.

Trace shoved away from where he leaned against the Yukon. "They should have let us go in with them. We've been inside. We know the terrain." His gaze went toward the location of the gate as if willing himself to see through the mountain. "What the hell is taking them so long?"

Skye gasped as a huge blast rocked the ground beneath her feet.

"Oh, my God!" Callie's gaze shot to the column of thick black smoke billowing up from the location of the third metal building. A second blast followed, shaking the earth, then a third, the explosions filling the air with dirt and debris.

The blast also set off the sirens in the compound.

"Fuck." Edge's hands balled into fists as he watched the heavy wall of smoke rising into the air.

"They . . . they blew up the lab," Callie said needlessly.

Skye gripped Edge's arm. "You think there were agents inside?"

His jaw went tight as they both imagined the hellfire the explosion had rained down on anyone who happened to be too near.

Callie started walking. "I'm not staying here any longer. My friend is in there. She might need my help."

Trace caught up with her and turned her to face him. "Let me take a look first, see if it's safe." He glanced at Edge, who nodded.

Trace grabbed a pair of binoculars and took off walking, heading for a gully that led up the hill, making his way to a vantage point on top where he could look down into the compound. He returned a few minutes later.

"DEA's got agents all over the place. No sign of the women or any of Henson's men."

"I'm tired of waiting," Edge said. "Let's go." They all piled into the Yukon, Trace behind the wheel. He pulled out from between two parked vehicles, drove back onto the main road, and headed the short distance to the compound.

As the Yukon reached the front gate, which stood open, agents swarmed the grounds inside, too busy to worry about a vehicle they had seen parked outside and figured was somehow connected to the raid.

Trace pulled through the gate, got as far as the church before two agents in black tactical gear ablaze with big yellow DEA letters stepped in front of the car, blocking their way.

One of them walked around to the window, an assault rifle slung across his chest. "Sorry, this area is closed. How did you get in here?"

"Edge Logan. We're working with SSA Cross." He flipped out his PI badge. "We saw the explosion and figured you might need some help."

"You can park over there." The agent pointed to a spot out of the way in front of the church. Trace parked, and all of them got out.

"Skye Delaney." Skye flashed her badge as she walked back to the agent. "We have women friends in here. We need to find them, make sure they're okay."

"Special Agent Joe Monroe." Of medium height and well-built, he had a hard, serious face under his black ballistic helmet. "The women are all in the church, but you can't talk to them until they've been interviewed and we've taken their statements. Sorry."

"I live here," Callie said, her chin lifting. "My name is Callie Delaney, and the women in there are my friends. I'm going in." Without waiting for permission, she whirled and marched off toward the wide front steps leading up to the front doors of the church.

The agent swore beneath his breath. Plucking his cell out of a pocket, he made a call, spoke briefly, then hung up the phone.

"Ms. Delaney can stay, but the rest of you need to leave. This place is toxic. We had guys in hazmat suits ready to go in, but the building turned out to be wired. The explosion nixed the plan."

Skye and Edge both looked past Agent Monroe to the thick smoke still climbing into the sky at the far end of the compound.

"Any casualties?" Edge asked.

"Lucky for us, the bomb went off before we entered the structure. Except for the women, the entire compound was empty when we got here."

"So no sign of Henson or his goons," Trace said darkly.

Edge softly cursed.

Henson was in the wind, just as Skye and Edge had feared. Skye prayed the forensic squad would find prints and DNA that would give the DEA the identities of the men and a way to track them.

She looked up to see Callie coming back down the steps, wiping a tear from her cheek. Worry slipped through her. They spoke for a moment, and the two of them walked back to the Yukon, Skye's arm around Callie's shoulders. Trace opened the rear passenger door, and Callie slid wordlessly into the back seat.

"What happened?" Edge asked Skye as she drew near.

"Of the twelve women who lived here, only six were in the church. Callie's friend Lila wasn't one of them."

"Molly's back in Denver. Callie's here. That leaves four of them unaccounted for."

"Two of the women had children with the men they were living with. According to Callie, she wasn't surprised they left with their men."

"That leaves two."

"Lila and a woman named Stella Beeker. Callie says Stella had nowhere else to go. She was willing to take any kind of abuse from her husband rather than be out on the streets again."

"What's her husband's name?" Edge asked.

"Riley. Apparently Riley Beeker and Molly's husband, Harley Purcell, are two of Henson's top men."

CHAPTER FIFTEEN

Daniel Henson opened the door to the safe house set up for exactly this purpose, a secure location to regroup and start the planning for a new operation. Driving all night, they had made the long trip from Blancha Springs to the small town of Hays, Kansas, without mishap. For the moment, they were safe.

Daniel's back teeth clenched as he thought of Callie Delaney and the trouble the girl had caused. Because of Callie, Callie's sister and Edge Logan had stumbled on their meth operation and brought in the law. He knew how the authorities worked, the slow-turning wheels that set an operation in motion. He and his men had been long gone by the time the DEA had finally arrived.

But the cost had been substantial.

Daniel stepped back to let Lila walk past him into the house. Dutch Hendrix and Harley Purcell followed, then Riley Beeker and his woman, Stella. Dutch, Harley, and Beeker were his most trusted men, the only ones who would be going with him to the new location. The rest had scattered like dust in the wind—exactly the strategy he had planned.

Lila walked over and sank down on the threadbare beige sofa. The nineteen-sixties, single-story tract house smelled like stale cigarettes and beer. The place turned his stomach, but it was just a short stay before he and his people would be on their way.

He cast a glance at Lila. Forced to come with him at gunpoint, Lila had been sullen and moody all the way to their destination.

Daniel didn't care. She wasn't there for conversation. She would learn her duties tonight in his bed.

He shouldn't have brought her, he knew, but he'd been wanting her for weeks. He'd sent her husband off to work somewhere else, then told her he had died in a car accident. Raul was dead. At least that part was true. He had given her time to grieve, hoping to find a new disciple in the meantime, someone to give him ease while he waited, but he had been too busy to find the right woman.

He glanced at Lila, his gaze going over her lush breasts, small waist, and full, tempting hips. He would begin her teachings tonight, make sure she understood who was boss. At the moment, he needed to call his employer, get final instructions.

Crossing the room to the kitchen, he opened the shallow drawer next to the sink and took out a disposable phone. Entering the area code for Las Vegas followed by the number, he pressed the phone against his ear.

"You in a secure location?" the deep voice asked after only two rings.

"We're here. Everything went exactly per the emergency plan. What are my instructions?"

"You'll be setting up in a spot in northern New Mexico, a parcel in the mountains outside the town of Chamaya. Basically, it's a large piece of land in the middle of nowhere. You'll be opening a halfway house, a rehab center for newly released prisoners, a place to help them make the transition from prison to civilian life."

Daniel smiled, though it was a damned long haul from their safe house in Kansas. "That's pure genius. Manpower in an operation like this is one of our biggest problems."

"We've got a contact in the Tierra Amarilla detention facility and one in the Corrections and Probation Department in Española. They'll be screening the prisoners being released, looking for the right fit. The men will understand the opportunity they're being given and what is required in exchange. You'll have all the manpower you need."

"There's definitely nowhere else they can earn that kind of money."

"They'll be needing women—best way to keep them happy and under control. Since you handled that before, I'm assuming you can manage it again."

"I'll make it work." New Mexico fronted the southern border. There were always people entering illegally, women desperate enough to do anything to keep themselves alive. Once they were inside the facility, they wouldn't be leaving.

"Any questions?" asked the man on the other end of the line. "Anything you need?"

"After I get there, take a look at the setup, and get things organized, there might be something I'll need. I'll keep you posted on our progress."

"You do that."

"Of course."

"And Henson?"

"Yes, Mr. Petrov?"

"Next time be more careful. Setting up a facility like the last one isn't cheap. If things go bad this time, you'll be paying the cost personally, if you know what I mean." The line went dead, and a chill slid down Daniel's spine.

Petrov's message was clear. Another failure and he was a dead man. Anger swept through him. The bastard had no right to threaten him after the millions of dollars Daniel had made for him over the years.

Daniel's hand fisted. He looked at Lila. He would never use his fists on a woman, but there were other ways he could vent his frustrations. His body hardened at the thought of the lessons he meant to teach her.

CHAPTER SIXTEEN

Skye rode with Trace and Callie back to Denver, while Edge followed in his Nissan. After a long night of dealing with the police, Skye was exhausted. Halfway through the journey, she fell asleep and didn't wake until Trace pulled up in front of her apartment building.

She waved as he drove away, undoubtedly as grateful as she was to be heading home and getting some badly needed sleep.

Molly was waiting when Skye and Callie walked into the apartment.

"Callie!" Molly rushed toward her, opened her arms, and enfolded her in a hug. "Thank God you're safe!"

Callie swallowed and hugged her back. "We're safe, but not everyone else made it out. Henson and his men were all gone by the time the DEA arrived. They took some of the women with them." Her eyes filled. "Lila didn't get away."

Molly hugged her again, then took her hand. "Come on. I'll help you get settled, and you can tell me everything that's happened."

"You need to call your mom, Callie," Skye reminded her. "Now that you're back in the city. You know how she worries."

"I'll call her right away," Callie promised as Molly led her down the hall to Skye's guest room. Since Callie didn't want to move in with her mother, the women would be sharing Skye's second bedroom while they looked for work and started putting their lives back together.

In the meantime, Skye had plans of her own.

She looked up as a firm knock sounded at her door. She checked the peephole and was only a little surprised to see Edge standing in the hallway. He wasn't there for her, she reminded herself. He would want to debrief, hear any other details Callie might have learned from the women inside the church.

"Everything okay?" he asked as Skye stepped back to invite him in. Both of them were still dressed in the black jeans and sweaters they'd had on when they'd gone into the compound the night before.

"The girls are getting settled. Callie needs a chance to digest everything that's happened."

Edge nodded. "I could use a little breather myself."

Skye watched him cross the room. His features looked tense, his broad shoulders tight as he took a seat on the sofa, resting his tall, hard body against the cushions behind his back.

It took a while to unwind after a mission. It had been a tough few days.

"You want a drink?" Skye asked, definitely needing one herself.

Leaning back, Edge spread his arms across the top of the sofa. "God knows I could use one."

"Whiskey, beer, or a glass of wine?"

"Whiskey."

"That makes two of us." She usually drank wine, but as she thought of Henson, the women in the compound, and the explosion that could have killed a lot of good people, a straight shot of whiskey seemed a better idea.

She headed for the ultra-modern stainless-steel kitchen that opened into the living room. After her very profitable trip to Mexico and her PI earnings, she had plenty of money, which her luxury high-rise apartment reflected.

The kitchen and cabinets were white, the countertops gray-and-white granite. Barnwood gray hardwood floors ran throughout the living room, two bedrooms, and two and a half baths. The apartment was sleek and modern, done entirely in white and dove gray with dark blue accents. The view of Denver through a wall of glass shared with the master bedroom was spectacular.

The apartment was walking distance to the office, not far from a similar apartment building where Edge lived. She had only been there once, when he'd had a party and invited the entire Nighthawk crew, as well as his two brothers and their wives.

Edge had been with a curvy redhead that night, but Skye had never heard him mention her again.

As she poured two fingers of Jack Daniels into a pair of heavy crystal tumblers, she glanced over and noticed Edge watching her. His gaze traveled slowly from her face to her breasts, then returned to settle on her mouth. The look in those amazing blue eyes sparked a fire low in her belly.

It had been months since her failed attempt to have sex with her fiancé, more months before that in the hospital. She might have been injured in the war, but from the sexual pulse she was feeling as she looked at the virile, blue-eyed male on the sofa, clearly she wasn't dead yet.

It was only natural, she told herself. She had seen his naked, hard-muscled torso when Edge had stripped down in the heat of Mexico, remembered the six-pack abs, the thick biceps, and heavily muscled shoulders.

Working at Nighthawk, she saw fit, good-looking men every day, but none of them made her feel the abdomen-clenching desire burning through her now.

"I've been thinking," Edge said, rising and making his way to the kitchen counter to accept the drink she offered. "After what they've been through, Molly and Callie could probably both use some space. My place is bigger than yours, so I've got plenty of room. Why don't you stay with me until the girls get things worked out and find places of their own?"

Everything inside her froze. For days, Edge had been tossing out not-so-subtle invitations to join him in bed. This one was more than clear.

He wanted her.

And heaven knew, she wanted him.

Her mouth dried up. Her heart was beating so fast she felt dizzy. "I don't . . . don't think that's a good idea."

He rounded the counter and walked up behind her. She felt his hands on her shoulders, lightly massaging away the tension in her weary muscles. He unfastened the clip holding back her dark hair and pulled it aside, pressed his lips to the nape of her neck.

The tension returned to her body, followed by a soft melting sensation that poured out through her limbs.

"Why not?" he asked softly, moving to the side of her neck. Another soft kiss, and his teeth grazed an earlobe. "You could come back here whenever you wanted."

Her knees felt weak. She couldn't believe this was happening.

He curled a finger in the neck of her sweater and drew it aside, pressed a damp kiss on the curve of her shoulder. A tremor ran through her. Heat slid into her core. She worked to stifle a moan.

"It's not that far away," he said, his mouth returning to the side of her neck, trailing hot, wet kisses over her skin, making her shiver. "Walking distance." Desire swept through her, need she hadn't felt in months, maybe years.

She swallowed as she forced herself to turn and face him, rested her palms on his wide, hard chest. "What's changed, Edge? We've been working together for more than a year. Now all of a sudden—"

He caught her hands and held them in place on his chest. "It's not all of a sudden. I've wanted you from the moment I first saw you. But, like you said, we were working together. At the time, I figured taking you to bed was a bad idea for both of us. But the wanting just got worse. In Mexico, I forced myself to focus on the mission. People's lives were at stake. But I wanted you then—same as I want you now."

She shook her head. She could feel his solid strength in the hard sinews beneath her fingers.

Edge bent his head, and his mouth settled softly over hers. She couldn't resist opening for him, inviting him in. When he deepened the kiss, a little sound slipped from her throat.

This was Edge, and he was kissing her the way she had imagined a hundred times, softly coaxing, nibbling and tasting, kissing her and kissing her as if he couldn't get enough.

Knowing she should stop him, Skye let the kiss go on, her arms sliding up around his neck, her fingers curling into his thick black hair as she tumbled deeper under his spell.

If she hadn't heard the sound of the guest room door opening and footsteps coming down the hall, there was no telling where the kiss might have led.

Edge must have heard, too. He gently broke away and took a step back. "They need space. I need you, and after that kiss, I think there's a chance you need me, too. Think about it."

She'd think about it, all right. She wouldn't be able to think about anything else. But the answer would have to be no. Edge meant too much to her to risk the kind of reaction she'd had from Brian. Just the thought made her stomach churn.

Callie walked into the kitchen. She was too upset to notice the heat still simmering between Skye and Edge.

"Henson forced Lila to go with him," Callie said. "There's no other explanation." She had changed into brown yoga pants and a pink knit sweater, clothes Molly must have purchased with the money Skye had given her. "We have to find them. We have to help Lila. I gave her my word."

Edge started shaking his head.

Callie ignored him. "You're detectives, right? You and Skye? Finding people is what you do. Once I get a job, I'll have money. I can pay whatever you want."

"It's not the money," Edge said.

"Edge is right," Skye said. "It's not the money. You don't have to worry about that. I've already decided I'm going to find Henson. He's not getting away without paying for what he did to Sarah, to you and Molly and the rest of those women."

Sometime over the past few hours, Henson's actions had become personal. He'd managed to escape the DEA, but Skye was going to find him. She was a private investigator, and she was a good one. She was going to hunt Daniel Henson down and bring him to justice.

"Both of you stop right there," Edge said. "This is DEA business now. You get in the middle of it, you'll be interfering in a federal investigation."

"I don't care!" Callie said, jamming her hands on her hips. "Lila needs my help. You don't know what Henson's like, what he might do to her. Sarah's dead. Lila could be next. I have to help her get away."

Callie's eyes filled, and Skye pulled her into a hug. "I'm going to find out where he's gone," Skye said. "Once I know his location, I can bring in law enforcement. The feds will be looking for him, too. If Lila's with him, they can help us get her to safety."

Edge blew out a breath, paced away to stare out the window, then walked back. "I had a bad feeling this wasn't over." He looked at Skye hard. "Dammit, are you sure about this?"

Skye felt the impact of those intense blue eyes, but it couldn't dissuade her. "I'm going after Henson. It may take me a while to find him, but once I do—"

Edge swore softly. "All right, fine. If you're that determined to do this, count me in."

Skye felt a rush of relief she wished she didn't feel. Not only would she be working with a partner she could count on, she would be spending more time with Edge.

It was early Monday morning. Conner Delaney's dark head bent over the wide oak desk in his office. He finished his call to Zoey Rosen, the office digital forensic expert, and hung up the phone, then looked up as a knock sounded on his door. The knob turned, and the door swung open without his permission.

Edge Logan walked into the room.

"Well, come right on in." Used to the aggressive males who worked in his office, Conn leaned back in his chair. "What can I do for you at this hour of the morning?"

"I need to talk to you," Edge said. He was as tall as Conn and as solidly built, but his hair was black instead of brown. Edge had been army, while Conn was a marine.

"I gathered that from the way you barged in here," Conn said.

Edge didn't smile. "It's about your sister."

Conn sat forward in his chair. "What about her?"

"I want to know what happened in Afghanistan."

Conn's shoulders stiffened. "She was wounded. They gave her a purple heart and a military discharge."

"I know that. I want to know what happened."

Conn just shook his head. "That's Skye's business. I don't talk about my sister. You want to know what happened, ask her."

Edge moved closer, flattened his palms on the desk and leaned forward, putting them face-to-face. "It's important, Conn. I need to know how badly she was injured."

"If you're worried about her being able to do her job—"

"It's nothing like that. I know how capable she is. This is personal."

Personal. For months, Conn had been watching the sparks building between Skye and Edge. But something always held them back. Since they were working together, he figured it was a smart move on both of their parts not to get involved.

"You can trust me," Edge said, pressing the issue.

One thing he knew—he could trust Edge Logan. He also knew Edge cut a wide swath through the female population of Denver. Conn didn't want his sister winding up on Edge's list of conquests.

On the other hand, after the accident, Skye's ex-fiancé, Brian Galen, had done a job on her self-esteem. Maybe Edge's attention would help her.

Conn settled back in his chair. "Skye enlisted right out of community college, probably influenced by the long list of family members who had served. She breezed through basic, excelled in marksmanship and hand-to-hand combat, wound up an army intel analyst stationed in Kandahar. She was good with languages, caught onto Farsi real fast. Skye was a good soldier, but you can't defend against an IED."

Edge remained quiet, silently urging Conn to continue.

"Skye was being ferried from one location to another when the Humvee she was riding in hit an IED. What was left of the Humvee landed upside down on fire, with Skye half dazed in the back seat. She was able to crawl out, but the guy next to her was pinned inside. Skye managed to pry him free, but the Humvee exploded as they were trying to escape. Flying pieces of hot metal knocked her unconscious. A heavy chunk landed on her left leg, causing third degree burns from mid-thigh to ankle."

Edge's blue eyes remained on Conn. "There's more. There has to be."

"The portion of her leg that was injured is badly disfigured. The doctors did a series of skin grafts, but they didn't do much good."

"What else? Skye was a soldier. She would have accepted the possibility she could be wounded when she joined the army. There's something else."

There was, indeed, something else. Resigned now and hoping he was making the right decision, Conn finished the story.

"Skye was engaged at the time she was wounded. Months later, after she got out of the hospital, the first night she and Brian spent together, he couldn't get it up. He said her leg was repulsive, said he couldn't handle it. Skye broke the engagement the following day and never saw the bastard again."

The look in Edge's eyes could have sliced a man to bloody bits. "*Brian*. What's his last name?"

Conn shook his head. "No way. He's out of the picture and no longer living in Denver. I've told you what you wanted to know—now leave it alone."

Jaw hard, Edge turned and strode to the door. "Thanks for telling me." He reached for the doorknob.

"One more thing," Conn said, stopping him. "Don't hurt her, Edge. Skye's been hurt enough already."

Edge's jaw hardened even more. Jerking the door open, he strode out of the office.

CHAPTER SEVENTEEN

Edge didn't work the rest of that day. Instead, he took time off to get his head on straight about a couple of things and recover from mission failure.

That was how he saw it. True, they'd gotten Callie Delaney out of the compound safely, as well as Molly Lockhart. Their work had managed to send Daniel Henson packing, which had freed most of the rest of the women, but it was more than likely Henson was still in business, just setting up shop somewhere else.

Trying to catch up on sleep lost during the all-nighter they had pulled in Blancha Springs, Edge caught a late-afternoon nap. It was dark when he awoke. He spent a little time on the computer, digging for info on Henson, came up with mostly old news.

The afternoon faded, and darkness crept over the city. He felt caged and restless, his mind going back again and again to the story Conn Delaney had told him about Skye. As he sprawled on the comfortable burgundy leather sofa in his living room, Conn's words echoed in his head.

Don't hurt her, Edge. Skye's been hurt enough already.

The last thing he'd ever want to do was hurt Skye. He wanted her, yes. More than any woman he could recall. And after that kiss in her kitchen, he was pretty damn sure she wanted him, too.

But there was no way to know if a relationship between them would work. Over the years, he'd dated plenty of women, but none of the affairs had lasted more than a few days or weeks. Everything about Skye felt different, his need for her somehow deeper, almost vital.

Still, there was no real way to predict what might happen, and he didn't want to jeopardize a friendship he valued so greatly.

Along with that, sooner or later, he'd find a way to clear his name and return to the Green Berets. It was what he was trained for, what he was meant to do. He'd rain justice down on Major Bradley Markham and get his life back.

What if they were together? He'd be deployed most of the year. It wouldn't be fair to Skye to tie her to a man who wouldn't be there for her.

It was dark outside the tall glass windows in the living room, the lights of the city sparkling for miles in all directions. Edge tried to motivate himself to go into the kitchen and fix something to eat, or at least call for a pizza delivery, but after his conversation with Conn, his appetite had waned.

He straightened on the sofa. Elbows on his knees, he sat with his head tipped forward into his hands. He'd leave Skye alone, he told himself. No matter how tough it would be, he'd stay away from her, do his best to put things back the way they were before that earth-shattering kiss.

He thought of Henson. Skye intended to find him. Edge had promised to help her, had given her his word. That meant more time together, more sleepless nights aching for her.

Maybe he could talk to Trace, convince Trace to take his place. Trace was smart, strong, and capable, and he'd do everything in his power to protect one of his best friends.

He was also a damn good-looking man, one any red-blooded female would find attractive.

A knot tightened in his stomach. Trace and Skye were just friends, but still . . .

And what about Henson? No matter how much he trusted Trace's abilities, Henson and his men were deadly opponents. Skye could be injured or even killed. Edge needed to be there to make sure she was safe.

His head came up at the sound of a knock on the door. It was getting late, and he wasn't expecting visitors. As he crossed the room, he flicked a glance at the drawer in the side table where he kept a little .380 semiauto. His job pissed off a lot of people. Better to be safe than sorry.

He checked the eyehole, felt a jolt when he saw it was Skye. For an instant, he couldn't look away. With her thick dark hair curling softly around her shoulders, a fuzzy pink cashmere sweater curving over her breasts, and a long, malt-brown wool skirt flaring around a pair of brown leather ankle boots, she looked luscious.

He stepped back as he pulled open the door. "Hi." He worked not to stare. She looked even more feminine than usual—and even more tempting.

"I didn't think you'd be asleep yet," she said as she walked past him into the apartment.

For the first time, he noticed the carry-on she rolled in behind her, and everything inside him went still.

"What's the matter?" She looked up at him with those pretty sea-green eyes. Then her gaze shot toward the hall leading to his bedroom, and a flush rose in her cheeks. "Someone's here. I should have called. I feel like an idiot. I'm sorry." She started to turn around, but Edge stepped in the way, blocking her retreat.

"No one's here. No one but you." He kicked the door closed with his boot as he backed her up against the wall and kissed her. He'd vowed to leave her alone, put things back the way they were before, but Fate had intervened. Since he was no match for Fate, he would follow the path that stretched out in front of him, find out where it might lead.

Edge gentled the kiss, coaxing now, his lips moving softly over hers. He could feel her response in the way she melted against him. She was here. *Finally.* He didn't want to ruin things by moving too fast. Reluctantly, he eased away.

"I'm glad you decided to come over." He glanced toward the bedroom. *Too soon. Take it easy.* "How are the girls doing? Are they getting settled in?"

"They're fine. Talking about the past and making plans for the future."

He nodded. "That's good. So . . . are you hungry? You want something to eat? We could call for pizza or have Chinese food delivered. I know you like Chinese."

Skye's tension eased. She relaxed and smiled. "You're nervous. You don't ever get nervous."

He smiled. "Maybe I'm a little nervous. You're here. I really wanted you to come stay with me."

She rested a hand on his cheek. He should have shaved, he thought, gotten rid of his days' growth of beard.

Skye didn't seem to mind. She went up on her toes and very softly kissed him. "I wanted to be here. It took a while for me to get up the courage, but I've wanted to be with you like this for a very long time."

"Yeah?"

She smiled. "Yeah."

Edge relaxed. He was good with women. He knew what they liked and how to give them what they wanted.

Still, this was different. This was Skye.

"So . . . pizza or Chinese?"

"Is that really what you want, Edge? Or is it me you want?"

He was already aroused. He went even harder. "You're what I want. I've wanted you for months, wanted you for what seems like forever. I just . . . I don't want to rush you."

Skye simply stepped into his arms. "I don't want Chinese."

Edge bit back a groan and kissed her. What started soft and gentle deepened and went hotter, wetter, mouths mating, bodies straining to get closer. Every second felt like an eternity—or an instant—he couldn't be sure. He wanted more, wanted everything. Wanted all of her, and he wanted it now.

Instead, he just kept kissing her. One of his hands fisted in her thick dark curls, and he tipped her head back to trail kisses along her slender throat. He could feel her heart beating, her pulse thrumming faster than his own.

He wanted to take her against the wall, drag her down on the floor. It didn't matter. He just wanted her.

His brain finally began to settle, to accept what was going to happen. Scooping her up in his arms, he carried her down the hall to his bedroom. They had all night, he reminded himself, as he set her on her feet next to his king-size bed and started kissing her again.

Soft pink lips, the scent of flowers on her skin, the sexy taste of her. God, he could kiss her forever.

He felt her palms on his chest as she eased a little away from him. "Before this happens, we need to talk."

He only shook his head. "I think we've talked enough. You're here. I'm here. We both want the same thing." He leaned over to kiss her again, but Skye moved away.

"It's about my leg. I need you to be prepared. I don't want this to go wrong." Her eyes filled, and he wanted to kill her ex-fiancé.

"It's not going to go wrong. I know what happened in Afghanistan. Your brother told me."

Her head came up. "Conn talked about me behind my back?"

"I forced the issue. I told him it was important. I needed to know what was holding you back. I know you were wounded. I know what the explosion did to your leg. I don't care."

She blinked away the wetness. "You might when you see what's left of me."

He caught her shoulders. "I've seen men blown in half right in front of me. I've seen men's chests ripped open by shrapnel. Your leg isn't the part of you I'm interested in." His hands slid down to cup the ripe fullness of her breasts. A thumb brushed over her nipple, which hardened into a tight bud, and a little sound escaped her throat. "Do you trust me?"

She moistened her kiss-swollen lips. "You know I do. I've trusted you with my life more than once."

"Then trust me with your body. Trust me to make everything come out right."

The uncertainty faded from her eyes, turned into a flash of the confidence that was so much a part of her. Reaching for the hem of her sweater, she pulled it off over her head and tossed it away, shook out her heavy dark hair. A lacy pink bra thrust up pale twin globes like a feast he couldn't wait to devour. He moved closer, pressed his mouth to the soft swell of one and then the other.

Skye unhooked her bra and tossed it away, and Edge groaned as the fullness spilled into his palms.

"Beautiful," he said, kissing her again, trailing kisses lower, till his mouth replaced his hands. He could feel her trembling as he suckled and tasted, laved and savored each delectable mound.

Things progressed more rapidly after that. Both of them stripped off their clothes and stood facing each other, Skye holding her skirt in front of her, the last barrier to her nakedness.

Edge eased the skirt from her hands and tossed it over a chair. Conn hadn't lied. The leg wound was severe, the burn scars ugly. Skye looked at him as he caught her hips and began kissing his way down her body, from her breasts to her naval, along her left thigh, crouching, moving lower, trailing kisses all the way to her scarred ankle. She made a little sound in her throat.

Edge rose and very gently kissed her. "Do you know what I see when I look at your leg?"

Skye swallowed but said nothing.

"I see a badge of courage. A mark of heroism. I see a woman who sacrificed herself to save the life of a fellow soldier." He drew her closer, till her body pressed the length of his. "You feel that?" He was hard against her belly. "That's how much I want you. Nothing is going to change that."

With a quiet sob, Skye went into his arms. He held her a moment before his mouth came down over hers. The kiss lingered, deepened. It didn't take long before both of them were panting, their hearts racing. Lifting her against his chest, he settled her in the middle of his big bed and eased down beside her. He spent time enjoying her breasts, ran his hands over her narrow waist and flat belly, began to stroke her.

Skye shifted restlessly, her arousal strengthening, growing hot enough to match his own. "I want you so much," she said. "Please, Edge."

"Soon, I promise." He kissed her again as he moved and settled himself between her legs. *Soon, but not yet.* Not until he had her stirring impatiently beneath him, not until her thighs parted even wider, urging him to take her.

He felt her fingers digging into the muscles across his shoulders. "Edge, please . . . I need you."

He needed her, too. She had no idea how much.

He took care of protection, then returned to kissing her, arousing her all over again, at the same time working to hold himself back. His jaw clenched at the pleasure sweeping through him as he slid himself inside.

He tried to give her time to adjust to his size, the depth of his invasion, but his control was rapidly slipping. He had just started to move when her body tightened around him, her muscles contracted, and the first ripples of climax struck.

Determined to make it good for her, he increased his rhythm, moving deeper, faster, taking her harder. Skye came again, and he could no longer hold back. He'd wanted her too long, resisted his need for what seemed ages. Clenching his teeth, every muscle straining, he felt the rush, felt the all-consuming pleasure as he reached the powerful release he had craved for so long.

Seconds passed while his body lingered in the warm sweetness of hers. Finally, he came back to himself enough to lift his heavy weight off her. He took care of the condom and returned to settle beside her.

"You okay?" he asked, pulling her close. She nestled her cheek against his shoulder, and he felt her smile.

"Better than okay. Thank you for making this so easy."

"The pleasure was all mine, believe me." He was already hard again. He had wanted her for months. A whole night of lovemaking would only be a start.

She traced a finger through the dark whorls on his chest. "So . . . if I'm staying, I should probably get up and get settled in the guest room."

Edge grinned. "Not a chance." Kissing her again put an end to the subject. She was his for now, his for as long as this thing between them lasted, and he meant to enjoy every moment.

Tomorrow they would start the search for Daniel Henson.

There was no way to know what the future might bring or what danger he and Skye might be facing, but Edge would do everything in his power to protect her.

CHAPTER EIGHTEEN

FAINT GRAY LIGHT SEEPED THROUGH THE CURTAINS OVER THE BIG glass windows in the bedroom. Skye had been awake for hours, thinking of last night and the huge mistake she had made.

She had known her feelings for Edge ran deep. She hadn't understood that she was falling in love with him. Not until last night. She had never imagined how tender he could be, that he could make her feel as if she were the only woman in the world. As if she were a beautiful temptress he couldn't resist.

Her leg didn't seem to matter. She had never felt sexier or more appealing than when Edge made love to her. After the second time, she'd told him she was on the pill, and he had told her he'd just had a physical and been pronounced fit.

Skye had no doubt of that. The man had the body of a warrior. Hard-muscled shoulders, six-pack abs, mouth-watering biceps—she couldn't get enough of him.

Without a condom, round three was even better than the first two times. Good Lord, she'd had no idea she was such a passionate woman.

As he lay curled around her spoon-fashion, she listened to his deep, even breathing, and almost smiled, would have if the truth weren't so frightening. She was already more than half in love with him, and there was no way it would last.

Edge wasn't into relationships. He wasn't a one-woman man—

at least not for long. She should have considered the consequences before she had thrown herself at him.

Not that Edge seemed to mind.

She felt him stir as he began to awaken, felt the thick ridge of his sex nudging her from behind. He wanted more of her, and as long as he did, she would give him what he wanted, give them both what they wanted.

Easing her legs apart, she encouraged him to take her, felt the glide of rigid heat as he slid himself inside. Soon work would intrude, her promise to Callie to find Daniel Henson and free Lila Ramirez.

In the meantime, Skye closed her eyes and felt the hot press of Edge's mouth against the back of her neck, felt the sweep of pleasure as he adjusted her position and came up on his knees behind her. Skye picked up the rhythm he set, felt the surge of hungry need as their bodies moved in perfect unison toward the peak.

There was plenty of time, she told herself. The day was only getting started. Her problems could wait a little while longer.

Still wearing her fluffy, pink flowered robe, Skye sat at the breakfast table in front of her laptop an hour later, working on leads that might help her locate Daniel Henson.

She heard Edge's footsteps approaching, felt his lips against the nape of her neck.

"Morning." He took her cup of cold coffee and handed her a fresh hot mug.

"Thanks." She took a sip, enjoying the rich, delicious taste that reminded her of Edge's dark, arousing kisses.

"Any luck?" he asked.

"Actually, I did have a bit of luck this morning. I found out who owns the property where Henson's compound was located."

"Sunstar Corporation out of Denver," Edge said, taking a sip of his coffee.

"That's right."

"Unfortunately, that's as far as I got."

Skye smiled. "I got a little further. Sunstar is owned by two corporations, each owned by two different companies. I need to look at the corporate filings, see who's listed on the board of directors, see if I can find a name or names that overlap. It's going to take some time."

"In other words, the actual ownership of the land is buried."

"Exactly."

"Which strengthens our theory that Henson works for someone else."

She took a sip of coffee and glanced up at him over her shoulder. "I'm calling Zoey Rosen. We'll see what she can find out. We've talked in the office a couple of times, but I've never asked for her help. Conn swears she's a miracle worker."

Zoe was a recent addition to the Nighthawk crew, a digital forensics expert. She had majored in computer science at the University of Colorado, was working as a computer analyst when Conn hired her. According to office gossip, Zoe had been fascinated with computers, gaming, and the Internet all her life and could find out just about anything—as long as no one asked how she did it.

"She's helped me a few times," Edge said. "Computer searches aren't my long suit."

Skye hid a grin. "I found out what your long suit is last night."

Edge laughed. "It's still early. We could go back to bed for a while."

She did smile then. "Tempting, but we have work to do—which you very well know."

He nodded, sipped his coffee. "I do." Edge padded off to shower and dress, and Skye phoned Zoe Rosen.

"Skye. Nice to hear from you. We still need to make time for lunch one day soon."

"We sure do," Skye said.

Zoey was a petite woman, cute and spunky, with a pixie face and short blond hair. Zoe's friend, Ellie Bowman, a PI with Nighthawk, now married to Edge's brother Kade, had told Skye that Zoe's nickname in college was Tinkerbelle. She looked the part.

"So what can I do for you?" Zoe asked.

"I'm investigating a guy named Daniel Henson. I'm hoping you can help." Skye filled Zoe in on Henson, the Children of the Sun, the DEA raid, and the missing woman, Lila Ramirez. She mentioned there could be other women with Henson and his men, but it was primarily Lila they were hoping to help.

"I dug around a little this morning," Skye said, then relayed the information she'd come up with on the Sunstar Corporation.

"A lot of stuff has been written about Daniel Henson," Skye continued. "Father deceased, no siblings, but father and son were both preachers. Nothing I could find that connects Daniel with drugs. The raid put him on the run. With the kind of money involved, there's a good chance he's setting up shop somewhere else."

"If Henson leaves any kind of trail," Zoe said, "I'll find him."

"It's just a gut feeling, but Edge and I both think Henson's working for someone else. We need to know the name of the guy at the top of the food chain."

"What about the men who worked for him? You have any names?"

"I got a partial list from my sister. She didn't know all of them. I did a little digging. A guy named Webb Rankin has a warrant out for armed robbery. Klaus Mahler is wanted for sexual assault on a twenty-two-year-old woman in Omaha, Nebraska. There was nothing on Harley Purcell or Riley Beeker, two of Henson's top men. I have a feeling a lot of the men were using aliases."

"What about the women?"

"I took a look. One had a history of drug abuse, another had a couple of arrests for prostitution. From what my sister said, some of them were living on the street, others were just misfits, people looking for a home. They all saw Henson as some kind of savior." Like Callie, who was grieving for her dead father.

"Scan the names and send them to me," Zoe said.

"Will do."

"If you think of anything else, text me."

"Thanks, Zoe."

"Thank me when I have something." Zoe hung up the phone.

In black jeans and a rust-colored Henley that hugged his wide chest, Edge walked back in, towel-drying his thick black hair. It was longer now than it had been in Mexico. Skye thought it looked even sexier than before. Her mind shot back to last night, the things he had done to her, the things she had done to him, and a flush rose in her cheeks.

"Do any good with Zoe?" Edge asked, hopefully oblivious to her thoughts as he tossed the damp towel over a kitchen chair. His galley-style, stainless-steel kitchen, done in white with black granite countertops, was as modern and streamlined as her own.

"Zoe's on it. I'm sending her the list of people who were in the compound. Unfortunately, it's incomplete. Nothing on Beeker or Purcell."

"DEA will have prints and DNA. They may be able to figure out who was there, but that doesn't mean they'll be able to find them." Edge's brilliant blue eyes moved over her. He caught her hand, pulled her up from her place behind the computer and into his arms.

"You have any idea how good you look in that fluffy little robe, your pretty curls mussed from what we did this morning." He smiled. "I had no idea what a distraction you were going to be." Then he bent his head, and his lips covered hers.

Skye kissed him back, fighting to ignore the melting sensation in the pit of her stomach. She managed to ease away before it was too late. "Work," she reminded him.

Edge threw up his hands. "Okay, okay."

Needing to shower and dress, Skye turned toward the hall leading to the guest bath just as Edge's cell began to ring. He pulled the phone out of his pocket and checked the caller ID.

"It's Akins," he said.

Barefoot, Skye padded back to him. She couldn't hear the other side of the conversation, but Edge's jaw looked tight.

"I'd appreciate if you'd keep us posted, Sheriff." He nodded. "Will do."

Edge turned to Skye. "They found Sarah's body. The coroner

hasn't ID'd her yet or specified official cause of death, but Akins said they could tell she'd been badly beaten, and there were signs of strangulation."

"Oh, God."

"It's going to be tough on Callie."

"Yes, and she'll be terrified for Lila."

"We're going to find her," Edge said.

Skye prayed it was true. "Callie only knew Sarah by her married name, Rankin, which could very well be fake. Once the coroner ID's her, we can start looking into her background."

"Be good if we could talk to some of the other women, but without Akins's help, it'll be tough to find them."

"Zoe's going to take a look."

He nodded. "In the meantime, let's talk to Callie and Molly again, see if there's something they might not realize they know."

"Good idea. I'll go take a shower." She started down the hall.

"Want some company?" Edge called after her.

Skye's insides clenched. "No," she said and wondered if Edge knew it was a lie.

CHAPTER NINETEEN

"READY TO HEAD OVER TO MY PLACE?" SKYE ASKED.

Edge's gaze ran over her. She looked good—too good—her dark curls loose around her shoulders, her cheeks still flushed from her time in the shower. He felt a familiar stirring in his loins, forced himself to ignore it.

"I thought about calling," she said. "But I'd rather keep it casual. No stress, just a few easy questions."

"Good idea."

They walked the few blocks to Skye's apartment building, and Edge pulled open the big glass front door. As they crossed the lobby, he looked up to see Trace walking toward them.

"I came over to check on Molly," he said, "but she isn't here. Callie says she packed her things and left early this morning."

"Oh, no," Skye said.

"I hope she knows what she's doing," Edge added.

"She's afraid of her ex," Trace needlessly explained, since they all knew exactly why Molly had run.

"Did she tell Callie where she was going?" Skye asked.

"She has friends somewhere in the Midwest," Trace said. "Apparently, that's all she was willing to say."

Edge set a hand at Skye's waist. "Let's go on up, see if there's anything else Callie can tell us."

Skye waived to the guard in the lobby, a pudgy guy who recognized her as one of the residents. The guard waved back, and they started for the elevators.

Trace's deep voice stopped them. "Ask Callie to tell Molly I stopped by to see if she was okay, will you?"

"You bet," Edge said. Trace was one of the good guys. He was worried about the young woman he'd helped rescue. If Harley Purcell decided to go after her, Trace might have good reason to be concerned.

They headed upstairs, and Callie opened the door to let them in.

"Molly's gone," she said first thing. "I tried to stop her, but she wouldn't listen. She's terrified Harley will find her."

"Trace told us," Skye said.

"You know where she was headed?" Edge asked.

"She said it was better if I didn't know. That way Harley couldn't force me to tell."

"Harley isn't coming near you," Skye promised.

"Not if we find him first," Edge added. "To do that we need your help." Their hope was that Purcell would be with Henson and they could round up the whole lot of them.

Callie sighed. "I've told you everything I know. What more can I do?"

"Maybe nothing," Edge said. "On the other hand, if we go over everything again step-by-step, maybe you'll remember some little detail, something that might turn out to be useful."

Callie nodded. "Sure. Okay."

"Why don't I make us a pot of coffee?" Skye suggested. "Then we'll talk."

As the women worked together at the kitchen counter, Edge heard Skye telling Callie that Sarah's body had been found, followed by Callie's quick intake of breath.

"Those vicious bastards," Callie said, wiping tears from her cheeks. "I can't believe the DEA let them get away."

"The investigation is only getting started," Skye reminded her as the coffee brewed.

"We'd like to talk to someone in Sarah's family," Edge said. "Any idea what her name was before she married Rankin?"

"After we got back to Denver, I remembered Lila mentioning it. Her name was Sarah Simmons. Mostly the women used their husband's names. It was what Daniel expected."

"Speaking of Daniel," Skye said, taking down some mugs. "Do you have any idea where he might have gone? What plans he might have made for an emergency exit?"

"Guy like him," Edge added, "odds are he'd have an escape plan all worked out."

"Special Agent Cross asked me that question. At the time, I couldn't think of anything. I was pretty shook up. I tried to imagine where he might have taken Lila, but my mind just went blank."

"And now?" Edge pressed, accepting the steaming mug Skye handed him.

"This morning while Molly was packing, I remembered a phone call Daniel made while I was with him in the rectory. I'm not sure where it came from, but he called the man on the phone Mr. Petrov. I remember how respectful he sounded. Now I'm thinking it was fear I heard in his voice, not respect."

"Petrov," Edge repeated. "Sounds Russian. Might link to something we turn up. Thanks, Callie."

"I want those murderers caught. I want Lila safe."

"We're going to find her," Skye promised, a vow they both hoped they could keep.

While Edge drank his coffee, they went over events in the compound one more time, but no new intel surfaced, and without Molly or one of the other women to provide a fresh point of view, it was time to look in another direction.

"I've got the address for Sunstar," Skye said. "It's on Sixteenth Street in the Market Square Center. We need to check it out."

"Definitely worth a look, but there's something I need to do first." Instead of walking back to his place, Edge called an Uber and they waited on the sidewalk for the vehicle to arrive.

"Where are we going?" Skye asked as they climbed into the back seat of a white Toyota Corolla.

"I told you I needed another vehicle." Even before their trip to

Blancha Springs, Edge had decided to buy a second vehicle, one more suited to his work as an investigator. He'd purchased the snappy little sports car thinking he'd soon be returning to the Green Berets.

He gave the Uber driver the address for the Ford dealership on East Evans.

"So you bought a new car?" Skye said.

Edge smiled. "Sort of." Once they arrived, he paid the driver, and they started across the parking lot. There were rows of cars, both new and used, every size, color, and shape. He stopped in front of a big, lifted black Ford truck. "So . . . what do you think of this little beauty?"

The look on her face was priceless. "I definitely did not see this one coming." Skye flashed him a grin. "I never knew you were a pickup man."

Edge laughed, getting the reference to one of Skye's favorite country songs. "I grew up on a ranch. I tried to convince myself I needed an SUV, but I just couldn't quite get there."

"One word," she said, checking out the chrome rims, heavy-duty bumpers, and gnarly set of all-weather tires. "Wow."

Edge grinned. "F-250 Lariat, power stroke 6.7. Four-wheel drive, extended cab, LED quad beams, black exterior package. There's a fiberglass tonneau cover on the truck bed you can lock down tight. Great place to store our gear."

"You ordered this?"

"Some other guy did. Before it arrived, he got married and was transferred to Manhattan, made the wise decision not to pick it up."

He walked around and opened the passenger door. An automatic chrome step extended, which would make it easy for Skye to climb aboard. Would have been a deal breaker without it.

A fact he ignored.

She winced as she put weight on her bad leg climbing into the cab.

Edge felt a stab of conscience. "Your leg. Did I hurt you last night? Dammit, I shouldn't have been so rough."

Skye just smiled. "You weren't rough. You were perfect."

But the idea he'd had of a sexy nap later in the afternoon slipped away. He'd have to be more careful, not tax her injured leg too much.

Skye settled back in the deep black leather seat. "I love it," she said, snapping her belt in place.

Edge found himself smiling. He'd been working with one of the salesmen to close the deal. The transaction was complete, the keys in the ignition. "Let's go for a ride."

Not the kind he had been thinking about all morning. He'd slow things down, save that for another day. The last thing he wanted was to cause Skye physical pain.

Edge fired the engine.

Skye had repeated the address on 16th Street she had given Edge earlier, but when they took the elevator up to what turned out to be a small interior office, the door was locked, no one there.

"I'm betting this is just a front for a company that doesn't actually exist," Edge said. "Let's go back and see if we can find any other properties Sunstar or one of its subsidiaries owns."

"You think this guy, Petrov, might be part of Sunstar?"

"If he is, his name is not going to show up on any corporate filings."

"Probably not." But they would take a look, just to be sure.

Edge headed for the Nighthawk office instead of returning to his apartment. Skye figured he wanted to check with Zoe, see if she might have come up with something. Skye told herself she wasn't disappointed he didn't want to spend part of the afternoon in bed.

The good news was, when they knocked on Zoe's glass office door and she invited them in, she did have news.

"So what have you got?" Edge asked.

"According to what Skye's sister, Callie, said, Riley Beeker and Harley Purcell were two of Henson's top men. I figured they should be our first priority." Zoe ran a finger under the neck of the black turtleneck sweater she wore with black yoga pants. She had tamed her short blond hair into a smooth, Peter Pan style befitting her Tinkerbelle nickname.

"You found them?" Skye asked hopefully.

"I found Beeker. I played around with the name a while, looking for a possible alias. It turns out that's exactly what it is. Riley Beeker, aka Richie Becker, also known as Riley Becker. Real name's Rolland Beekman. As a kid, they called him Rollie."

"That's good work, Zoe," Edge said.

"What can you tell us about Rollie?" Skye asked.

Zoe turned back to the computer screen and pulled up a mug shot. Shaggy dark hair, thick dark eyebrows, a tattoo of a skull and crossbones on the side of his neck.

"Born in Oroville, California," Zoe said. "Thirty-eight years old. Dad died in prison while Rolland was doing time for grand larceny. Raised in foster care, in and out of juvey half a dozen times before he turned eighteen. Cleaned up his act for a while after that and got married."

"I'm betting that didn't last long."

"My guess is Rollie couldn't handle the money pressure of having a wife, and that's when he started dealing drugs. Wife divorced him while he was in prison. She's living in Tulsa, Oklahoma, is married to a lawyer, and they have a couple of kids."

"Good for her," Skye said.

"Rollie served his time and got out of prison five years ago. No record of arrests after that."

"Probably when he went to work for Henson," Edge said.

"That would be my guess," Zoe said.

"He's got a woman with him now," Edge said. "Goes by the name Stella Beeker. Can you look for a record of their marriage?"

"Skye mentioned her. No record of marriages between any of the men and women on the list."

"Fake marriages to men with fake names," Edge said darkly. "Henson's a real piece of work."

"No record of their marriage, but I found a photo of him with a woman named Stella Walker. Middle name is Marie. She was born in New York City, arrested for shoplifting when she was twelve years old, lived on the streets for a while, and eventually just disappeared."

"How about Harley Purcell?" Skye asked. "Were you able to come up with anything on him?"

"No. Probably an alias, too. I'll work on the list, see if I can learn anything else. I've got some things to do for other people. As soon as I get caught up, I'll take a look at Sunstar."

"Thanks, Zoe," Skye said.

They left the office and went back out to Edge's truck, which was parked in the lot. Skye climbed in, this time without a problem, and realized she was already getting used to the big black beast.

"*Beast*," she said. "That's what I'm calling this thing."

Edge's blue eyes crinkled at the corners. He flashed her a smile and fired the engine. "I like it."

From Nighthawk, they decided to put the truck to the test and drive out to one of Edge's favorite spots for a late lunch, a local tapas restaurant a couple of miles away.

"I'm starving," Edge complained. "I need to refuel. This place has really great food, and you'll love the view."

It was a sales pitch she couldn't resist, and she was actually hungry, herself. They'd gotten about halfway to their destination when Skye's cell phone started to ring.

CHAPTER TWENTY

WORKING ON HER RÉSUMÉ, CALLIE SAT AT THE KITCHEN COUNTER, trying to come up with words that would convince an employer to hire her. She finished her opening, but it didn't seem quite right. She hated to bother Skye, but she needed more input, and it seemed as if Skye was good at just about everything. She pressed her sister's contact number, hoping for some suggestions.

Skye picked up just as footsteps sounded in the hall outside the apartment. The knock came swift and hard.

"Hang on a second. Someone's at the door." Setting the phone on the counter, she crossed the living room, wondering why the guard in the lobby hadn't called ahead.

When the knock came again. Her pulse took a leap. What if it was Daniel or someone he'd sent after her? Maybe Daniel was afraid she knew something that would help the police.

"Open the door, Callie! Open up, or I'll break the fucking thing down!" Klaus's angry voice sent an icy chill down her spine.

She ran back and grabbed her cell phone. "Klaus Mahler's here! He's trying to break in!"

She heard a loud thump as Klaus's thick shoulder pounded against the wood. The door shuddered but held, then crashed open beneath the weight of Klaus's heavy boot. The blond giant and his friend, Cisco Vasquez, burst into the apartment.

"They're inside!" She grabbed the phone as she raced down the hall toward the bedroom to lock herself in. She was almost there when Klaus caught up with her. The phone went flying as he gripped her shoulders and dragged her backward. Callie whirled and tried to knee him in the groin, then kicked him hard in the shin and rushed into the bedroom.

"Fucking bitch!" Klaus was right behind her. She tried to close the door, but he blocked it with his boot. Big and strong, he shouldered his way inside.

"Get away from me, you pig!"

Klaus's eyes narrowed. "That's no way to talk to your future husband." His mouth looked like a hole in his thick blond beard. "You're going with me, Callie—one way or the other. You can make it easy or hard."

"This is kidnapping, Klaus! The police are already looking for you and the rest of Henson's men. You won't get away with it!"

Klaus's big hand swung out, and he slapped her so hard she flew backward across the bed. She tried to roll away, but he grabbed her ankle and hauled her toward him, yanked her to her feet, and slapped her again, then dragged her out of the bedroom and down the hall.

Dark and menacing, Cisco Vasquez stood next to the splintered front door, which hung on its hinges at an odd angle. His one good eye focused on the activity in the hall.

"We need to go, *ese.*"

Klaus nodded and hauled her across the room. *Where were the police?* She trusted that Skye would have called them, but police departments were shorthanded. Lately, everyone was shorthanded.

Callie stumbled as Klaus yanked her through the broken front door and down the main corridor toward the elevator, his grip so tight she hurt from elbow to shoulder. Her face burned where he'd slapped her. Her lip felt puffy and swollen.

As the elevator doors parted, the emergency exit door leading to the stairwell flew open, and a big, dark-haired man stepped out. He was wearing a tactical vest and leather boots. A black semiautomatic pistol gripped in both hands pointed directly at Klaus.

"Let her go! Do it now!"

Holy hell—her half-brother, Conner Delaney! She barely knew him. She started shaking.

Vasquez jerked his pistol. He stepped out from behind Klaus and fired. At the same time, Conn ducked, moved, and returned fire. Vasquez went down.

Klaus shoved her forward hard enough to send her sprawling, jerked his weapon, and ran for the elevator, but Conn was already firing. Klaus pulled off a wild shot as he darted inside and the steel doors slid closed.

Ears still ringing, Callie struggled to sit up and saw Conner striding toward her. "You okay?" he asked, crouching beside her.

Callie swallowed, managed to nod. Conn gently took her arms and helped her to her feet. "You sure?"

"I-I'm okay."

Conn looked at the marks on her face, and his features hardened. He walked over to Vasquez, unmoving in a spreading pool of blood, and kicked his pistol away. Conn knelt and pressed two fingers to the side of Vasquez's neck. Callie felt a sinking feeling as he rose and walked back to her.

"Is he . . . is Cisco dead?"

Conn nodded. "He made a bad choice, and he died for it." He shoved his pistol back into the holster at his waist.

"What . . . what are you doing here?"

"Skye called," he said simply. Sliding an arm around her shoulders, he guided her back down the hall, through the broken front door of the apartment. "Skye couldn't get here in time to help. My office is only two blocks away." He glanced toward the door. "With any luck, the cops'll have a nice little welcome party waiting for your boyfriend in the lobby."

Callie stiffened. "Klaus isn't my boyfriend. He's a pig."

"Sorry," he said. "It was a joke. Not a very good one." Conner must have noticed she was trembling because he drew her across the living room over to the sofa, eased her down, and sat down beside her. "You're safe, Callie. Mahler's gone, and everything's okay."

Her eyes filled. She barely knew her half-brother. He was years older than she. But he had risked his life to save her.

"Thank you for coming."

Conn reached down and caught her hand, gave it a gentle squeeze. "We're family. I'm glad I could help."

Family. She was beginning to understand she had a family she had never known.

Her sister appeared in the doorway and rushed toward them across the room. Callie noticed the slight limp, which was rarely visible. It occurred to her that she wanted to know what had happened to Skye when she was in the army, wanted to know more about these people she was coming to care for.

"The police are in the lobby," Skye said. "Edge is with them. Klaus assaulted the guard—that's how he got in."

"Is the guard all right?"

"They're taking him to the hospital. Looks like he's got a concussion, but they think he'll be okay."

With a deep breath, Callie stood up from the sofa. "What about Klaus? Did they catch him?"

"Not yet," Skye said. "But they've put out a BOLO, and they've set up a perimeter around the neighborhood. They'll get him."

She thought of Klaus's determination. He wasn't a man who accepted failure. "What if they don't?"

Skye's gaze flashed to her brother, and a look passed between them. "Edge and I are going to keep working the case. Until we get things figured out or Klaus is arrested, you can stay at Conn's house."

Callie started shaking her head. "I can't do that. It's too much of an imposition."

"You need protection," Conn said. "I own a security firm. I'll be with you—or one of my people will—twenty-four seven."

"But—"

"The house is big, and my housekeeper has an apartment over the garage. Isabella does all the cooking." He smiled. "You'll be more than comfortable."

"Conn's right," Skye said. "We can't be sure Henson didn't send Klaus and his one-eyed sidekick—"

"Cisco Vasquez," Callie supplied.

"We can't be sure Henson didn't send Klaus and Vasquez after you. He may think you know something that could lead to his arrest."

"I have no idea where he is."

"Henson might think you do."

She looked up as Edge and two men in dark suits walked into the apartment and headed in her direction.

Edge introduced them. "Callie, this is Detective Zach Powers and Detective Lee Chen. They're going to need statements from you and Conn."

Powers was young for a detective, maybe twenty-five or -six, muscular and good-looking, with dark brown, buzz-cut hair and blue eyes. Chen was a few years older, lean, with high cheekbones and very smooth skin.

"Why don't we go into the kitchen?" Detective Chen suggested.

Conn squeezed her hand. "I'll be right here if you need me, Callie."

Her half-brother had saved her today. Edge and Skye had rescued her from Henson's compound; now Conn had rescued her from a fate she didn't even want to think about. She had misjudged both her siblings from the start.

As she walked into the kitchen with Chen, Conn sat back down on the sofa and started talking to Skye and Edge. They were there to help. They weren't going to abandon her even after her disaster with Daniel Henson.

Callie felt a soft pang in her heart.

The afternoon slid away. It was dusk when the big Ford truck pulled into the parking space next to Edge's flashy sports car in his underground garage.

"Two spaces came with the unit." He grinned, a blaze of white in a face so handsome Skye's pulse kicked up just looking at him. "Might as well use them."

Skye smiled. "Well, you really did need a bigger vehicle." And the pickup definitely fit him. The sports car suited the dangerous, outlaw side of his personality, while the truck screamed macho as nothing else could. There wasn't a man alive more masculine than Edge.

He hit the elevator button, and her stomach lifted. She was going up to Edge's apartment. There was nothing more they could do on the case until morning, and Callie was safe. As she rode up to the tenth floor, her body tingled with anticipation.

The elevator arrived. They headed down the corridor, and Edge opened the front door. Across the living room, outside the big glass windows, the lights of the city were beginning to flicker on, faintly illuminating the apartment.

As the door closed and Edge joined her, Skye slid her arms around his neck. "It's been a long day." Going up on her toes, she kissed him. She'd been thinking about him all day, imagining the evening they would be spending together.

Edge kissed her back with all the passion she remembered from last night. Walking her backward till she came up against the wall, he pressed his hard-muscled body intimately against her, his knee between her legs. Everything inside her began to burn. She could feel his erection straining toward the zipper of his snug black jeans, and hungry need poured through her.

Edge groaned and pulled her even more firmly against him. The kiss went on and on, soft and coaxing, then hot, wet, and demanding. She was panting for breath, Edge's heart pounding as fast as her own, both of them desperately wanting more. Edge gripped her hips and pulled her injured leg up around his waist—then he froze.

"What . . . what is it?" She could barely breathe. Her skin was on fire, her body damp and aching.

Edge swallowed and released her. "I just remembered something I have to do. Just . . . umm . . . give me a second, and we can start over in the bedroom." He took off down the hall, disappeared into his study, and closed the door.

What the hell had just happened? Skye wasn't sure but whatever it was, it wasn't good. Willing her heart to slow, she took several calming breaths and walked over to her laptop, sitting open on the dining room table.

She sat down and stared at the dark computer screen, her mind and body still fighting a haze of lust and need. She tried to focus on the work she needed to do on Sunstar, or maybe she could find something on Sarah Simmons. But her thoughts remained muddled, work the furthest thing from her mind.

She stood up as Edge walked back into the living room. All she could think of was how tall he was, his wide shoulders, and the six pack beneath his black T-shirt. It was embarrassing.

"Did something happen?" she asked. "What's going on?" His face was still flushed, his skin damp. At least she'd had some effect on him.

"I . . . umm . . . thought we should slow it down a little."

"Slow it down?" A tendril of uneasiness slipped through her. "Why is that?"

He glanced off toward the window as if deciding how much he should say. "Earlier I noticed you favoring your leg. I figured it would be easier on you if we waited until we went to bed."

Disbelief warred with anger. "Wait a minute. That's the way this is going to be? You holding back because you don't want to hurt me?" She looked him straight in the face. "Or is it something else? What happened between us last night, Edge? Was that you being kind to a woman with a disfigured leg? Was it some kind of pity fuck?"

"What!"

"Well, I'm not interested." She started for the door, but Edge strode in front of her, blocking her way.

"What the hell are you talking about?" He gripped her shoulders. "I haven't been able to think of anything but having you again since we got out of bed this morning. I've wanted you all day, but—"

"But what? You backed off because you think I'm too fragile to handle it? I don't want a man who holds back. That was one of the things that attracted me to you in the first place. Everything you do, you don't hold back. You're all in. That's the way it was last night. That's what I want from you—all or nothing. Let me know if you change your mind."

She barely got the words out before Edge shoved her up against the wall and his mouth crushed down over hers. The kiss was scalding, deliciously wet, and deep. It was everything she wanted and not nearly enough.

"The way I want you . . ." He nipped the side of her neck. "I'm afraid of what will happen if I let go completely."

Skye went up on her toes and kissed him. "I want you, Edge—all of you—and I'm not afraid."

His eyes darkened to blue black pinpoints. He unbuttoned her blouse and dragged it off her shoulders, unfastened her bra and tossed it away. Big hands cupped her breasts, thumbed her nipples, tugged hard enough to give her a shot of pleasure/pain.

Skye moaned. Her hands trembled as she unbuckled his belt and worked down his zipper. She pulled his black T-shirt off over his head as she toed off her sneakers and Edge worked her stretch pants down over her hips.

Mouths fused together, they stripped off the rest of their clothes and stood naked in the sparkling lights of the city. Skye smoothed her hands over the solid muscles across Edge's chest, down his flat belly.

God, she loved touching him. A sound escaped from her throat.

"You want everything?" he said, wrapping her legs around his waist. "I'm going to give you everything I've got and more." And then he buried himself inside her, taking her hard against the wall.

She climaxed almost immediately. This was Edge. He was so beautiful, so totally male. He drove her up again, sparing nothing, pounding hard, taking what he wanted, sending her over the edge before allowing his own release. Then he held her tight against him as they both spiraled down.

Seconds ticked past. Little by little, their heartbeats slowed, and they drifted back to earth.

He cupped her jaw and softly kissed her. "Better?"

Skye gave him a drowsy smile. "Much."

Edge shook his head. "Nope, still not good enough. Maybe I can improve with practice."

Skye laughed. This was the Edge she wanted, the man who gave all he had.

Carrying her into the bedroom, he settled her on his big bed and came down on top of her. "Practice makes perfect," he said and started kissing her all over again, trailing little love bites down the side of her neck.

Skye gave herself up to the melting sensations. Tomorrow she would worry about the consequences of her deepening feelings for Edge.

Tomorrow she would worry about Callie, figure out a way to locate Daniel Henson and Lila Ramirez. Tomorrow—not tonight.

CHAPTER TWENTY-ONE

Lila sat in the back seat of the black SUV, while Daniel rode in the front passenger seat next to Harley, who was driving. Dutch drove the second SUV, accompanied by Riley and Stella Beeker. The six of them were off to a location where Daniel planned to start a new drug operation.

Lila suppressed a shiver. The more she learned, the more danger she was in.

They had spent three days at the safe house, waiting for Daniel to get everything ready for the trip to wherever they were going. She had overheard bits and pieces of conversation, not enough to know their final destination.

Since that first night, she had been sleeping in Daniel's bed, going along with his dominance-and-discipline sex games, trying to stay alive. It wasn't as bad as it could have been. Daniel wasn't that much of a man.

Still, she understood the risk of defying him, remembered Sarah and what had happened to her. Lila vowed to stay strong, do whatever she had to in order to survive. Sooner or later, she would find a way to escape.

Lila knew Callie had made it out. The night Daniel had dismantled the compound, she had heard him talking. She knew Callie's sister, Skye, and two other men had come to rescue her.

She was pretty sure Molly had also managed to escape.

The other women had been left behind, but as Callie had warned, Henson wanted Lila for himself. At gunpoint, she had been forced to go with him.

As the vehicle continued down the highway, she rode in silence, quiet but alert to any possibility for escape that might arise. In the meantime, as long as she held Daniel's interest, she would stay alive. As long as she was alive, she could find a way out of this nightmare.

She thought of Callie. Her friend had promised to come back for her. Lila believed Callie would press the authorities to search for her, believed she would not give up.

Neither would Lila.

She rested her head against the back of the seat and watched the changing landscape. They had been heading west, traveling along I-70 through open, rural country; then Dutch had turned on US 40. They'd passed through a few small towns, but again the land was mostly open and rural. She wondered at their final destination. They would get there eventually.

In the meantime, she needed to keep Daniel Henson happy long enough to get away.

Edge sat at his desk at Nighthawk. He worked better here. Easier to keep his head in the game and not get sidetracked by his pretty roommate.

Skye was staying in his apartment—which should have messed with his head. Instead, he was looking forward to going home tonight with a beautiful woman and a chance to compare notes after what he figured would be a very long day.

He glanced over to where she sat at her desk, clicking away on the keyboard as she studied her laptop screen. Her thick dark hair hung in soft curls around her shoulders, and he remembered the silky feel of it draped across his chest that morning.

His body stirred. Edge forced himself to ignore it, but the lady sure did turn him on. Skye was deep in concentration, focused on her search. Edge hoped she was making some progress. He sure as hell wasn't.

He looked up to see Nighthawk's computer whiz Zoey Rosen walking toward him.

"I've got something for you," Zoey said, her slightly tilted cat eyes crinkling at the corners.

Edge stood up from his desk. "What is it?"

"I found Rolland Beekman's mother. She lives in Colorado Springs. Been at the same address for the last fifteen years." Zoe handed him a slip of paper with the address. Edge yanked it impatiently out of her hand, then flashed an apologetic smile.

"Sorry, this is the first break we've had in days."

"I hope it helps," Zoe said, smiling. "I tracked down Sarah Simmons. After her parents died in a house fire, she wound up in the system. One day she just disappeared."

"So no family left to notify," Edge said.

"Doesn't look that way. I'm still working on Sunstar, but so far, I haven't found anything useful."

"You'll get there." Edge hoped it was true. Along with finding Lila, they needed to find the guy at the top of the organization—assuming Edge was right and it was someone other than Henson. Sunstar was their best chance.

As Zoe walked back to her office, Edge headed over to Skye's desk. "We caught a break," he said.

Skye rose from her chair. She looked more relaxed today, soft color in her cheeks, her shoulders less tense. He thought of last night and figured he deserved some credit for that. He managed not to smile.

"We got a lead?" Skye asked.

"Rollie Beekman's mother lives in Colorado Springs." He held up the paper Zoe had given him. "Got the address right here. We can be there in a little over an hour."

Skye reached for her purse, slung the strap over her shoulder. "Let's go talk to her."

Edge went back to his desk, grabbed his black leather jacket and shrugged it on, and they headed out the door. It was the third week of September, the weather in the low seventies, but a storm was brewing. A stiff breeze shifted the branches of the trees, and a bank of clouds hung over the city, turning the sky pewter gray.

They crossed the parking lot to Edge's new black pickup, and both of them climbed in. Following Siri's directions, he drove south on I-25. The seventy-mile trip took them to the address Zoe had given him in the 2600 block of East Yampa, an older area of small, wood-frame houses, many of them in rough condition.

The paint was peeling on Mrs. Beekman's dilapidated dwelling, the asphalt roof tiles missing in several places. A broken-down sofa sat on the covered front porch, springs protruding and stuffing coming out. A junk car on blocks rested in front of a detached garage that leaned precariously sideways.

"Doesn't look like Rollie comes around very often," Skye said.

"If he does, he's not much of a handyman."

Edge drove past the house, turned at the corner, and continued down the alley. It was overgrown with weeds, the fences along the lane falling down in places. He circled back to East Yampa, stopped at the end of the block and turned off the engine.

Skye reached for the door handle, but Edge caught her arm. "Let's watch for a while, see who comes and goes."

But half an hour later, only the mailman had approached the shabby white house. An older, heavyset woman in baggy jeans and a printed blouse had opened the door and taken the mail. She nodded her thanks, and the mailman walked away.

"You think Rollie stays in touch with his mother?" Skye asked.

"According to Zoe, he's an only child. From his mug shot, he looks more like a transient than a mama's boy, but you never know. At the moment, she's all we've got." He flicked Skye a glance. "Be better if she doesn't know who we are."

Skye nodded. They waited another half hour. When no one else appeared, they got out of the truck and walked down the block to the front door. Edge knocked, then stepped back out of the way to let Skye do the talking.

The door swung open, but the screen stayed in place. "May I help you?"

"Mrs. Beekman?" Skye asked.

"Yes . . . ?"

Skye smiled. "I'm Carol, and this is Mark. We're friends of Rollie's. He asked us to stop by and say hello while we were in town, make sure you're okay."

The woman's plump lips spread into a wide, bright smile. "Well, that's very nice of you. Rollie is always so thoughtful. Tell him I'm fine. I got the money he sent. It wasn't expected, but it's always appreciated."

"I'll be sure to tell him," Skye said.

Edge moved out of the shadows. "Rollie asked us to find out if there's anything you need, but the two of you probably stay in touch."

"Not as much as I'd like." Mrs. Beekman pushed open the screen door. "The house is a mess, but you're welcome to come in. How about a nice glass of iced tea?"

"That would be great," Skye said, following the woman into the house. Edge walked in behind them.

Mrs. Beekman rushed around, plucking supermarket newspaper advertisements off the sofa, which was covered by a brown fringed throw. She straightened a pair of small pale blue pillows and indicated they should sit down.

"I'll get you that tea, and you can tell me how the two of you know Rollie." She started for the kitchen.

"Why don't I help you?" Skye suggested, giving Edge a chance to prowl the living room.

"That would be nice, dear."

As soon as the women disappeared into the kitchen, Edge went to work. An old TV sat on a wooden table. Beside it, there was a photo of baby Rollie in a silver-plated frame tarnished with age. In a knickknack cabinet, he noticed a couple of plastic high school basketball trophies above a more recent photo of Rollie with his mom. Same shaggy brown hair that looked like it needed to be washed and a tattoo crawling up the side of his neck. Edge used his phone to snap a shot.

A stack of bills on the lamp table next to the sofa caught his attention. Hearing the clink of glasses and the women still conversing, he quickly sifted through the stack, but found nothing that had anything to do with Rollie.

He was moving toward a set of bookshelves against the wall when he spotted Mrs. Beekman's cell phone on the coffee table peeking out from under one of the supermarket advertisements.

His adrenaline took a leap. Grabbing the phone, he went to Contacts and found Rollie's name. He memorized the number, then went to recent text messages and quickly scrolled through them.

And there it was, a text from Rollie's phone.

STILL IN KANSAS. HEADING OUT IN A COUPLE OF DAYS. WILL CALL WHEN WE GET THERE.

Below it was Mrs. Beekman's reply.

DRIVE SAFELY. LUV U. MAMA.

Damn! It was almost too easy. *Scratch that.* Nothing they'd done so far had been easy. He quickly checked the date, slid the phone back under the newspaper ads, and sat down on the sofa just as Mrs. Beekman and Skye walked back into the living room.

He accepted the glass of iced tea with a smile. "Thanks."

Anxious to get back to the office, he drank half of it in one swallow. Skye picked up on his urgency and drank hers rapidly as well.

"Thanks, Mrs. Beekman," Edge said as they carried their glasses into the kitchen and set them down in the sink. "The tea was great."

"It was nice of you to stop by."

"Anything you want us to tell Rollie?" Skye asked.

"When are you planning to see him? I know he's traveling. Are you meeting him in New Mexico?"

Edge's pulse spiked again. He managed to smile. "He's sending us the details, but sooner or later we'll be in touch."

"Well, tell him to call his mama as soon as he gets the chance."

"Will do," Edge said, and they left the house.

Back in the truck, they clicked their seat belts in place, and Edge fired the engine.

"New Mexico," Skye said. "You think Beekman could be meeting Henson?"

"Or they could be traveling together." Edge flashed a satisfied smile. "I found Mrs. Beekman's cell phone. She got a text from Rollie a couple of days ago."

Skye's green eyes widened. "You got Beekman's cell number?"

"Yup. He was in Kansas when he sent the text two days ago, but he was getting ready to leave. With any luck we can track him all the way to New Mexico."

"That's great news!" She cut him a sideways glance. "Of course, Henson might be somewhere else entirely."

"Maybe. But Rollie's text said, 'Will call when we get there.' *We.* He might be referring to Stella, but his mother didn't mention her, and I didn't get the impression these guys consider a woman worth including in their business. If Beekman was one of Henson's top men, good chance they're heading someplace together."

"True," Skye said. "And it's the only viable lead we've got." Her eyes met his. "What if Mama Beekman calls Rollie and tells him two of his friends dropped by to say hello? It might put him on alert and blow all his New Mexico plans to hell."

"We had nothing before. It's a chance we had to take."

CHAPTER TWENTY-TWO

THEY MADE A STOP AT A BURGER KING ON THE WAY BACK TO DENVER and ate on the road.

"I'm surprised Beekman isn't using a disposable phone," Skye said, plucking a French fry out of the bag and popping it into her mouth. The salty taste elicited a moan.

"At this point, there's no reason he'd be worried," Edge said. "Rollie's served his time in prison. He's got no new warrants, and he's not even using his real name."

"So he feels pretty safe."

He nodded. "At least for the moment."

As soon as they got back to Nighthawk, Skye headed straight for Zoe's office, Edge right behind her. Zoe was on the phone when they walked in. She must have read something in Skye's face because she ended the call and sat up straighter in her chair.

"What is it?"

Skye smiled. "We got Rolland Beekman's cell phone number."

"Wow, that's great. Why don't we find out where he is?"

Edge rattled off the number, and Zoe went to work. It didn't take long to ping the nearest cell tower. It was in Boise City, Kansas, a small town on Highway 56.

Skye used her cell to pull up Google Maps. "Highway 56 runs northeast/southwest across Kansas. You think they traveled from Blancha Springs all the way to Kansas?"

"It's not that far," Edge said. He checked the distance on his phone. "Only two hundred and seventy miles from Blancha Springs to the Kansas state line. Be as good a place as any to hole up."

"Makes sense they would want to leave Colorado," Skye said. "The state police are looking for them." She glanced at Edge. "So why did Beekman head for Kansas instead of going directly to New Mexico?"

"That's where he's going?" Zoe asked.

"According to his mother," Skye said.

"We don't know his motivation," Edge said. "But, more importantly, we need to know if Henson and Lila are traveling with Rollie, and if they are, where exactly they wind up."

Zoe whirled her chair back toward her computer screen. "I'll set up a program to mark their route as the cell phone changes location. I can send a map to both your phones showing their progress."

"They would be great," Skye said, more than a little impressed.

They left Zoe to her task and went into the employee lounge. Neither of them wanted to leave the office until they knew for sure the direction Beekman was heading. Skye brewed a fresh pot of coffee. They each filled a mug and sat down at the Formica-topped table.

As the afternoon slid toward evening, the map of Beekman's travels on Skye's phone continued to show a southwesterly journey, and soon the phone was pinging on the other side of the New Mexico state line.

"Looks like Mrs. Beekman was right," Skye said. "The route they're taking . . . I think they're purposely avoiding Colorado."

"Be the smart move," Edge said.

"You think we should notify the authorities? Bring them up to speed on what we've found out?"

Edge shook his head. "We don't have anything solid, just a lot of speculation and a phone pinging its way across the country. Add to that, if Beekman is traveling with Henson and Lila and we bring in the police, there's no way to control the situation. Lila could end up dead."

"So what do you suggest?" Skye asked.

"I suggest we keep watching Beekman's progress, see where he ends up. Once he's settled somewhere, we go after him. We find out if Henson and Lila are traveling with him. If they are, we'll have a better idea what we're up against. Once we have enough intel, we can go to the police. The DEA still wants Henson. Maybe we'll be able to help them get him."

Morning sun filtered through the curtains in the windows of Edge's bedroom. He'd been awake for a while, lying contentedly in his big bed with Skye draped over his chest. They'd had a bout of early-morning sex and now drowsed peacefully. He'd get up soon, he told himself. They both had work to do.

Then his cell signaled, the ringtone jarring him fully awake. Skye rolled off him with a yawn as he leaned over and grabbed the phone off the nightstand.

He was too groggy to recognize the number. "Logan."

"Edge, it's Grease. I got news you'll want to hear."

Swinging his legs to the side of the bed, he pressed the phone against his ear. "Grease. Hey, buddy, what's going on?"

"Word's going round a certain army major is getting ready to turn in his papers. He's getting out, Edge-man. And it's happening soon."

Edge's whole body tightened. "Where's he going?"

"I hear he's heading south, not sure where. That's all I know."

"Keep me posted, will you?"

"You know I will, Sarge." The line went dead.

Edge felt the bed move as Skye came up on her knees behind him. She rested her hands on his shoulders. "What's going on?"

"That was Grease. His real name's Gill Franklin. He's one of the guys in my old unit."

"How'd he get a name like Grease?"

Edge smiled to think of it. "Gill loves junk food—the greasier the better. The nickname stuck."

Skye must have felt the knot of tension in his shoulders. She started kneading them softly. "Gill must not have had good news."

"In a way it was."

She waited for him to continue. When he didn't, she didn't press him for more. "So what was your nickname?" Her talented hands kept moving, and some of his tension slid away.

"Sometimes they'd call me Fast Eddy. Kind of a takeoff on Edge. Mostly they just called me Fast or Edge-man."

"Is Edge your real name?"

"Edgerton. It was my grandfather's surname. My mom saw it as a tribute to her father, but my dad never liked it. He always just called me Edge."

She kissed the nape of his neck, and a sliver of heat wound itself around his groin.

"So you're not going to tell me what the call was about?"

"Keep those talented fingers working, and I'll tell you anything you want to know."

Skye laughed, and more of his tension slid away.

"The man who got me tossed out of the army is resigning. Probably to spend the illegal money he's made trafficking military weapons."

Her fingers froze. "You knew about it?"

"I heard rumors, stumbled across a cache of guns that was part of a deal he was making. I went to the higher-ups. I thought they would at least look into it, but by then the guns had disappeared. Instead of investigating, they gave me a choice: resign or face disciplinary action for making false accusations against a highly respected officer. I should have considered Major Bradley Markham's connections. His dad was a full bird colonel on his way to becoming a brigadier general. No way were they taking my word without any proof."

"So now Markham is retiring."

"That's right."

"And that's important because . . . ?"

"Because he's the kind of guy who'll never have enough. He's got valuable contacts, the sort that can be extremely profitable. I don't think he'll get out of the weapons trade. The money's too tempting. I think he'll just move his business somewhere else, somewhere he can live the high life he believes he's earned."

She mulled that over, returned to kneading away the tightness in his shoulders. "Kind of like Daniel Henson."

Who was likely starting up in a new location.

Edge turned his head to look at her over his shoulder. "Now that you mention it, yeah. And if that's what Markham does, this time I'm going to nail him. I'm going to prove I was right and make sure he gets the justice he deserves."

He pulled her around and into his lap and took her mouth. The kiss deepened, and things got heated, as they always seemed to when they were together, and they ended up back in bed.

Afterward, they showered together and got dressed. Skye pulled a brush through her long, dark hair and drew it back in a low ponytail, held in place with a scrunchy. He loved her hair, the way the soft curls slid like silk through his fingers.

"So if you catch him," Skye said, "you plan to make the army grovel and welcome you back?"

His jaw tightened just thinking about it. "That's the general idea. The army's been my dream since I was a kid. It's my life. It's where I belong."

Skye's gaze found his, locked, and she didn't look away. "Is it?" Turning, she set the brush down on the dresser and walked out of the bedroom.

Edge realized his stomach was churning. What the hell had just happened?

Things were finally going his way—Markham was leaving the army, and there was every chance he would continue his illegal activities somewhere else. If he did, Edge would catch him. He'd prove he'd been right from the start, and the army would let him rejoin his old unit.

He should be ecstatic. Instead, he felt sick.

It was Skye, he knew. He was getting in too deep, beginning to care for her too much. He needed to pull back, put some distance between them.

Conn's words echoed in his head. *Don't hurt her, Edge.* Easing things back would be best for both of them.

In the meantime, while he waited for news, he had a job to do. Skye's family was still in danger. Callie's friend Lila was in danger.

He walked into the living room, ready to talk to Skye, go over their plans for the day.

There was a brief note on the kitchen counter.

But Skye was already gone.

Lila wrapped her arms around her waist, trying to stop the shaking. She stood in the shadows of the Sundowner Motel, the run-down establishment they had stayed in last night. The morning was chilly. The moist air seemed to stick in her lungs. A few feet away, Daniel loaded her carry-on into the back of the SUV.

She squeezed her eyes shut as Dutch and Beeker loaded the second SUV, sliding a rolled-up blue plastic tarp in the back that Harley and Dutch had stolen last night from a True Value hardware store in Angel Fire, a town twelve miles away.

They'd also taken cleaning supplies: a mop, bleach, and paper towels to clean up the blood on the floor of the room where Riley and Stella had been staying.

The room where Riley had killed her.

Lila's throat swelled. She shuddered at the memory of the argument that had gone on in the room next door in the middle of the night. She was sure Beeker had started it. Stella was too cowed to stand up for herself, and Beeker had a mean streak far more dangerous than any of the other men.

He would stir up trouble on purpose just to have an excuse to hit her. Stella didn't mix his drink the way he wanted it. He didn't like the way she was wearing her hair. It could have been anything. Beeker was all about using his fists, even though Daniel disapproved.

Quiet returned after the argument, but Lila was wide awake when the knock came at the door. Daniel slid out of bed and went to open it. She caught a glimpse of Riley, Harley, and Dutch standing outside. Daniel spoke to them for a moment, his voice low but hissing with displeasure.

"What happened?" Lila asked when Daniel returned.

"There's been an accident. Harley's handling it. They'll need your help when they get back."

"An accident? What kind of accident?"

"Riley and Stella got into an argument. Stella fell and hit her head on the bathroom sink. I'm afraid she's dead."

"Oh, my God!"

Daniel gripped her arms and shook her. "Pull yourself together. Dutch and Harley are going after supplies. They'll deal with the problem when they get back. They'll need your help cleaning up, but aside from that, this has nothing to do with you."

Lila bit her tongue to keep the scream locked in her throat. Sarah was dead. Now Stella. Who knew how many other victims there had been—or would be?

She could be next.

And something else had happened. In the chaos since the raid on the compound, worry about being late for the last two months had slipped her mind. But as she got back into bed, she couldn't deny it any longer. She was pregnant with Raul's child. She was carrying her husband's baby.

Whatever had happened to him, whatever his reasons for abandoning her, once she had loved him. She wanted his baby. She would protect it with her life.

Curled up in the darkness, she pulled up the covers and pretended to sleep. An eternity later, a second firm knock sounded.

"Get dressed," Daniel said. "You're needed next door."

Lila pulled on her jeans, sweater, and boots with trembling hands. When she walked into the seedy motel room next door, the coppery smell of blood hit her like a brick. She gagged, ran to the toilet, and threw up the cheeseburger she'd had for supper earlier that night. Threw up again before she regained control.

"We'll leave you to it," Dutch said, his red hair flaming in the harsh overhead light. "Let us know when you're done." Dutch went outside and closed the door.

Lila swallowed against a fresh round of sickness. She could do this. She had to. She had a child to think of now.

Fresh tears blurred her vision as she got down on her hands and knees on the cold tile of the bathroom floor. There was blood everywhere: in the shower, on the walls, a spray of it across the sink. From the corner of her eye, she could see a rolled-up blue tarp in the other room that contained Stella's body.

She stifled a whimper and wiped the wetness off her cheeks. Holding her breath against the smell of death, she went to work. Stella never had a chance. Not with men like these.

But Lila was tougher. Smarter. No matter what it took, she was going to stay alive for her baby. She wasn't going to let Daniel Henson win.

CHAPTER TWENTY-THREE

THE MORNING WAS SLIPPING AWAY AS SKYE DROVE HER METALLIC red Subaru Forester over to her brother's apartment. She wanted to talk to Callie, make sure she was holding up all right. Last night, Edge had texted Callie the picture he'd taken with his cell phone, the photo of Rolland Beekman, aka Riley Beeker, with his mother.

Callie had replied that Beekman looked pretty much the same as he had at the compound, though his mouse-brown hair was even longer, and now he wore a close-cropped beard.

All the way there, Skye thought of her conversation with Edge. Edge Logan wasn't a man who gave up on what he wanted. He had mentioned before that he hoped one day to return to the Green Berets. At the time, she'd hadn't paid much attention. They were somewhere in the Mexican tropical dry forest, and people's lives were at stake.

Now that she understood the circumstances that had caused him to leave the army, she realized he was going to continue his pursuit of Major Bradley Markham, and knowing Edge as she did, sooner or later he would find the proof he needed.

And he would leave.

An ache slid through her. She had known she was playing with fire from the start. Beyond a working relationship, she never should have gotten involved with him. She'd been dangerously attracted to Edge from the beginning. Now her heart was in peril, and when he was gone from her life, it was going to hurt badly.

Better to end things now, she told herself, before she got in any deeper.

She blew out a breath. On the other hand, they were teammates. They worked well together, and they had a job to do. She'd made a promise to Callie, and she meant to keep it. She was going to find Daniel Henson, find Lila Ramirez and bring her home. They were making headway.

The hard truth was she needed Edge's help.

One thing was sure. It was past time she moved back into her own apartment. She would take care of that today.

She rang Conn's doorbell. He lived in an old Victorian in a historic neighborhood on Vine Street. Conn had moved into the home after their father had died and their mother had remarried and moved to California. Skye hadn't wanted the big old financial albatross, but Conn loved the place.

He worked on the house every time he got the chance, originally to get it ready for the woman he planned to marry. Unfortunately, his fiancée had broken their engagement. Conn was still reeling from the blow.

Skye walked along the cement path, climbed the steps to the covered front porch of the two-story red-brick home, and rang the bell. The housekeeper, Isabella Rossi, answered the door.

"*Buongiorno,* Izzy," Skye said, smiling. "It's good to see you."

"*Si, si,* you as well. *Vieni, dentro*!" She smiled and motioned Skye forward. "Come in. Come in."

Isabella was a plump woman in her fifties with silver-streaked heavy black hair and an easy disposition. On a more leisurely day, the two of them would speak Italian while Izzy worked in the kitchen.

Skye had always had an aptitude for languages. By the time she'd graduated from college, she spoke Spanish, French, Italian, and enough German to get by. In the army, she'd added Farsi to her list.

They talked for a while, catching up a little. Izzy was a real sweetheart, and she took great care of Conner, mothering him as if he were her son.

"I am sorry, your brother is not home."

"Actually, I came to see Callie."

Izzy nodded, moving strands of hair that had escaped from the neat black bun at the back of her head. "She'll be glad to see you, I think. She is upstairs in the guest room working on her computer."

"Thanks, I'll go on up."

"I have cookies and coffee in the kitchen when you come back down."

Skye's mouth watered. "What kind of cookies?" Not that she didn't like them all.

"Chocolate chip."

Skye grinned. "My favorite. I'll be down in a minute." Her brother was lucky. Izzy was a fabulous cook.

Heading toward the stairs, she admired Conner's handiwork. The refinished hardwood floors gleamed. The white-painted moldings against the soft beige walls set off the cream sofa and chairs in front of a fireplace nestled between two old-fashioned leaded-glass bookcases.

She reached the second floor and knocked on the guest room door. Callie pulled it open.

Skye smiled. "I thought I'd stop by, see how you're doing."

Instead of a return smile, Callie's blue eyes filled with tears.

"Hey, everything's going to be okay." Skye stepped into the room and pulled her into a hug.

Callie hugged her back. "I know. I'm sorry. It's just . . . you and Conn, you've both been so nice. I wouldn't have made it without you. There's a chance I might even have been dead by now."

Skye gripped Callie's hand. "Don't say that. You were halfway to saving yourself when we found you."

Callie just shook her head. "You saved me. And the worst part is I always resented you. I always thought of you and Conner as

Dad's real family. It's taken all this bad stuff to figure out that you are part of my family, too."

Skye hugged her again. "Well, now you know. That's what matters."

Callie took a deep breath and brushed away the wetness on her cheeks. "Conn's not here. A guy named Morgan Burke is downstairs in the study. He's a friend of Conn's. Conn said he was a marine before he went into security. I guess something happened when he was working in the Middle East, and he quit the job and came back to the States. He just started working for Nighthawk."

Skye nodded. "I heard there was a new guy coming in. I haven't met him yet. You like him?"

"He's . . . umm . . . he's really hot."

Skye grinned. "Yeah?"

Color rose in Callie's cheeks. "Yeah. Very."

"How old?"

"Early thirties, maybe."

"Single?"

"I think so."

"He's a little old for you."

Callie grinned. "Doesn't make him any less hot."

Skye laughed.

"You don't have to worry; he seems very professional," Callie said.

"I'm glad to hear it. I'll say hello on my way out." Skye checked the time on her phone. "I've got to get back. I've got a ton of things to do. As I said, I just wanted to be sure you're all right."

Callie glanced away, and Skye frowned. "You are, right? You are okay?"

"I just . . . I still have nightmares about him, Skye. I keep asking myself how I could have been so stupid."

Skye understood bad dreams. They didn't come as often, but every once in a while, she still relived the nightmare explosion that had destroyed her leg.

"Daniel is a good-looking man. He managed to charm you into believing he was something he wasn't. He did the same thing to other women with a lot more experience than you."

"That's what I tell myself. But in the middle of the night, it's like he's there in bed with me. Like he's making me do . . . things to him again. It makes me sick."

Skye looked at Callie, and worry filtered through her. "Maybe you should see someone. Talk to someone about what happened."

Callie shook her head. "I'm mostly okay. It's just knowing he's still out there. And I'm worried about Lila. Once Daniel's in jail—"

"Oh, he's going to jail. We're getting closer to finding him every day." Last night, before she had gone to bed, she had checked Beekman's location. His phone had pinged in a tiny town called Eagle Nest. With luck, Daniel was with him.

Callie relaxed enough to smile. "I know you'll get him." She walked Skye to the door. "Thanks for coming. Thanks for everything."

Skye left the guest room and headed back downstairs. As she reached the bottom step, a man stepped out of the study, a semiautomatic pistol on his hip as if it belonged there. He was dark-haired and handsome, with chocolate-brown eyes that seemed almost black, a solid jaw, and a cleft in his chin. Like a lot of the men she knew, there was a hardness to his features that said he wasn't someone you wanted to mess with.

"Hi, I'm Skye Delaney." She offered her hand. "I hear we're going to be working together."

"Morgan Burke." He accepted the handshake. "I prefer working alone, but you never know."

"No, you don't." She glanced up the stairs. "Take care of my sister. The guy who's after her will do just about anything to get his hands on her."

Burke's jaw hardened. "That isn't going to happen. Not on my watch."

"I'll hold you to that, Burke. See you back at the office."

Skye walked out and couldn't help wondering what the new guy's story was.

As long as he kept Callie safe from Klaus Mahler and his no-good friends, it didn't really matter.

CHAPTER TWENTY-FOUR

SKYE CHECKED HER PHONE AS SHE CLIMBED INTO HER COMPACT SUV. Three texts from Edge.

WHERE ARE YOU?

The second read, I'M AT THE OFFICE. CALL ME.

The third said, WHAT'S GOING ON?

Instead of answering, she looked at the program on her phone that showed the location of Rollie Beekman's cell. Beekman must have spent the night in Eagle Nest because when she'd checked this morning, his location was only a few hours down the road.

She pushed through the office door and started across the room. She could feel Edge's intense blue eyes tracking her all the way. The muscles across her abdomen tightened with pure animal lust. After last night and this morning, she could hardly believe it.

Edge came up out of his chair and strode toward her, a hundred percent of his brooding male attention focused directly on her.

"What's going on?"

"What do you mean? I left you a note. I said I was going over to see Callie."

"We could have gone together," he said.

"I needed a little space."

Black slashing brows pulled into a frown. He glanced away. "No problem." But when he looked back at her, his taut features said he didn't like it.

"Have you checked the map on your phone?" she asked, aiming the conversation in a different direction.

"Yeah. Looks like Beekman stayed in Eagle Nest last night."

"I took a look at the area. There are a few cheap motels—that's about it."

"He's traveling again this morning, still on Highway 64. Cell service is spotty. Last time I looked, the nearest cell tower was Tres Piedras."

Skye sat down and opened her laptop. The place was only a dot on Google Maps.

"He's still moving," Edge said. "Looks like he's taking mostly back roads."

By late afternoon, the movement of the phone had stopped. The closest cell tower was in a town called Chamaya. An hour passed. Still no movement. Maybe they were just having a late lunch.

Or maybe they had reached their destination.

Skye googled everything she could find on Chamaya and the area surrounding it.

"It's in the Rocky Mountains of Arriba County. The population is only about twelve hundred. There's a steam-driven, narrow-gauge railway that attracts tourists in the summer. The scenery and the chance to explore the outdoors is the primary reason people visit. That and big-game hunting. Apparently elk are plentiful in the region. Hunting is a big money earner for locals in the fall."

Edge came up behind her and looked over her shoulder at the map she'd pulled up on the computer screen. She could smell his cologne, a woodsy scent that was a perfect match to his fierce masculinity. She tried not to breathe.

"Looks like a nice little town," he said.

"It's definitely rural. There are some large properties in the area, farms and ranches way up in the hills. Setting up a meth lab on a piece of ground somewhere a few miles out of town would be pretty easy."

"You know we could be way off base," Edge said. "Rollie might have just gone on the run and randomly picked New Mexico as a place to lie low. Henson might not even be with him. He might be somewhere else entirely."

"Could be. Or we could be right on Daniel's tail."

"My gut says they're together. Henson and his top men, including Riley Beeker/aka Rollie Beekman and Harley Purcell."

Molly's ex-spouse. Skye wanted him off the streets almost as badly as she wanted to take down Daniel Henson. Klaus Mahler was also on her list, but she trusted Conn to handle him.

"That meth operation was a real money maker," Edge was saying. "It's unlikely whoever's behind it is just going to quit."

"We need to know who owns that property in Blancha Springs. If we find a connection to any of the landowners in the Chamaya area, we'll know we're on the right track."

"Let's talk to Zoe."

"You go ahead. There's something I need to do." She closed down her laptop, stuffed it into its case, and slung the strap over her shoulder.

"What about supper?" Edge called after her as she crossed the room. "You want me to pick up something on my way home?"

Skye turned and walked back to him. "The door's been repaired on my apartment, and the cleaning crew's put everything in order. I'm going to move back home this afternoon."

Something flickered in his eyes, but Edge said nothing. It was exactly what Skye had expected. A little piece of her heart crumbled.

"What about Callie?" he asked.

"If it turns out Beekman is staying in Chamaya, we'll be traveling there ourselves. Callie's better off staying with Conn."

He nodded. "We'll give it till morning. If Beekman's cell location doesn't change, we'll drive on down." He took out his phone and brought up Google Maps. "Chamaya's a little over three hundred miles from here. If we get an early start, we can be there before dark."

Skye's mind leaped ahead. They were still working together. Assuming they were right and Henson was setting up a meth lab somewhere near Chamaya, she and Edge would be staying in the area, checking into a local motel to set up operations.

Her body heated at the thought. She wanted more of him, and yet she knew the danger. Should she take the risk? Or end things now, before her heart got even more battered?

It was just before seven the next morning when Edge tossed his gear into the truck bed of the Beast, including the long canvas bag that carried an AR-15 semiautomatic rifle, his Smith and Wesson .38 ankle gun, the Mossberg twelve-gauge, and two spare semiauto handguns. His M9 Beretta rode up front in the cab, and he trusted Skye would also be well armed.

He checked his black combat watch as he loaded the last of his gear—the FLIR Black Hornet drone. Surveillance was a necessity. The drone had done a great job before.

Time to pick up Skye. A tightness invaded his chest. She hadn't stayed in his apartment last night. The pervasive sense of loneliness had driven him down to the Fainting Goat for a nightcap. Which turned into three and didn't make him feel a damn bit better.

He hadn't slept well. He missed her. It was as simple as that. Missed the warmth she exuded, the companionship they shared after working together for so long. He missed her sexy little body nestled against him in the night and the passion she stirred without even trying.

He slid behind the wheel of the truck and fired the engine. It had taken him months to get past the wall Skye had built around herself. One lousy phone call had her walls right back up again.

He tried to tell himself it was for the best. Sooner or later, he would be going after Markham. He'd find a way to prove the major was guilty of weapons trafficking, prove he'd been right from the start. He'd return to the military life he had carved out for himself.

Skye needed a man who would be there for her, and he couldn't be that man.

His stomach knotted. She was better off without him.

But what about him?

The truth was he'd been lonely most his life. He'd barely been a teen when his mother had died. Kade had had their dad and the ranch for solace. Gage had focused on his dream of traveling the world. Somehow Edge had just accepted that loneliness would be part of his existence.

Then he'd joined the army, and the Green Berets had become the close-knit family he had lost years ago. He'd be okay once he returned. He'd have his friends, his sense of worth, his life back again. It was exactly what he wanted.

Wasn't it? He didn't like the nagging feeling that he could be wrong.

Parking in a yellow zone in front of Skye's apartment, he took the elevator up to her floor. As she'd said, the door was back in one piece. Still, there was a chance Mahler would return in search of Callie, and Skye would be forced to deal with him.

The thought sent acid into his stomach.

Skye opened the door and walked out towing her carry-on. She smelled like cinnamon and sugar, and he fought the urge to lean down and bury his face in her silky dark hair.

"Anything else?" he asked a little gruffly. "Your weapons?"

She tapped her purse. She usually carried a .380 in her handbag or wore it in an ankle holster. "My Glock and a spare are in my carry-on. I've got a stun gun in there, too."

He nodded, not surprised she was prepared. Edge loaded her stuff into the truck bed, locked down the tonneau cover, and they set off down I-25. They didn't talk much. The subject of last night rode the tip of his tongue, but he didn't bring it up. Had she called a friend to come over? She'd mentioned the new guy at Nighthawk, Morgan Burke. Edge hadn't met him, but he'd heard the guy had a big reputation with women.

He'd been a marine, so Skye's leg wouldn't be a problem. Hell, it wouldn't be a problem for any man with half a brain.

A couple hours into the trip, Skye rested her head against the window and fell asleep. He tried not to wonder if she'd had as much trouble sleeping last night as he had.

He tried not to think of the night ahead. Beekman's phone still pinged off a cell tower near Chamaya. They'd be setting up operations in a motel somewhere in the area. One room or two? That was the question. He'd let her make the decision. And prayed it was the one he wanted.

With Edge driving, they made the 310-mile journey to Chamaya in under five hours. A couple of pit stops and a drive-through food run at a Mickey D's added another twenty minutes. They came in from the north via NM-17 and drove down Main Street, basically all there was to the tiny town.

The old Hotel Chamaya dominated one block, a two-story wooden, false-fronted structure with a balcony running the length of the second floor. The place looked like it came right out of an old western movie. Down a ways, there was a co-op called the Chamaya Mall made up of vendor stalls.

Other businesses included the Evergreen Book Store and Thrift Shop, a grocery store attached to an Ace Hardware, a Family Dollar store, and a Speedway convenience store and gas station. For food, there was a pizza parlor, Jose's Tacos, Josephine's Espresso and Bakery, the Chamaya Café, the Buckhorn Bar and Grill, and the Franklin Family Diner.

A couple of motels sat along NM-17 at the edge of town, but Skye had booked one of the cabins at a place called the Antlers Lodge, which was west of town on Highway 84. Beekman's phone continued to ping in that area. It was just a matter of tracking the signal down.

First, they wanted to get settled in.

Edge pulled up to the manager's office. Skye went inside and got the key to their cabin, one of only five, from a grizzled old man named Charlie, who walked her back out to the truck and introduced himself.

"Nice to meet ya," Charlie said to Edge through the rolled-down pickup window, his thin white hair wafting in the breeze. "You're in cabin five. Best we got. It's just down yonder."

He pointed toward the wooden building at the end of the row, farthest away from the road. "Got nice views off the porch toward the mountains. Two bedrooms, so there's plenty of room, and a wood-burning stove. Got a kitchen, fully equipped. If you need anything else, just come see me."

"I'm sure we'll be fine," Edge said, still contemplating the fact Skye had booked a cabin with two bedrooms.

They unloaded their gear from the truck and went inside. The cabin was neat and clean, the kitchen compact but, as Charlie had said, fully operational. The sight of a coffeepot on the counter next to the sink was the best news yet.

"Let's see if Zoe has any updates," Edge said. "Then we'll go to the grocery store and buy a couple days' worth of supplies. If Zoe can find the exact location of Beekman's cell, we can head out there tonight and take a look."

"Sounds good."

Edge watched her haul her carry-on into one of the bedrooms. It took every ounce of will not to follow, toss his canvas bag up on the bed in the same room. Instead, he stood in the doorway looking like a fool, hoping for an invitation that never came.

A disappointed breath whispered out. Turning, he carried his gear bag into the other bedroom, then returned to the living room.

"Decent place," he said, surveying a dark brown sofa and chair with tan and burnt-orange throw pillows.

"Plenty of room to set up," Skye said. They both had laptops, iPads, comms, and weaponry, including guns and tactical vests, and gear for colder weather. The altitude here was 7,800 feet, a high mountain valley surrounded by craggy, pine-covered peaks. The days were still warm, but the nights could drop into the twenties.

They were just about finished getting organized when Skye's cell phone rang.

"It's Zoe." Putting the phone on speaker, she set it on the round pine kitchen table.

"I've got something for you," Zoe said.

"You've pinged Beekman's final location," Edge guessed, hoping he was right.

"Sorry, he's dropped off the grid. No cell service as of the past half hour. His last location was about ten miles west of Chamaya. But I've got something almost as good. I've found a connection between Sunstar and a corporation called Orion Properties, Inc. Dig deep enough, plow through enough companies owned by other companies, you come up with two names that appear in both ownership chains—an attorney named Carl Wisen and a CPA named Oscar Andreyev. They're both located in Las Vegas."

"Vegas," Edge repeated. "That's interesting."

"Sunstar owns the property in Blancha Springs," Zoe said. "Orion owns seven hundred acres west of Chamaya off Highway 64. Bought it last year. Before that, it was the Pine Tree Ranch, owned by the Miller family. When Thomas Miller's wife died, he sold the ranch to Orion and moved to Santa Fe. I'll text you a map of the site."

Edge's gaze shifted to Skye. "If the property ownership connects Blancha Springs and Chamaya, and Beekman is already here, there's a damned good chance that's where Henson is setting up next."

"Limited cell service out there," Zoe said. "But Beekman's last ping was in the area."

"That's where we'll find him," Edge said, certainty settling in his bones.

Skye's gaze shot to his. "Which means there's a very good chance Daniel is with him—or already out there."

CHAPTER TWENTY-FIVE

After Zoe's call, Skye climbed into Edge's truck for a run to the local grocery store. They picked up coffee, breakfast goodies, sandwich stuff, and a frozen pizza they could bake for supper before they headed out.

Neither Beekman nor Daniel had ever seen Edge's black Ford pickup, so they decided to drive west on Highway 64 toward the Orion property and do a quick recon of the area before it got dark.

Thirteen miles west of Chamaya, a dirt lane off Highway 64 led to the site on Zoe's map. The road was a barely visible line a little before the turn onto Highway 84 heading north to Pagosa Springs. Like the rest of the area, it was a land of high mountain valleys, golden this time of year, surrounded by rolling hills and tall, forested peaks.

Skye rode in silence, tense as they neared their destination. The open grassland on both sides of the unpaved road heading to the property was uninhabited—until the pickup rounded a bend and a two-story log house came into view.

Edge slid to a halt and quickly backed up around the bend out of sight. Turning the pickup around, he drove to a narrow dirt track peppered with potholes he had spotted on the way out, turned down the road, and backed into a place where they couldn't be seen.

Skye joined him at the rear of the truck and watched as Edge assembled the drone on the tailgate, hooked it up to his iPad, and launched it into the air.

It didn't take long for the device to reach its destination.

"Looks like just the log house and garage, plus a couple of wooden outbuildings," Edge said. The drone moved toward the wooden buildings. "Dilapidated barn with a few old stalls and what looks like a bunkhouse." The drone hovered close to the windows of the second building.

"Got bunk beds lining the walls." Edge moved the drone higher. "There's a black SUV in front of the house. Garage door is open. Another black SUV's parked inside."

"So far no sign of Henson or Lila," Skye said, her gaze glued to the iPad screen.

Edge changed direction and flew the drone closer to the house, staying just above the windows.

"There! Two men in the kitchen." She pointed at the screen. The drone hovered, giving them a better view.

"Worker bees," Edge said. "Ex-cons, street thugs, or mercenaries from the look of them."

"Just like before," Skye said.

Edge moved the drone to a different set of windows. Three men sat on overstuffed sofas and chairs in the living room. One of the men was Daniel Henson.

Edge grinned. "Bingo."

"See the guy with the red hair?" Skye pointed at the screen. "That's Dutch. He drove me out to the vegetable garden where Callie was working."

"The butt-ugly guy with the shaggy, mouse-brown hair is Beekman," Edge said. "I recognize the tat on the side of his scrawny neck."

"The third guy fits Molly's description of Purcell."

Edge nodded. "Around six-three. The pointed beard is a dead giveaway."

Skye's heart was racing as she stared at the screen. "Where's

Lila?" So far they'd seen no sign of her or Stella or any other woman.

"Let's try upstairs." The drone shot up to the second floor and cruised by the windows. In a bedroom at the back of the house that looked out toward the mountains, a beautiful, black-haired woman with a curvy figure sat on the side of a queen-size bed, staring into space. The despair on her face tugged at Skye's heart.

"Got to be her," Edge said.

From Callie's description, there was no doubt about it. "I wish there was a way to let her know we're here for her."

Edge shook his head. "We can't risk it. We only have Callie's word that Lila went with Henson against her will. Henson's a charming bastard. Maybe he convinced her to go with him. If he discovers we've found him, he'll run again. The next time we might not be so lucky."

"You're right. We need to wait, get more information, find out what we're facing."

"It might be better to let Henson settle in for a day or two, see if he's planning to set up another lab. In the meantime, we'll recon the area, figure a way to get in and get Lila out."

"Assuming she's willing to go."

"Yeah. That could definitely pose a problem. We'll just have to deal with it as it plays out."

They decided to walk the hills at the edge of the open land surrounding the house. Skye suggested they split up, but Edge refused.

"We don't know how many more men he might have out there. We stick together until we have more intel."

Skye reluctantly agreed. Edge was overly protective. There were times she found it annoying. Most of the time she found it endearing. Another quality she liked about him.

Her heart squeezed at the thought.

A three-strand, barbed-wire fence ran along the boundary line of the property, matching the map Zoe had sent. The intriguing thing was the huge stack of metal on the ground a half mile from the house.

"What is it?" Skye asked.

"Same stuff he used to make the Quonset-style buildings in Blancha Springs. He's got the metal framework for the lab all set to go. He just needs the labor to build it."

"He's got a few men already."

"He'll need more to cook the meth once the lab's set up."

"I wonder where he plans to get them?"

"Good question. Maybe we can get some answers in town. The house looks like it's been here a while. Let's see what the locals know about it."

They waited till dark to make the trip into town. First, they stopped at the Chamaya Café and had supper, a steak for Edge and grilled salmon for Skye. Before they left, Edge talked to the owner, a friendly, gray-haired man who seated people and worked the register while his wife and son did the cooking.

Jedediah Austin told him the old Pine Tree Ranch had been purchased by some big company, but they'd never done anything with it.

"Leastwise not till lately. Word is they're gonna use the property as some kinda halfway house, a place for ex-cons to make the transition from prison to civilian life. Nobody 'round here's too keen on the notion, but that's the way it goes."

Jed finished ringing him up, and Edge paid with his credit card. He opened the door for Skye, and they walked out into the night.

"A halfway house," Skye said. "That sounds exactly like something Henson would do. He can play preacher again, or something close to that."

"He's probably got somebody on the inside sorting through the prisoners being released, picking the ones who'll do his dirty work for him."

From the café, Edge drove to the opposite end of town and

parked in front of the Buckhorn Bar and Grill, which was more a saloon than a restaurant. Just a long bar lined with stools and a room full of battered wooden tables. There was a big-screen TV behind the bar, so the stools were all taken.

A couple in black motorcycle leathers waved goodbye to the bartender and headed for the door, leaving two empty spaces halfway down the row. Edge set a hand at Skye's waist, urging her forward, and they bellied up to the bar.

The crowd at the tables was a little on the rough side, a mix of men and women, a few more bikers, a couple of guys in cowboy hats. The bartender who mopped the place in front of them had slicked-back brown hair pulled into a man bun on top of his head. "What'll ya have?"

"I'll have a beer," Skye said. "Got anything local?"

Eyes the color of ink ran over her head to toe, rested for a moment on her pretty breasts. Edge clamped down on the urge to grab the guy by the throat and pull him across the bar.

Inwardly, he sighed. How had he ever convinced himself he wasn't the jealous type?

The bartender flashed Skye a lecherous smile. "Got a Metal Snake Stout that'll put hair on your chest. Comes from the Turtle Mountain Brewery down toward Santa Fe."

There was a hint of challenge in his words. It was clearly a potent brew, but Skye didn't back away. "I'll try it," she said, looking the bartender straight in the eye.

Edge's fake smile was brittle, though he couldn't hold back a touch of amusement. The Delaneys were Irish. Skye Delaney could drink any ten men under the table.

"I'll have a Bud," he said.

The bartender drew two tall tap beers and set them down on the counter. "Where ya'll from?"

Edge tipped up his beer and took a long swallow. No way was he mentioning Denver, not with Henson being chased by half the Colorado State Patrol.

"Kentucky," he said. Fort Campbell was home to the 5th Special

Forces Group, US Army Green Beret. It still felt more like home than Denver.

The bar towel made circles in front of him. "I don't hear no southern accent."

Edge just shrugged and took another drink of beer.

Next to him, Skye's eyes were locked on the TV screen behind the bar. "Can you turn that up?"

The bartender grabbed the remote and raised the volume. The local news was on, or at least as local as it got in Chamaya. Channel 2 News in Santa Fe.

"The body of a woman was found this morning in a ravine off Highway 64, west of Angel Fire. The victim, identified by fingerprints as Stella Marie Walker, was discovered by a hiker at the bottom of a ravine off the Elliot Barker Trail. Animals had apparently dug up the partially buried remains, discovered when the hiker left the trail to take a photo. If you have any information, please contact the Colfax County Sheriff's Department."

The department's number scrolled along the bottom of the screen. As the newscaster began to shuffle a stack of papers, Skye turned to Edge. "Did you hear that, Edge? Stella Marie Walker. That's her, Edge. Stella Beeker."

"Yeah, and now she's dead." Edge looked hard at Skye. "We can't wait to go in. Not if we want to get Lila out of there alive."

The jukebox started playing a country song as Skye slid off the barstool. A big guy with a ball cap covering most of his stringy blond hair walked toward them, blocking their exit. A dirty black T-shirt that read FUCK OFF stretched over his massive chest, and his thighs were the size of tree trunks.

His eyes swept over Skye's sexy curves. "Wanna dance, sweet thing?"

"Thanks, but we were just leaving." Skye smiled and tried to brush past him, but the guy caught her arm. "Come on, darlin'. Don't be that way." His grip tightened, and he started hauling her back toward the jukebox.

Edge clamped down on a rush of temper, caught a thick-muscled shoulder, and spun the guy around. "The lady said she was leaving. We don't want trouble. We just need to go."

The sound of chairs sliding back cut through Willie Nelson singing "Poncho and Lefty." Three of the big guy's friends stood up and surged forward, leaving them no escape.

Edge could feel it coming. Like a freight train roaring down the tracks with no way to stop it.

He looked at Skye.

"Let's make this quick," she said. "We need to leave." She cast him a look. "Just don't kill anyone."

Edge couldn't stop a grin.

When the dude with the ball cap and the FUCK OFF T-shirt swung the first punch, Edge ducked and stepped out of the way, letting the guy's momentum carry him forward, then delivering a kick in the ass that sent him sprawling into a table. His cap went flying. He swore foully and struggled to get back on his feet.

The second guy, in a leather biker vest and greasy jeans, was smaller, thinner, but sinewy and tough. Skye turned as he approached and shoved an elbow into his stomach, eliciting a grunt, then shot out with her good leg and sent him flying into a chair that tipped over backward, knocking his head against the scuffed wooden floor.

"We just want to leave," Edge said to the remaining two men.

As the big guy got back on his feet, the third guy jumped into the fray. Lowering his shiny bald head, he charged like a bull in an arena. Edge caught him around the neck and turned, slamming him headfirst into the wall. The bald guy slid down to the floor, his eyes rolling back until only the whites showed.

Hearing a commotion, Edge turned to see Skye boxed in by the fourth guy, pale-faced and ugly, and the big dude in the FUCK OFF T-shirt.

Time to get serious.

He caught Skye's glance, and she nodded, dropped to the floor on her back, and rammed her boot into the pale-faced guy's kneecap. With a scream, he twisted away, grabbing his leg and whining like a baby. Edge stepped in and used the side of his hand in a quick carotid chop to the big guy's neck. He dropped like a stone, and the fight was over.

"We just want to leave," Skye said, and then she smiled. "Okay with you gentlemen?"

The kneecapped dude made a whimpering sound, but none of them moved. Edge ushered Skye to the door, and they stepped out into the night. No one followed.

"No idea why that felt so good," Skye said.

"It's been a while. Maybe you needed the practice."

"Maybe," she said with a grin.

His gaze ran down her body. "How's your leg?"

"I'm wearing my brace." She smiled as she climbed into the truck. "It feels just fine."

Ten minutes later, they were back in the cabin, both of them still pumped. A hot look passed between them. There was something about standing up to a challenge and winning that heated your blood.

Edge reached for her at the same time Skye stepped into his arms. His hand slid into her thick dark hair to anchor her in place as his mouth crushed down over hers. The kiss was hot, wet, and deep. He told himself it didn't mean anything. It was just the heat of battle that had them both desperate for release.

"We don't have time for this," he said when they came up for air.

"We'll have to hurry." Skye reached for his belt buckle, then unzipped his fly while Edge unfastened her jeans. In seconds, her boots were gone and her jeans with them. A wet kiss kept them both occupied while Edge eased her panties down over her brace, turned her around, and bent her over the arm of the sofa.

Skye moaned and arched her back, and Edge took her deep. He took her hard, and she came the same way, groaning his name as she reached release. He didn't have time to wait, just gripped her hips and followed, his own release mind-blowingly intense.

Drawing her back against him, he held her while they drifted down again. He kissed the nape of her neck, and Skye turned into his arms, her face flushed, her pretty breasts still quivering.

"We . . . umm . . . have to go get Lila," she said.

"I know." Already wanting more of her, he kissed her one last time and let her go. "We need to make a plan."

CHAPTER TWENTY-SIX

EDGE MADE A CRUDE SKETCH OF THE PROPERTY LAYOUT ON THE side of a cardboard box he found in the trash and tore apart. The drawing showed the house and garage, the bunkhouse, and what was left of the dilapidated barn.

"I'll fit the drone with night vision, and we'll locate each man's position. With any luck, at least some of them will be asleep in the bunkhouse."

"Henson might post guards," Skye said.

"Could be. With Stella dead, the sheriff may come sniffing around looking for leads. Henson will figure on that."

"The sheriff probably won't come at night."

"Probably not. At least not as late as we'll be going in." Three to four a.m., prime time for a snatch-and-grab. Which, at this point, was the mission. They needed to get Lila out before she ended up as dead as Stella.

They talked through the details, but the plan had to remain fluid until they had more intel. They loaded their gear into the bed of the pickup beneath the tonneau cover and headed out a little before midnight. That gave them roughly three hours to collect information and figure out how to get Lila out without getting anyone killed—including themselves.

Not that he'd feel a lot of remorse if one of Henson's stone-cold killers strayed into the line of fire. They'd murdered Sarah Simmons and Stella Walker and buried them like heaps of trash.

Still, killing them wasn't his job. Not anymore. If everything went as planned, they could notify the DEA, let them handle Henson and his men.

Maybe the feds wouldn't botch the takedown this time.

As before, the drone was invaluable. From what Edge could see on the iPad screen, there was only one man standing guard. He patrolled the area around the house, staying some distance away, mainly keeping an eye on the road.

Two more men were asleep in the bunkhouse. He wondered if Beekman was one of them. The guy might have fallen out of favor when he'd murdered his common-law wife.

No way to know for sure.

The drone displayed a swamp-green image of a man in each upstairs bedroom. In a larger room at the other end of the hall, two images shared the same bed, presumably Henson and Lila.

Two men in the house plus Henson to deal with. If they timed it right, they could avoid being spotted by the guard or waking the men in the bunkhouse. With luck, they would be long gone by the time the DEA or the sheriff got there to round them all up.

They went over the plan for the third time before Edge was satisfied they were ready to go. The first guard had been relieved at midnight and returned to the bunkhouse. Three hours later, the second guard was relieved.

Probably rotating in three-hour shifts. They waited until the guard who'd just finished his turn was back in his bunk and a new guard was on duty, then, staying in the shadows, made their way down the slope, through the pine forest that surrounded the house. Edge used a lockpick to open the back door, and they slipped silently inside.

They would be saving Henson for last, taking down the other two men first, since they were the bigger threat. These guys were streetwise and tough. From what Molly had said, Harley Purcell was former military and mean as they came. Sarah Simmons and Stella Beeker had both been murdered.

Fortunately, none of the men were expecting visitors that night. They were miles from Blancha Springs, in a completely different state. Edge drew his Beretta, while Skye pulled a stun gun from its holster on her belt next to her Glock. At her nod, he quietly opened the door of the bedroom at the far end of the hall.

In the dim rays of moonlight coming in above the curtains, he caught a glimpse of red hair and a short red beard on the man asleep in the double bed. *Dutch.*

Skye moved, her hand shooting out to jab the stun gun into Dutch's ribs. Electricity crackled and popped. Dutch's eyes flew open, and his whole body shook. Muscles locked, teeth clenched. Dutch couldn't move, and in seconds, Edge had him on his stomach, his hands behind his back, cuffed with nylon zip ties.

Skye slapped a piece of duct tape over his mouth, and together they duct-taped his ankles. On a count of three, they quietly lifted him off the bed onto the floor so he lay facedown, then bent his legs back and taped them to his arms. Dutch was no longer a threat.

To be sure he stayed quiet, they dragged him into the closet and closed the door.

One down.

As they eased along the hall, Edge heard movement in the second bedroom. Someone was stirring, but there was no sound of footfalls on the floor. Skye pulled her Glock and held it two-handed. Edge opened the door and rushed forward, recognized Purcell from Molly's description, shoved his pistol into the flesh beneath Purcell's jaw before he was fully awake.

"Make a sound and I pull the trigger," Edge softly warned. Next to him, Skye kept her Glock pointed at the middle of Harley's barrel chest.

"Sit up, Purcell," Edge commanded. "Very slowly."

Harley's jaw clenched in fury as he sat up on the bed. "It was Molly, wasn't it? That bitch heard us talking. When I find her, I'm going to kill—"

Edge pressed the barrel deeper, tipping Purcell's head back. "I told you not to open your mouth." Harley fell silent, but the fury in his face didn't lessen.

"Hands behind your back."

Harley complied, his dark eyes tracking their every move. Skye slipped a nylon tie around his thick wrists and cinched it tight, then tore off a strip of duct tape and sealed it over his mouth.

Edge rolled him over, and Skye began duct-taping his ankles. When Harley jerked and started fighting, Edge did a quick tap with the gun barrel to the back of Harley's head, and he collapsed face-first on the mattress. Not dead, but definitely out for a while.

Skye finished tying him up, and they left him on the bed.

"Now Daniel," Edge said. Skye followed him out into the hall, both of them two-handing their weapons. He turned the knob on Daniel's bedroom door, but it wouldn't open. Pulling the lock-pick out of his pocket, he quickly worked the rudimentary lock. Daniel was fast asleep, one arm draped over Lila's middle. When Edge glanced at the woman's face, he found eyes as dark as midnight open and watching him.

This was the moment their well-thought-out plan could rapidly turn into a shitstorm. Lila didn't move as Edge approached the bed.

"Callie sent us," he said just above a whisper, and shoved the gun barrel against the side of Daniel's neck. Henson jerked awake.

"What the . . . ?" His whole body went rigid. "You!"

"We meet again," Edge said. "Be smart, Daniel, and don't make any sudden moves."

"Lila, are you coming with us?" Skye asked. "Or staying with him?"

Lila shoved Henson's arm off her and came to her feet beside the bed. She was wearing a man's white T-shirt, nothing more, while Henson wore a pair of men's red plaid flannel pajamas. She leaned over Daniel and spat in his face.

Edge flashed a grin at Skye. "Well, I guess we have our answer."

"Get dressed," Skye said to Lila. "Put on a jacket and some shoes you can walk in, and let's get out of here."

Wiping the spittle off his face with a shaking hand, Henson glanced wildly toward the door.

"Afraid they're out of commission for a while."

Henson's furious gaze fixed on Skye. "I remember you. You're Callie's sister. I was hoping my men would deal with both of you in Denver."

"If you didn't know," Skye said, "your man Vasquez is dead, and Mahler is on the run."

Henson turned back to Edge. "You want money? I'll pay you. I'll give you both a percentage of the operation."

"We don't want your money," Edge said.

"And your operation is just about finished," Skye added.

They bound Daniel's wrists and duct-taped his mouth and ankles. By the time they were done, Lila was dressed and ready to go.

A sound from outside the house caught Edge's attention. Hurrying to the window, he looked down to see the guard running toward the bunkhouse.

Time was up.

He looked at Henson. The cops were too far away to get there in time. Daniel would escape again.

"Change of plans," Edge said, jerking Henson to his feet. Pulling his knife from his boot, Edge cut the duct tape binding Henson's ankles. "You're going with us."

The slack-jawed surprise on Daniel's face gave Edge a shot of satisfaction.

"That's right. You're going down, Henson. You're going to get what you deserve for what you've done."

Skye moved ahead to clear the way as Edge dragged Daniel barefoot along the hall and down the stairs. Outside the dining room window, Edge spotted the guard and saw two men rush out of the bunkhouse to join him.

Edge hauled Henson through the kitchen and opened the back door.

"Cover me," he said to Skye, firing a series of shots toward the men, who scattered and ducked out of sight. Edge dragged Henson out of the house, then locked an arm around his neck, jerked the duct tape off his mouth, and pressed the barrel of the Beretta against the side of his head. "Tell them to hold their fire."

Daniel swallowed.

"Tell them!"

"Stop shooting!" Daniel shouted. "Don't shoot!"

The gunfire ceased.

"Tell them to stay back or I'll pull the trigger," Edge commanded, moving slowly across the yard.

"Stay back or he'll kill me!" There was a frantic note in Henson's voice.

Edge kept moving, dragging Daniel along as they headed into the forest. Skye and Lila rushed past them, racing toward the pickup, parked out of sight over the ridge. Henson's goons dogged their every move, prepared to shoot.

By the time Edge reached the truck, the engine was running, Lila in the front passenger seat, Skye waiting for his arrival, holding open the rear passenger door. Edge shoved Henson into the back seat, and Skye followed him in, jamming her pistol into his ribs, then pointing it down at Henson's crotch.

Edge managed not to grin as he slid behind the wheel. He shoved the pickup in gear, and the big truck leaped forward. Tires spun and gravel flew as the pickup shot down the narrow lane, slid around the turn onto the dirt road, and raced for Highway 64. A few miles down the highway, he made a sharp right onto Highway 84 and hit the gas, heading for Pagosa Springs, across the state line about forty miles away in Colorado.

"Everybody okay?" Edge asked, keeping his speed as high as possible through the dangerous mountain curves. He checked his rearview mirror for any sign they were being followed. Skye's glance connected with Lila's.

"Lila?" Skye asked.

"I'm fine," she called back.

Edge checked the rearview again. With a Colorado warrant out for Henson's arrest, his hired goons wouldn't have much trouble figuring they were headed to the nearest town across the line. But at the speed they were traveling, catching up to them wouldn't be easy.

As soon as the pickup rolled into cell range, Edge called up his voice-activated contacts and phoned DEA Supervisory Special Agent Derrick Cross.

A groggy voice came through the hands-free speakers. "Logan."

He must have recognized the caller ID. "What the hell do you want at this time of night?"

"I've found what you've been looking for. Daniel Henson and five of his men were setting up a new meth operation in New Mexico, at a place called the Pine Tree Ranch. It's thirteen miles west of Chamaya. Skye will text you the details. I've got Henson, but the rest of his men have scattered. Good chance they'll come after him. I'm hauling ass to the sheriff's office in Pagosa Springs."

"I'm on it," Cross said, his tone sharper now. "I'll have agents meet you there. I can't believe you managed to get yourself involved with Henson again."

"Believe it. Rolland Beekman is one of Henson's goons. Looks like he killed a woman named Stella Walker near the town of Angel Fire."

"Jesus."

"I've got to go. Be best if you didn't waste any time." Edge hung up the phone and checked his mirror. No sign of the men. He didn't let up on the gas.

CHAPTER TWENTY-SEVEN

It was quiet in the pickup, just the darkness and the curves ahead, lit by the wide white beams of the headlights.

Daniel's voice, a low whine, drifted over the back seat. "You don't understand what you've done. The man I work for . . . he's a very powerful figure. If you take me in, he'll think I'm going to talk. He'll find a way to kill me."

"That's your problem," Edge said.

Henson shifted his attention to Skye, whose pistol still pressed against his balls. "Please. I'm begging you. Let me go, and I'll give you all the money I have. There's at least a couple million in my account in Grand Cayman."

"If you turn state's evidence," Skye said, "the police will keep you safe."

"He's got cops on his payroll. Once I'm in the system, he can get to me wherever I am."

"What's your boss's name?" Edge asked, tossing out a line just to see if Henson would bite.

"I can't tell you that."

Edge turned the mirror a little to look at him. "You want to disappear? Tell me your boss's name, and I'll pull the truck over and let you out. You can keep your money and take your chances."

"You can't just let him go!" Lila looked ready to attack Daniel herself—or him.

Henson ignored her. "Why do you want his name?"

"That's my business," Edge said. "Do we have a deal?"

Daniel made no reply.

Five miles out of Pagosa Springs, Edge spotted a dirt road and pulled off the highway, drove around the first bend out of sight. He killed the engine, popped his seat belt, and turned to Henson.

"Your freedom for a name."

Daniel swallowed. His face glistened with sweat.

"We're only a few miles from town. You want to make a run for it, give me a name."

Henson smoothed a hand over his mashed-down, bed-head hair. He blew out a shaky breath. "Ivan Petrov. His name is Ivan Petrov."

Edge remembered what Zoe had told him. "He in Vegas?"

Daniel nodded. "That's him. Now let me out of here."

Edge grinned. "April Fools."

Skye laughed. Lila gave a teary chuckle of relief.

Daniel twisted and kicked his feet against the front seat in outrage. "We had a deal! Let me out of here!"

Skye pressed the gun deeper into his crotch. "Take it easy, Daniel. There's nothing I'd like to do more than pull this trigger."

Daniel stopped fighting. "You lied! You said you'd let me go."

Skye scoffed. "Yes. Just like you lied to all those women you convinced to join your so-called church."

Daniel fell silent. Ten minutes later, they drove up in front of the Archuleta County Sheriff's Office on Hartman Park Road. This late, the building was closed, but a pair of white-and-gold-striped sheriff's SUVs waited in front. The doors on both vehicles opened at the same time, and four uniformed deputies climbed out.

Edge walked around to the rear passenger door of the pickup, hauled Daniel out, and dragged him toward the deputies. His wrists were still bound, his feet bare. Duct tape clung to the legs of his plaid pajama bottoms.

"I'm Edge Logan. I'm a PI at Nighthawk Security in Denver. I imagine you got a call from the DEA regarding this man, Daniel Henson."

"I'm Sheriff Lassiter." Tall, lean, gray-haired, and hard-mouthed. "I received a call from Supervisory Special Agent Derrick Cross. We've been instructed to take Henson into custody on an outstanding warrant and hold him until the DEA arrives to pick him up."

Edge shoved Daniel forward. "He's all yours, Sheriff." Edge started back to the truck.

"I'm afraid we're going to need a statement from you and the other people involved."

Edge turned back and pulled a Nighthawk business card out of his wallet. He handed the card to the sheriff. "I was hoping the statement I gave Agent Cross would be enough for now. Agent Cross knows the details and where to find me."

The sheriff looked at the card. It was late, it was dark, and the temperature was below freezing. Clearly, the sheriff had been dragged out of a nice warm bed to take Henson into custody.

Lassiter tipped his head toward the truck. "What about them?"

"Skye Delaney is also a PI at Nighthawk. Lila Ramirez is a civilian. She's prepared to give a full statement, but only to Agent Cross."

The sheriff released a slow breath. He was looking for a way to lessen his paperwork and get back to bed. "I suppose as long as Agent Cross knows where to find you . . ."

Edge nodded. Skye had texted Cross the basic info, along with her home address in Denver, where Lila would be staying. "Thanks for the help, Sheriff." He turned to the other men. "Deputies."

Glad to be rid of their unwelcome cargo, they headed back to Denver, almost three hundred miles away. Ironically, Skye thought, by taking the route through Blancha Springs, they could shave off thirty minutes.

"Why don't you let me drive for a while?" Skye suggested when Edge yawned for the third time since they'd left Pagosa Springs.

He glanced at her over his shoulder. "You sure?"

"Absolutely. You may have been raised on a ranch, but I've got a brother who taught me how to drive, and he owned a big Dodge truck. To say nothing of my time in the army."

"Okay, great."

Dawn was breaking when they reached the next convenience store to change places.

While Edge gassed the pickup, the women made a quick pit stop. Then Skye climbed in behind the wheel, Edge took the back seat, and Lila continued to ride up front. Within minutes, Edge was asleep. It was a handy soldier's trick, one Skye had also learned. Both of them could fall asleep in minutes just about anywhere and still keep an ear cocked for danger.

As Skye drove the truck back toward the city, Lila's voice drifted over from the passenger seat. "Thank you for coming to get me. I was waiting, praying for a chance to escape, but I was . . ." She swallowed. "I was beginning to lose hope. I will never be able to repay you for what you both have done."

"Callie made you a promise. We're just helping her keep it."

Lila's eyes welled with tears. "Stella's dead. Riley Beeker killed her."

Skye's hands tightened around the steering wheel. "I know. It was on the news. His real name is Rolland Beekman. Most of the men in Blancha Springs were using aliases. Their marriages weren't real."

Lila sniffed and wiped away the wetness. "Mine was. Raul Ramirez is my husband's real name. My real name. We were married in St. Mary's Church two weeks before Daniel hired him. We were both excited about his new job."

"Callie said Daniel told you Raul was dead."

Lila gazed out the window. "To me, he is dead. Raul left me with Daniel and never came back. I was a fool to believe he loved me."

"Maybe Daniel's men killed him," Skye said. "Maybe that's why he never returned."

Lila turned to stare out the window at the dawn beginning to lighten the horizon. "It doesn't matter. Not anymore." Her hand curved over the front of the yoga pants and sweater she had put on, along with a pair of sneakers. The heater was running to keep her feet warm. "Raul abandoned me—and his child."

Skye's attention shot to the woman in the passenger seat. "You're pregnant?"

"I have been late for two months in a row." A faint smile touched her lips. "And something inside me feels different. I pray it is true." Lila didn't say more, and silence filled the truck cab.

A full hour passed before Edge awoke and demanded to take back the wheel.

This time Skye napped in the back seat. Or tried to. She kept thinking of everything that had happened since she and Edge had gone to Chamaya. She was supposed to be pulling away from him, protecting herself. Instead, she had given in to the wild hunger stirred by the fight in the bar. Whatever her intentions, her body had refused to listen.

She'd wanted Edge. Needed him. She still did.

Her thoughts went to Lila and Raul Ramirez, the man she had married, the man who had left her alone to bear and raise his child. One thing she knew—Edge might move on with his life, but if something happened, he would never abandon her. It just made her care for him more.

Not *care*, she corrected herself. She was way beyond that. She was in love with him.

Skye closed her eyes and managed to force thoughts of Edge from her mind. It was late morning when they arrived in Denver. Lila was exhausted, and the brief nap Skye'd had in the back seat of the truck hadn't done much good.

Carrying her bags, Edge followed her and Lila up to the apartment, said a brief farewell, and disappeared. Though he lived only a few blocks away, Skye felt strangely bereft.

Once they were settled, she pulled out her cell and phoned Callie.

"I'm coming over right now!" Callie said. "Tell Lila. I'll ask Conn to drop me off at your place."

During the women's tearful reunion, Lila told Callie about Stella and that Riley Beeker, aka Beekman, had killed her. She explained that Daniel had forced her to accompany him and service him in bed.

"I did what I had to do to stay alive. Then I realized I was pregnant with Raul's child, and I was even more determined. I was so afraid they would kill me. If I died, so would my baby. Then your sister and her friend Edge came to the ranch."

Lila explained to Callie about the shootout, how Edge had forced Daniel to go with them, then turned him over to the sheriff in Pagosa Springs.

"I will never forget what your sister and her Edge did for me," Lila said.

Callie leaned in and hugged her. Both of them cried.

Lila believed Skye and Edge were a couple. Skye didn't bother to correct her. She didn't think Edge would ever belong to any woman. He was too much of a loner to open up in the way that was necessary for a relationship to work.

Leaving the women alone in the guest room to catch up and try to figure out which paths their future should take, Skye was surprised when Edge showed up at the apartment that evening carrying two large pepperoni pizzas.

"I figured after such a long day you'd all be hungry," he said.

Skye smiled as she took the pizzas and set them on the kitchen counter. "Thanks, these smell great. I thought you'd be ready for some down time by now." *Some time to yourself*, she meant.

Edge's blue eyes fixed on her face. "I guess I'm getting used to having you around."

Ignoring the little thrill that slipped through her and refusing to read too much into the words, she went to work. In the cupboard, she found some paper plates and set them on the counter, then called Lila and Callie to join them.

"Callie's here?" Edge asked.

"I called to let her know Lila was safe, and she wanted to come over. Conn dropped her off. He'll come back for her in the morning."

She turned as the women walked into the kitchen. "Edge brought pizza. There's soft drinks and beer in the fridge." Grabbing a Bud Light for herself and one for Edge, she handed him a bottle.

Callie grabbed a beer. "I turned twenty-one while you were gone." She cranked the cap off the bottle and held it up. "I'm finally legal."

"Oh, that's right! Happy birthday!" Skye smiled. "We need to celebrate. You can't have a twenty-first birthday and spend the night at home."

"I . . . umm . . . went out with Detective Powers that night."

Skye remembered him. Buzz-cut brown hair, muscular, and good-looking.

"He convinced Conn I'd be safe with him," Callie said.

"Or maybe not," Edge drawled, a protective note in his voice.

Callie laughed. "He's only twenty-five, and he was a perfect gentleman. But thanks for your concern."

Lila smiled softly as she picked up a soda. "No alcohol for me. Not for a while."

By now, everyone, including Edge, knew about the baby. "Congratulations," he said.

Callie reached over and squeezed Lila's hand. "I know it must be scary, but whatever happens, we'll figure it out."

Lila smiled.

They finished the pizzas. The girls helped pick up the trash, then disappeared back into the guest room.

"We need to talk," Edge said, as soon as they were alone.

CHAPTER TWENTY-EIGHT

WITH SO MUCH UNSETTLED BETWEEN THEM AND NO IDEA WHERE the conversation was headed, Skye just looked up at him.

"About Petrov," Edge added. He grabbed another beer out of the fridge and handed her a second one.

Skye cranked off the cap and took a swallow. At least they were back on familiar ground. "I assumed you would turn that information over to Agent Cross."

"I'm thinking about it. But if Henson's right and this guy, Petrov, has law enforcement on his payroll, the investigation might not go anywhere. Petrov could walk, and before long he'd be starting his drug operation all over again."

"So you're thinking . . . what?"

"I'm thinking I might go to Vegas, do a little digging myself. The idea of Petrov just finding another stooge and starting all over doesn't sit right with me."

Skye had been thinking the very same thing. "Doesn't work for me, either."

"I'm not asking you to go. I'm just telling you what I'm going to do."

"Don't insult me."

His sexy mouth curved. "Sorry." He took a drink of beer. "So I guess we're both going to Vegas."

Which meant this thing between them wasn't over. Skye

thought of Edge's hot kisses in the cabin in Chamaya, thought of his lean, strong hands moving over her body, and heat slid into her core.

Oblivious to her thoughts—thank God—Edge tipped up his beer and took a swallow. "After I left the office this morning, I talked to Zoe about Petrov."

She nodded. "I was planning to call as soon as things settled down."

"Zoe called me back just before I got here. Ivan Dmitri Petrov's his full name. Russian parents. Petrov owns a fancy supper club in Vegas called the Four Winds, which is where he generally hangs out. But he also owns strip clubs in Vegas, Reno, all over Nevada."

He pulled out his cell and brought up the photo of Petrov that Zoe had texted. Six feet tall, thick-shouldered and barrel-chested, slicked-back black hair and hard features.

"He lives in a house worth somewhere close to fifteen million dollars. Italian style. Calls it Villa Milano."

Skye took a sip of her beer. "Guy definitely lives the high life. Did Zoe find any connection between him and Carl Wisen or Oscar Andreyev?"

"She's on it. She's got other stuff to do, so it may take a few days."

"You know, there's always the chance Henson served Petrov up to the DEA in order to save his own rotten skin."

"Yeah, I thought of that. Daniel's afraid of Petrov, but working with the feds is probably his best chance of getting a lesser sentence."

"I've been expecting to hear from Cross," Skye said. "Sooner or later, he's going to want a statement from Lila."

"He knows where to find her."

She nodded. "Meanwhile, we're off to Vegas. What's our objective?"

"For now, we just sniff around, get the lay of the land. Maybe check out Wisen and Andreyev, see how they fit into the scheme of things."

"Sounds good. Are we driving or flying?" Skye asked.

"Too far to drive, and getting our weapons through the airlines is too much trouble. Better to fly private. I've already made the arrangements for a charter to leave in the morning, if that works for you."

"I'll be ready."

"We don't know what we'll be facing so prepare for anything."

"Okay."

"We'll need accommodations. I was thinking the Bellagio." Hot blue eyes ran over her, scorching in their intensity.

"Nice place," she said.

He nodded, took another drink of beer. "So the only question is . . . one room or two?"

Silence fell. Skye looked up at him, her insides churning. Surely, he could read in her face what she wanted. With his black hair, blue eyes, and perfect features, he was so handsome it made her breath catch. To say nothing of his sculpted, amazing body. She knew he was going to leave. It was only a matter of time.

Still . . .

His phone rang before she could answer.

Edge took the call and walked a few paces away to speak. He looked different when he returned. Harder. Darker. She knew what he was going to say before he opened his mouth.

"That was Grease. Bradley Markham's discharge came through. He's moving to San Diego."

Her insides tightened. "San Diego? Why San Diego?"

"Grease says he's bought a house there. Tract house, nothing special. Word is he's got another place under a different name in Cabo San Lucas. Grease says it overlooks the ocean. Says the place is worth millions."

Skye finished her beer. "Smuggling weapons pays a lot better than a major's salary."

"That's for sure."

She arched a dark eyebrow. "So . . . are you heading for California or are we still going to Vegas?"

Edge set his empty bottle down on the counter. "First things first. We look into Petrov, then I tackle Markham." Skye didn't resist when he eased her into his arms, bent his head, and very softly kissed her.

His eyes locked on her face, and she could feel the heat. "You didn't answer my question."

She told herself to say no. She was setting herself up for heartache. *One room or two?* She swallowed. "One . . ." she whispered. "One room."

Edge kissed her again, slowly, intimately, making all sorts of unspoken promises. He glanced down the hall, his thoughts more than clear, but the apartment wasn't empty.

"What about tonight?" he asked, his eyes never leaving her face.

Going home with him was exactly what she wanted. But if she was going to do this, she needed time to collect herself, get herself back under control.

"I've got to get Lila settled in, and Callie's here. Police still haven't picked up Klaus Mahler. Conn will be back in the morning. I'll see you then."

Edge nodded, but she didn't miss the regret in his face. "Whatever you want."

Far from it, she thought, wishing she could change her mind. Knowing it was the wrong thing to do.

Skye slept fitfully. So much had happened in the past few days. So much remained unfinished. It was two o'clock in the morning when she heard a sound in the guest room where Callie and Lila were spending the night. After all they had been through, they were a comfort to each other. And they had a lot to catch up on.

Skye sat up in bed, heard a scream, followed by the door bursting open down the hall.

Callie's voice rang out. "Skye! Come quick! It's Lila! Something's wrong with the baby!"

She was already on her feet. Ignoring thoughts of Mahler, she left her gun in the drawer next to her bed, grabbed her terry robe and pulled it on, stuck her cell phone in her pocket, and raced down the hall.

Lila sat up in the twin bed, bent double, clutching her abdomen.

"She's bleeding," Callie said, her voice shaking. "And she's in a lot of pain."

Pulling out her phone, Skye punched in 911.

"This is police dispatch. What's your emergency?"

"We need an ambulance. There's a woman—she's pregnant. She's bleeding and in pain. Please hurry!" She rattled off the address of the apartment building, including the unit number. "Hurry—please!"

"Ma'am, stay on the line."

Bent over on the bed, Lila gripped her stomach. "My baby . . ." Tears rolled down her cheeks. "Please . . . I don't know what to do."

Skye's heart clenched. "The ambulance is on its way. Try to stay calm. How badly are you bleeding?"

"Not . . . not too much, but the cramps, they are really bad." A deep groan of pain escaped her throat as another vicious stab struck.

Callie rushed into the bathroom for towels, returned, and pressed them between Lila's legs. Her flannel nightgown was spotted with blood, and she was trembling. Skye pulled the blanket up over her, but it didn't stop her body from shaking.

Every minute seemed like an eternity. *Where was that ambulance?*

"I can't lose my baby," Lila said. Fresh tears welled. "I have already lost Raul. I cannot lose my baby, too."

Skye's own eyes filled. Lila had suffered so much. She didn't need this, too. Skye found herself stepping into the hall, taking a shaky breath, and punching in Edge's number. She couldn't stop a sob at the sound of his voice.

"Skye! What is it? Skye? Honey, tell me what's wrong!"

She swallowed back another sob. "It's . . . it's Lila's baby." A sound slipped from her throat, but knowing Edge was on the other end of the line somehow steadied her. "The ambulance is . . . is on its way. I just . . . there's nothing you can do. I don't know why I called."

"I'm coming over. I'm on my way. If the ambulance isn't there when I get there, we'll drive her to the hospital ourselves."

Her throat closed. She felt better just hearing his voice. "Yes. All right. I'll tell her." She hadn't realized she was crying. Wiping tears from her cheeks, she took a deep breath and hurried back into the bedroom.

In an emergency, she was usually the strong one. The thought of Lila losing her precious child touched a place inside her, a secret feminine place she hadn't been sure existed until now.

She reached for Lila's hand. "Edge is coming. If the ambulance isn't here when he arrives, he's going to drive us himself."

The tears in Lila's eyes rolled down her cheeks, followed by a deep moan of pain. "I can't . . . can't lose my baby."

"Everything's going to be okay." Skye squeezed Lila's hand and prayed it was true. Inside her chest, her heart beat dully. Lila wanted this baby so badly. She had already lost so much. Skye prayed she wouldn't lose her unborn child, too.

The intercom buzzed, and Skye hurried to answer it.

"Your ambulance is here," the guard in the lobby said. "Paramedics are on their way up."

Her voice shook. "Thank you." Skye rushed to the door. "Please come in. Hurry. Mrs. Ramirez is just down the hall."

Two paramedics in dark green uniforms wheeled a gurney into the living room. Edge walked in behind them. When he reached for her, Skye went into his arms. She found herself clinging to him as if his presence could somehow save her.

"Lila's going to be okay," he said, holding her even tighter. "So is the baby." He eased back and caught her chin, forcing her to look at him. "You need to believe that, honey, for Lila's sake."

A trembly breath whispered out. "You're right." She leaned into him, felt his solid strength. "I shouldn't have called. It's not your problem."

Edge caught her shoulders. "If it's your problem, it's my problem. We're friends, aren't we? That's what friends are for."

Her throat tightened. She nodded. They *were* friends. When had she started wanting more? Edge pulled her back into his arms, smoothing a hand up and down her back. The sound of the gurney wheels churning down the hall had them stepping apart. The gurney rolled toward the front door.

Callie followed a few feet behind, already dressed to leave. "I'm going with her."

"I'll put on some clothes and meet you there," Skye said.

"I'll drive you," Edge said.

Skye shook her head. "You don't have to do that."

"Just get dressed, okay?" There was command in his voice. It wasn't up for negotiation.

She managed to nod. "Okay."

A few minutes later, they were on their way to St. Joseph's Hospital on East 19th Street, not too far away.

The three of them spent the balance of the night in the waiting room, while doctors checked for complications that could threaten mother and baby.

The hours seemed to stretch endlessly.

Dawn was breaking when the doctor, a slender Hispanic man, came in to tell them they had things under control. There was no hemorrhaging. It was not an ectopic pregnancy, and there was no life-threatening rupture.

"We've given her some medication to help with the pain," the doctor said. "It's already beginning to fade, but we'll keep her a few more hours to be sure everything is okay. As long as Mrs. Ramirez takes it easy for a while, there should be no reason she can't have a normal, healthy baby."

Relief hit Skye hard. Edge's arms went around her from behind, pulled her back against his chest, and she drew a steadying breath. Apparently, the motherly instincts she'd never realized she had were alive and well inside her. She got an odd sense of comfort from that.

She had no idea why. Her biological clock was ticking, and there was little chance she would marry and have children. Certainly she wouldn't be marrying Edge, who wasn't a one-woman man. Even if he were, his dream was to return to the Green Berets. Which meant he would be gone well over half the year. She wasn't interested in a part-time husband.

Another half hour passed before they were allowed to see Lila, who was drowsy but smiling. It occurred to Skye that Lila Ramirez was a very brave woman.

They were ready to leave. Callie was planning to stay until Lila was released. Conn would be picking up both women and taking them back to his house, where he insisted they stay until things went back to normal. Lila was dozing when Skye and Edge slipped away.

Callie walked them down the hall. "Are you still going to Vegas?" Though Skye hadn't gone into detail, she had mentioned the trip. Too much was going on to simply disappear.

"We'll only be there a couple of days. We're staying at the Bellagio. If you need anything, call me."

"I will." Callie leaned over and hugged her. "I'm lucky to have a sister like you."

Skye smiled. "I think that goes both ways." She had learned the same lesson Callie had. Family meant everything. And Skye had a good one.

Callie disappeared back down the hall, while Skye and Edge headed for the elevator.

"I guess we've missed our plane," Skye said as they made their way out the glass front doors into the late-morning sunshine.

"I called and had the flight put back a few hours," Edge said. "Now that we know Lila's okay, we can still make the flight."

Skye nodded. "I packed last night. Callie and Lila will be safe with Conn until I get back."

"Great, let's grab our stuff and head for the airport."

And the room they would be sharing at the Bellagio hotel.

CHAPTER TWENTY-NINE

EDGE HAD JUST PARKED HIS TRUCK AT THE PRIVATE TERMINAL AT Centennial Airport when his cell phone rang. He pulled out the phone and checked the caller ID, flicked a glance at Skye, and put the phone on speaker.

"Agent Cross. I've been expecting to hear from you." At the very least, Cross still needed a statement from Lila.

"We need to talk," Cross said simply.

"Sorry, I'm on my way to Vegas. After recent events, I figured I deserved a little time off."

"Vegas, huh? What a coincidence. That's where I'm headed."

Petrov. Had to be. So Daniel had rolled on his Russian boss after all.

"Where are you staying?" Cross asked.

"The Bellagio."

"Nice. I assume Ms. Delaney is with you."

"Not that it's any of your business, but yes."

"Even better. We can meet in the hotel, somewhere we can speak privately."

"All right. You can come up to the suite. I'll text you the room number once we've checked in."

"Seven o'clock work for you?"

"Fine." Edge ended the call and shoved the phone back into his pocket.

"What do you think Cross wants?" Skye asked as Edge unloaded their bags and they started toward the terminal.

"No idea. But if he's coming to Vegas, it's something to do with Petrov."

"I guess we'll find out tonight."

"Yeah, I guess we will."

The just over two-hour chartered jet flight from Denver to Harry Reid International in Las Vegas was uneventful. A black Lincoln SUV limo waited at the executive terminal to carry them the five miles through traffic to the Bellagio.

There were newer resort/casinos on the Vegas Strip, but Edge had stayed at the Bellagio before and knew his way around. He could easily afford the luxury one-bedroom suite he had booked.

He clamped down on where that thought led.

Years ago, he had sold his share of the Diamond Bar Ranch, his family home, to his oldest brother, Kade. In the army, he'd had no real place to spend the money, so most of it still sat in the bank. Add to that his share of the gold bullion he had helped Gage bring back from Mexico, and he had no real money worries.

He checked in at the front desk using an app on his phone, and a bellman brought up their luggage, all but his suitcase, which held their semiautomatic pistols and other miscellaneous weapons and gear. That big wheeled bag he brought up himself.

When the bellman opened the door to the suite, he heard Skye's intake of breath. She crossed the white marble floor in the entry, noticed the powder room for guests off to one side, and turned to survey the living room, the plush, gray-patterned carpet, the pale blue velvet sofa and chairs.

"I certainly didn't expect this." She walked over to the big plate-glass windows that wrapped around both the living room and dining area. "This is fantastic. Look!" She pointed. "You can see the fountains from here!"

Edge smiled. "I'm glad you like it."

Smiling, Skye walked back to him. His heart kicked up when she set her palms on his chest. Wisps of silky dark hair clung to her cheeks, and he could smell her soft perfume. He pulled her closer. He could feel her breasts pressing against him, and his body stirred to life. In an instant, he was hard. He couldn't remember a woman who aroused him the way she did.

"You know, I'm the one who should be paying for this," Skye said, still smiling. "Going after Daniel Henson was my idea."

Edge forced himself to concentrate. "Yeah, well, going after Ivan Petrov is my idea."

Skye laughed. "I guess it really doesn't matter." She glanced around the suite. "Neither of us is hurting for money." She started to turn away, but he pulled her back into his arms.

"The thing that matters is there's only one bedroom in this suite, and as soon as we get back to the room tonight, we're going to make use of it."

Skye flushed. Edge bent his head and softly kissed her, forcing himself not to linger. "Until then, we have work to do." He eased away before his body took over and said to hell with waiting for tonight.

"What's on the agenda?" Skye asked.

"After we get rid of Cross, we're going to supper at the Four Winds. According to Zoe, Petrov's practically a fixture. With luck, we'll get a look at him, see what we're up against. I checked the place out on Tripadvisor. It's first class all the way. If you didn't bring the right clothes, you can probably find something in one of the shops downstairs."

"I'm fine. You said to come prepared."

He smiled. "So I did."

As evening approached, the expression on his face changed to one of awe as Skye walked into the living room. He had never seen her in a dress. With her leg injury and the brace she sometimes wore, pants were typically the best option.

Or so he had believed.

Tonight she wore a floor-length gown made of sleek bronze fabric that clung to her curves and gleamed like burnished gold. Thin spaghetti straps held up the front, which draped so low he could see the tempting swells of her breasts. She turned in a circle so he could see the back, which matched the front, draping almost to the crack in her perfect little ass.

He wanted to lock her in the suite, keep her all to himself, keep her from wearing that sexy dress in front of a roomful of randy men.

Edge silently cursed. He had no idea where the thought had come from and no right to think it. They were sleeping together, but there were no strings attached, nothing permanent, nothing that would last.

His insides tightened at the thought.

As Skye walked toward him, his gaze went to the knee-high slit in the right side of the dress that revealed a gold sandal, a trim ankle, and a portion of shapely feminine leg.

It occurred to him that he never thought of Skye's scarred limb. It never entered his head. She was just Skye, one of the most beautiful women he had ever seen, one of the smartest, the sexiest, and by far the bravest.

She had swept her silky locks up in a twist, but wispy strands floated beside her ears, where long gold earrings dangled. The gleaming bronze gown set off the same rich highlights in her hair.

He was hard as a brick by the time she reached him, rested her hands on the lapels of the black, custom-tailored suit he was wearing with a black shirt and black tie. Leaning up, she settled her mouth very softly over his, and those damp, full lips set him on fire.

He caught her waist, pulled her in and deepened the kiss, let it go on as long as he dared, finally forced himself to pull away.

He ran a finger down her cheek. "I'm hanging on by a thread here. This stops right now, or we're heading for the bedroom."

Skye laughed. It was a sexy, crystalline sound he had never heard before. She was reclaiming her feminine power, he realized, finally understanding that her injury did nothing to blunt the sharp stab of sexual desire he felt for her, that any red-blooded male would feel for her.

"You look beautiful," he said gruffly.

Sea-green eyes ran over him, from his freshly trimmed black hair to his polished black shoes. "You look amazing. That suit fits those wide shoulders of yours perfectly."

He smiled, pleased by her approval, grateful for his mother's sense of style and the manners she had drilled into him. "It should, for what I paid for it."

Skye returned his smile. "I've never seen you this dressed up before."

"Yeah? Maybe we should have done this sooner." His gaze went to her breasts, getting a tantalizing glimpse of plump, satiny flesh, and his arousal strengthened. "Room service is beginning to sound a lot better than a night in a crowded restaurant."

The laughter came again. Edge felt a sliver of sexual heat that tightened every muscle in his groin. He cleared his throat. "We need to leave." *Now. Before it's too late.*

The doorbell rang. *Saved by the bell.* He had completely forgotten his appointment with Cross. He flicked a glance at Skye. He had placed his backup weapon in a drawer in the entry table within easy reach, but after a quick check of the peephole to confirm who it was—dark brown suit, pale yellow shirt, spit-shined shoes, and perfectly styled brown hair—he relaxed and pulled open the door.

"Agent Cross. Right on time. Come on in."

Cross walked into the suite with another man, taller, broader, African American. with very dark skin and intelligent black eyes.

"Edge Logan and Skye Delaney, this is Special Agent Oliver Jackson. As I said on the phone, we need a word with you."

Edge led them farther into the living room, and they all sat down on the L-shaped pale blue sofa.

"All right," Edge said. "You're here. We're here. What can we do for you?"

"I'm going to jump right in and guess you didn't just come to Vegas for a vacation. You were hunting Daniel Henson in Denver. You were hunting him in New Mexico, where you managed to find him and turn him over to law enforcement. I figure you're also hunting the man who was paying him—Ivan Petrov."

"So Henson rolled on his boss. Is Daniel in protective custody?"

"Henson's clammed up tight. He's lawyered up and not saying a word. We got the name from a different source. Now answer the question."

"And if we're here for Petrov?"

"Then we have the same goal. Petrov's running the show. Put him out of business for good and his whole empire comes crashing down."

Edge said nothing. He wanted to know Cross's plan.

"I assume the idea appeals to you," Cross said.

"Of course, it does," Skye answered. "Petrov has ruined thousands of lives with the drugs he manufactures, to say nothing of the people who die from using them."

"Getting Daniel Henson off the streets isn't enough," Edge said. "It's Petrov who needs to be put away."

"Exactly." Cross's shrewd gaze ran over the black suit Edge was wearing and Skye's long, sexy, body-hugging gown. "You wouldn't be going to the Four Winds tonight, by any chance?"

Edge stiffened. He didn't like the idea of being dogged by the DEA. On the other hand, Cross might prove useful. "Actually, we are." He flashed a phony smile. "Five stars on Tripadvisor."

The corner of Cross's mouth curved up. "You've already agreed our goals are the same. If we work together, we can make this happen."

Edge hadn't planned to take on Petrov this soon, but if the opportunity was here, he intended to grasp it. "What, exactly, do you have in mind?"

CHAPTER THIRTY

THEY POSTPONED THEIR DINNER RESERVATION. TWO HOURS LATER, they were finished with agents Cross and Jackson and were ready to leave for the second time that night.

Edge straightened his black suit coat, custom designed to allow for the shoulder holster he was wearing. He and Skye were both legally permitted to carry. The rest of their weapons and the disposable phone Cross had given them were locked in the room, safe in the closet.

"I'll get my bag and my wrap." The temperature in Vegas the first of October was in the low 80s during the day, but it was cool at night. Edge watched Skye cross the room to the bedroom, the dress hugging her slender curves. He closed his eyes against a fresh rush of heat.

She returned with a small gold bag and a black lace shawl he draped over her bare shoulders. He wanted to press his mouth against her sun-bronzed skin, kiss his way up the nape of her neck, and inhale the scent of her soft perfume. He wanted to cup those delectable breasts, feel her nipples harden in his hands. He wanted to do a whole lot more.

Turning away from her, Edge narrowed his focus on the task ahead. The mission came first. They were there for Ivan Petrov. He wanted to wrap the Russian up in a shiny red bow and hand him over to law enforcement. He hoped to hell Petrov would be at the restaurant tonight. If not, they would need to try a different approach.

He smiled to himself. Staying in Vegas wouldn't be tough duty in a luxury suite with Skye in his bed. His smile slowly faded. Whatever happened, the task they'd undertaken was infinitely more complicated now that the DEA was involved.

His phone rang just then. Edge checked the number, saw it was Zoe. "What's up?"

"You can cross Wiser and Andreyev off your list. They work for Petrov, but they're just placeholders. They do menial work, mostly get paid for signing their names to whatever papers Petrov shoves in front of them."

"Like corporate land-ownership documents."

"That's right. Petrov wants to keep things anonymous, but in the case of the property in Colorado and New Mexico, Wiser and Andreyev's names on the corporate filings worked against him. We were able to connect the ownership of both properties to Petrov."

"The DEA probably has the same info by now. Thanks, Zoe. Saves us a lot of leg work." The call ended, and Edge looked up to see Skye walking toward him.

"Ready?" With every step, the dress slid sinuously over her body, and Edge felt another sexual kick.

"The hotel limo's waiting out front," he said, forcing himself to concentrate on the task ahead.

In theory, the plan was simple. Get a meeting with Petrov and convince him to bring the two of them into his organization. By now, Daniel had no doubt reported who they were. Petrov would know Edge Logan and Skye Delaney were the ones who had destroyed his meth operation in Blancha Springs. Odds were, he also knew they had turned Daniel in to the Colorado authorities, destroying any plans to rebuild in Chamaya.

Simple in theory. In reality, dangerous as hell. He had no idea what Petrov would do to them once they made contact. Would he hear them out or just want them dead? Edge didn't like bringing

Skye into such a volatile situation, but she had been in it from the start. He knew she wouldn't back off now.

Skye slipped her arm through his, and they left the suite. As they stepped out of the elevator, the clank and clatter, bells, whistles, and flashing lights of gaming machines, along with the roar of the crowds at the dice tables, followed them toward the front door. If Petrov was at the Four Winds tonight, they could launch their campaign.

If not, they would find another way to reach him.

Edge thought of the big bed waiting for them when they got back to the hotel—assuming they managed to stay alive—and his blood rushed south. Either way, the night would not be boring.

The hotel limo dropped them off at the Four Winds Supper Club, which was even more stylish than advertised on its web page. The two-story, free-standing building was designed with an art deco theme, the interior entirely done in black and white.

The restaurant itself was a circular room with linen-draped tables on raised daises surrounding a glossy-black dance floor. A three-piece orchestra played 1940s music, and a bar ran the length of one curved wall.

Edge set a hand at Skye's waist to guide her over to the bar, then helped her up on a stool with a curved black leather back. The waiters all wore tuxedoes, including the bartender who arrived in front of them.

"What can I get you?" He was mid-forties, dark-haired with a neatly trimmed mustache and pointed goatee.

"I'll have a vodka martini," Skye said. "Two olives. Beluga, please. Gold if you have it."

Top-line Russian vodka. Edge flashed her a look of approval. She was casting a lure for Petrov, and as beautiful as she looked tonight, it might just work.

The bartender made a brief nod of his head. "No problem." He turned to Edge. "And for you, sir?"

"Glenfiddich. Neat." The bartender slipped silently away, and a few minutes later, reappeared. He set their drinks on the bar in front of them.

Skye took a sip of her long-stemmed, chilled martini. "Delicious. I love martinis, but I rarely drink them. I like to save them for special occasions."

Edge thought of what he had in mind for her in the suite later that night—hopefully after they'd made contact with Petrov. He definitely intended to make it special.

The restaurant was packed, every white-draped table filled with elegantly dressed men and women. It was a mixed crowd of older and younger successful businessmen and women, and hip, monied late-twenty, early-thirty-year-olds in outrageously expensive designer clothing.

Edge spotted a couple of muscle-heads in white dinner jackets who looked more like cage fighters than doormen. Skye's gaze followed his, and she cast him a knowing look. These were the same type of goons who'd worked for Henson.

Her glance slid off to one side. "Edge, we've got company."

He spotted the red-haired, red-bearded man walking toward them. *Dutch.* The guy knew who they were. He had been in Blancha Springs, as well as New Mexico. Two of Petrov's thugs fell in behind him as Dutch skirted the dance floor, made his way to the bar, and stopped right in front of them.

Edge just smiled. "Well, look who's here. If it isn't our old friend, Dutch."

He was as tall as Edge, with wide, thick shoulders. Skye tipped her head back to look at him. "You never know who you're going to run into in a place like this," she said.

A knot bunched in Dutch's cheek. "Mr. Petrov wants to see you."

Well, that didn't take long. Hell, they hadn't even gotten to finish their drinks.

Edge took a sip of his scotch. "Tell him we'd love to have him join us. Tell him we'll buy him a drink."

"Let's go," Dutch said. The other two men moved closer, boxing them in. "Now."

Edge stood up and helped Skye down from the barstool. In one way, he couldn't have planned it better. He figured Cross would be doing a happy dance. In another way, they were walking a very thin line.

According to Cross, the DEA had people in place in the restaurant, but at this point there was no way to contact them. He hoped wherever they were, they were prepared to step in if the whole thing went south.

"This way." Dutch led them up the center aisle into the impressive, black-and-white, marble-floored entry. A staircase wound up the wall on the right.

"Upstairs."

They headed in that direction, reached the landing at the top, and started down the hall. Dutch paused in front of a pair of closed, ten-foot-tall doors and did a quick pat down, found the gun in Edge's shoulder holster, removed it.

"Got anything else?" Dutch asked.

"Nothing you'd be interested in." Which wasn't exactly true since he had a knife strapped to his calf just above his ankle.

"What about her?" Dutch asked.

Edge's gaze ran over Skye's shapely curves outlined by the body-hugging, sleek bronze dress. He cocked an eyebrow. "Seriously?"

Dutch turned and rapped on the door, then reached for the knob and opened it. "Go on in."

Edge walked past Dutch into the room, then stood back to allow Skye to enter. Petrov's office, complete with wide mahogany desk, green-shaded lamps, ornate bookcases filled with gilt-trimmed, leather-bound volumes and tufted, red-leather chairs, might have belonged to an old-time cattle baron.

"Have a seat." The big Russian looked exactly like his photo: linebacker shoulders, slicked-back black hair, a hard face that looked as if it had been pounded with a meat tenderizer.

Dutch shoved Edge down in one of the two, high-backed red-leather chairs in front of the desk, and Skye sat down beside him in the other one.

"You and your woman have caused me a great deal of trouble," Petrov said calmly, though Edge didn't miss the angry flush beneath his cheekbones.

"We did our best," Edge agreed.

"You have some big stones coming here. You must know this place belongs to me."

"We're aware. That's why we're here. We wanted to talk to you."

Petrov leaned back in his chair. "Is that right?"

"That's right." From the corner of his eye, Edge caught movement, a woman with platinum blond hair in a low-cut, long, white-satin dress.

"And what, exactly, is it you want from me?"

"We want to make you a business proposition. Enter into an employment contract, in a manner of speaking."

Petrov scoffed. "You want to go to work for me—you and your woman?"

"That's right. We're a team. We'll be happy to give you a little background information if you need it."

"I know everything about you. I know you both work private. Hired help, so to speak. I know that you, Mr. Logan, were forced out of the army. No golden boy, are you?"

Irritation trickled through him, but he managed to tamp it down. In this case, the bogus charges worked in his favor. He wondered how Petrov knew. But Henson had said the man had contacts everywhere.

"You're well-informed," Edge said. "Considering the scope of your operation, I'm not surprised."

"By now, you must have guessed Dutch doesn't work for Henson. He never did. He works for me. The moment you showed up at the compound in Blancha Springs, I knew you were trouble. Unfortunately, there was nothing I could do about it at the time." Petrov leaned over and plucked a cigar out of the humidor on his desk but made no attempt to light it. "Chamaya is another story. You're lucky you made it out of there alive."

"It wasn't luck," Edge said.

"That's the thing," Skye added. "We're obviously good at what we do. We zeroed in on Daniel Henson's operation and shut him down, found him again and shut him down a second time."

"Henson was a clown," Edge added. "He thought with his dick instead of his brain. We're both former military, both professionals. We can make sure your interests are secure. And if you have a problem with the competition, we can keep them out of your hair."

Petrov fingered the cigar, rolling it between his thumb and forefinger. "You destroyed two of my operations. You cost me an absurd amount of money. Did you think shutting down my lab was going to keep some spoiled kid out there from buying drugs?"

"It wasn't about the drugs," Edge said. "We didn't even know about the drugs. It was about the women. Skye's sister and her friend were in that compound. We got Callie out of Blancha Springs, but Henson forced her best friend to go with him to Chamaya. Family comes first. We had no choice but to go after her."

Petrov said nothing, but something moved across his features.

"Here's the deal," Edge continued. "If you hire us, we can help you get back everything you lost because of Henson's incompetence."

"You think so, do you?"

"We know it," Skye said.

Petrov leaned back in his chair. "You make it sound easy. We both know it isn't."

Edge shifted forward in his seat. "Pay us enough and it doesn't matter if it's easy or not."

"I could kill you right now. You know that, right? I could have your dead bodies dragged out of here, and no one would ever know."

Edge's gaze zeroed in on Petrov's face. "There's a certain amount of risk involved in everything. You could kill us. Or you could take advantage of our skills."

Petrov rolled the cigar back and forth. "How would I know I could trust you?"

"You can trust that we want to stay alive badly enough to obey your orders."

Intrigued, one of Petrov's black eyebrows inched up. He was clearly a businessman before anything else. Killing the two of them wouldn't get him back the money he had lost.

"You're right," he said. "If I hire you and you make one move out of line, Dutch and his men will drive you and your lady friend out into the desert and make you disappear."

Edge said nothing.

Neither did Petrov.

Edge took a chance and rose from his chair. "Why don't you take some time to think it over." He pulled out a Nighthawk business card with his cell number on it. "We're staying at the Bellagio. You can reach us there."

Skye rose to join him, and they started for the door. Dutch stepped in front of them, blocking their way. Edge turned back to Petrov. Black eyes locked with blue.

"Perhaps we might be able to do business," the Russian said. "I will be in touch."

Dutch stepped out of the way, and Skye walked past him out the door. Dutch returned Edge's Beretta as he walked out behind her.

In front of the restaurant, Edge helped Skye into the first cab in line and followed her into the back seat. They didn't speak until the taxi rolled off toward the Bellagio.

"You think Petrov will go for it?" Skye asked.

"From what I can tell, he's a very practical guy. I'm thinking there's a chance he might."

They didn't say more until they reached the hotel and rode upstairs in the elevator. You never knew who was listening.

"We need to talk to Cross," Skye said as they walked out into the hall.

Edge nodded. "We'll use the disposable, fill Cross in on where we are with Petrov."

"So what's our next move?" Skye waited while Edge flashed his key card to unlock the door.

Edge thought about the big bed in the suite. "If Petrov wanted us dead, we'd be dead. Until we hear from him, we might as well relax and enjoy ourselves."

Skye's slow smile said she agreed. Edge felt the heat of anticipation all the way to his groin.

CHAPTER THIRTY-ONE

THE EXCITEMENT SKYE WAS FEELING DISAPPEARED AS THEY WALKED inside. She was too much of a professional not to notice the room had been searched.

The subtle shift of a magazine on the coffee table. Drawers in the bedroom that hadn't been completely closed. Toiletries in the bathroom moved from one side of the sink to the other.

"Well, he wasn't subtle about it," Edge said, his gaze following hers as they checked each room.

Skye looked up at him. "Doesn't look like anything's missing. You think Petrov was delivering a message? Telling us he can get to us whenever he wants?"

"Probably—and looking for anything that might indicate we were lying or working with the cops."

"Which we aren't," Skye said clearly in case the room was bugged.

Edge just smiled. Skye went with him as he opened the safe in the bedroom and took out the disposable phone and a handheld bug finder. She knew the device was standard equipment in Edge's gear bag. He held it up, and she nodded.

As he moved through the rooms, she watched the surface of the black plastic device to see if any of the lights lit up, but no warning colors flashed.

"Nothing," Edge said. "But I didn't really expect there would be. Petrov's all about muscle and intimidation. He's used to winning by force. I don't think he's a techie kind of guy."

He set the device on the dresser, closed the bedroom door behind him, and made sure it was locked.

Skye's anticipation returned. She glanced at the bed. "I wouldn't want them to hear us. Are you sure your device is working?"

Edge's gaze heated. "Sure enough." Reaching out, he eased her into his arms. "Jesus, I've been hard for you all night." Tipping up her chin, he settled his lips over hers and sank in, claiming her in a hot, wet kiss that melted her bones.

"Shouldn't . . . shouldn't we call Cross?"

"Later." Damp kisses fell onto the side of her neck and over her shoulders. "That dress should be illegal." Sliding off the narrow straps, he peeled the top away to expose her breasts. "I can't stop wanting you." He cupped the weight in one of his big hands, and Skye moaned.

Edge reached up and took down her hair. Skye shook her head, sending dark strands tumbling around her shoulders.

"Damn, I'm crazy about you." Edge lowered his head to kiss her again, then paused. "I didn't mean to say that, but I guess it's no secret." He kissed her before she had time to process the words.

Until that moment, she'd had no idea what Edge felt for her. Now she knew he cared about her—maybe more than cared—but the sad truth was, it didn't matter. They had what they had for as long as it lasted. That was all.

Still, her heart had squeezed at his words.

The kiss deepened as Edge stripped her out of the dress, stopping at the sight of the little .380 semiauto strapped to the inside of her thigh.

"What is there about a woman wearing a gun?" he mused, his eyes hot as they roamed over her.

Skye leaned down and ripped off the Velcro tabs holding the holster in place, set the little pistol on the nightstand.

Edge leaned down and kissed her. Lifting her into his arms, he carried her across the room and set her down on the side of the bed.

A long, slow kiss, and he knelt in front of her, eased her back on the mattress. She was naked, Edge fully dressed. His broad shoulders wedged her legs apart, the fabric of his suit coat rubbing against her thighs. Delicious ripples of pleasure slid into her core.

"Your leg," he whispered. "Am I hurting you?"

She swallowed, barely able to force out the word. "No . . ."

His hands moved down her body, stroking, soothing. Damp kisses roamed over her skin, moving lower, making her burn. When he reached his destination, everything inside her went white-hot with need.

Her mind went blank. They were in the middle of a dangerous operation that could get them both killed, and all she could think of was Edge and her need to feel him inside her.

"Please . . ." she whispered, moving restlessly on the mattress.

"Soon, baby." Edge was relentless, using his hands and his mouth to drive her to the peak. In minutes, she was on the precipice, then tumbling over, crying his name as she reached release.

His zipper buzzed, then he was sliding in, driving deep. "God, I need you. I can't get enough of you."

Her eyes filled. This wasn't supposed to happen, this overpowering hunger for a man she could never have. But the agonizing truth was, she loved him. And because she loved him, she wanted every moment she could get with him.

Skye gave herself up to the powerful emotions she didn't want to feel, let Edge drive her up all over again, then joined him in a spectacular release.

Another hour passed before Edge made the call to Cross. Skye was lying in bed, her eyes heavy-lidded and drowsy, a faint smile on her lips. Standing a few feet away in one of the hotel's white terry robes, Edge felt a shot of male satisfaction.

Cross picked up the phone on the first ring. "Why the hell haven't you called? Our man followed you to the Bellagio and watched you go into your suite. I figured I'd hear from you a couple of hours ago."

Edge's gaze went to Skye. "I was busy."

"Yeah, I'll bet. You better start taking this more seriously, Logan. Petrov's nobody to fool with."

He straightened. "I get it. Believe me." He shifted the phone closer to his ear. "The meeting went better than expected. Petrov's a businessman. He liked what we had to say. He's already had us vetted. Since we've got no connection to law enforcement other than the raid in Blancha Springs and handing his boy, Daniel, over to the county sheriff, I think he might go for it. The question is, what happens if he does?"

"We need him to corroborate the information our informant has already given us."

"I thought you said Henson wasn't talking."

"This is someone else. But we need more info. A wire would be best, but we can't risk it. If Petrov found out, you'd be dead before we had a prayer of getting you out."

"So what's the alternative?"

"One of our inside people put a bug under Petrov's private table. He eats in the club almost every night. Always sits there. He and his latest mistress."

"Platinum blonde? Big tits and too much makeup?"

"That's her. Name's Sasha Jankova. See if you can get him to invite you and Skye to supper. Then bait him, get him talking. Like you said, he's a businessman. He likes to brag about how he came from nothing and how much he's worth now. If you can get him to incriminate himself, we'll get it recorded. Combined with the informant's testimony, we'll have enough to nail him on drug and racketeering charges."

Charges that carried very long sentences. Just what Petrov deserved. "We'll see what we can do."

"Keep me posted—for both our sakes."

"Will do." Edge ended the call and set the phone down next to the bed. Skye drew back the covers, inviting him to join her.

Edge tossed the robe and climbed back into bed. They still had hours until morning.

Enjoying the luxurious suite, they slept late, then ordered room service for a breakfast of coffee, eggs Benedict, and fresh-squeezed orange juice, which they enjoyed in front of the windows overlooking the Bellagio fountains. The sun was well up by the time Skye dressed for the day in khaki cargo pants and a pair of sneakers, a white tank, and white jeans jacket.

She glanced over at Edge, who wore jeans and a light blue, short-sleeved button-down. He tossed a navy blue windbreaker over the back of a chair to cover the shoulder holster he planned to wear when they went out.

Cross was right, Skye thought. Petrov was a dangerous enemy and not to be underestimated. Edge would be armed with his Beretta, while Skye carried her little .380 semiauto in her purse.

They were ready to prowl the shops, have lunch at Mon Ami Gabi in the Paris Hotel and Casino, maybe gamble a little, whatever it took to pass the time until Petrov called.

Or didn't.

Edge grabbed his windbreaker just as Skye's cell phone rang. Worry rushed through her as she recognized Conn's number. "Hey, what's up?"

"Good news."

"Really? I could use some." She flicked a glance at Edge, who'd moved a little closer. "It's Conn." She put the phone on speaker.

"The good news is the police arrested Klaus Mahler last night. He and a guy named Webb Rankin."

"Wow, that is good news. According to Callie, Webb Rankin was Sarah's supposed husband. He was one of the men who killed her. I'm glad they caught him."

"Callie's safe," Conn said, "but even so, she and Lila are going to stay with me a little longer. Both of them are anxious to get back to work, so they'll be looking for jobs. Apparently, Lila has some experience as a bookkeeper. Callie's looking for a job in a restaurant. She's decided to go back to community college in the spring, pick up where she left off, maybe even continue, get her bachelor's degree."

"That's great."

"They want to share an apartment as soon as they have enough money."

"Tell Callie I'll loan her first and last month's rent and whatever else she needs. She can pay me back once she's settled."

"Okay, I'll tell her."

"Thanks for everything, Conn. You went way above and beyond. I know Callie and Lila appreciate it."

"Actually, it was kind of fun having some female company again."

Skye felt a twinge of regret. Conn still missed his ex-fiancée. Rebecca was never right for him, which she had finally figured out and Conn had reluctantly accepted. But living by himself in a house that size had to be lonely.

The call ended, and Skye tucked the phone into her purse.

"With Mahler in jail, that's one problem solved," Edge said. "Too bad the cops didn't round up Harley Purcell along with him."

Skye thought of Purcell and the threat he still posed to the woman he considered his wife. "I hope Molly's okay."

"Yeah. I wonder where Purcell went after he left Chamaya? No sign of him among Petrov's crew so far."

"From what Molly said, he was Daniel's man all the way. With Daniel under arrest, he could have gone anywhere."

"Let's hope Molly keeps her head down long enough for Harley to lose interest."

Skye felt a chill. In her work as a private detective, she had known men like Harley Purcell. Brutal and unrelenting, some of them stalked their wives or girlfriends for years, just waiting for the chance to make them pay for whatever imagined crime they had supposedly committed.

She felt Edge's hands on her shoulders, turning her around. "You can't save everyone, Skye."

She looked up at him. "I know."

"Come on. Let's get something to eat. Maybe by the end of the day we'll hear from Petrov."

Skye just nodded. Petrov was their target now.

Her resolve strengthened. Sooner or later, they were going to bring him down.

CHAPTER THIRTY-TWO

IT WAS LATE IN THE AFTERNOON WHEN EDGE GOT THE CALL. THEY were walking along Las Vegas Boulevard, on their way back to the hotel. Tourists packed the sidewalks, a sea of people flowing from one casino to the next.

Mixed into the crowd were jugglers and mimes, dog walkers, and showgirls in skintight costumes and silver, thigh-high boots. Bright feathered plumes on their headdresses waved in the breeze. There were street people dressed as animated characters and a guy in a spiderman outfit.

Since it was too loud to hear the phone ring, Edge had set it to vibrate. When he felt the buzz, he grabbed Skye's hand and hauled her around the corner, into an alcove where he could talk. "Logan."

"Mr. Petrov wants to see you. You and the woman."

Recognizing the voice, Edge flicked a glance at Skye and mouthed the name *Dutch.* "All right. How about supper? We can meet him at his place."

"You don't give the orders, Logan. Mr. Petrov does."

"Sorry."

"Be at the Four Winds at eight p.m."

"For supper?"

Dutch grunted his agreement, and Edge almost smiled.

"Fine. We'll be there." The line went dead, and Edge turned to Skye. "Petrov wants to see us. Dinner at his place, eight p.m."

"That should make Cross happy."

"Yeah, but it doesn't leave us much time. Or should I say, it doesn't leave Agent Cross much time."

As soon as they got back to the suite, Edge called Cross's cell. "We're on for tonight," Edge said. "Eight p.m. at the restaurant. Will your people be ready?"

"We'll be ready. Just get him talking. We'll do the rest." The call ended, and Edge turned to Skye. Their eyes met. Both of them were hoping it wasn't some kind of trap.

Back in the suite, the next few hours seemed to drag. Edge thought about making use of the big bed in the other room, but the mission kept intruding. He could tell Skye felt the same.

They dressed down a little for the evening. Edge chose a gray tweed sport coat and black jeans while Skye wore a white jumpsuit with wide legs and a halter top. His eyebrows shot up when she reached into the left pocket, which apparently wasn't stitched at the bottom, and pulled her little pistol from the holster strapped to her thigh.

Edge grinned. "Very clever, sweetheart. You never cease to amaze me."

"We pull this off, I promise I'll amaze you even more when we get back to the room tonight."

His mouth went dry at the hot promise in those sea-green eyes. He didn't dare touch her. "Work first," he said gruffly. "Then we celebrate."

Skye just smiled.

They left for the Four Winds in the Bellagio limo. He was wearing his shoulder holster under his sport coat, figuring Petrov would expect it. The place was packed when they arrived five minutes early, showing the Russian respect. Dutch waited in the entry, his red hair and short red beard freshly trimmed.

"Weapons," Dutch demanded. Edge reached inside his coat, pulled out the Beretta, and handed it over. Dutch flicked a glance at Skye, but she ignored him. Being a typical male, he assumed she would defer her protection to the man she was with.

Big mistake, Edge thought.

Dutch led them up to Petrov's private table on the third tier, the top level of the dining room. There was extra room on each side of the table so their conversation couldn't be overheard, and the location provided a view of the dining room, bar, and dance floor below.

Petrov sat at the head of the table. He rose at their approach. "Good of you to come." The greeting held a hint of sarcasm. He turned to the woman seated to his right. "This is Sasha. She will be joining us."

Up close, she was in her early thirties, her skin nearly as pale as her gleaming platinum hair. A fuchsia dress, cut low in front and covered with silver spangles, displayed her voluptuous cleavage. Edge caught a glimpse of exposed thigh beneath the table, so it was a short skirt tonight.

Petrov finished the introductions. Edge seated Skye, then took a seat himself. They made light conversation until the waiter arrived with an ice bucket and champagne, Cristal, which the server opened and poured into tall crystal flutes.

Petrov lifted his glass and took a sip. "Six hundred a bottle and worth every dime." He smiled at the woman beside him. "The rosé is Sasha's favorite."

The blonde took a sip and made a little sound of pleasure in her throat. "Thank you, darlink." Edge had noticed the Russian accent earlier. It definitely sounded real. He figured Petrov wouldn't settle for a fraud, not even one who gave a better-than-average blow job.

They all sipped their champagne, which Edge had to admit was first class. Beluga caviar was brought out and served to enjoy with the bubbly. Edge wasn't a connoisseur, not even really fond of the stuff, but he figured it was probably as extravagantly expensive as the liquor.

Petrov's black eyes went to Skye, slid over the creamy swells of her breasts. He practically licked his lips. "Do you like it?"

Edge clenched his jaw. He noticed Sasha hadn't missed Petrov's interest either. Her tight lips said she wasn't pleased.

"You have very good taste in champagne," Skye said. "And the caviar is exquisite."

"Thank you." He set his crystal flute on the table. "First, we eat. Then we talk business."

Orders were taken. Skye chose duck a l'orange, while Edge selected a peppercorn filet mignon. The salad was chosen by Petrov: cranberry, goat cheese, and pistachio. Every time Petrov looked at Skye, Edge's appetite waned.

Their meals arrived. Like everything else, the food was extraordinary. Not surprising, Edge thought, considering the possible consequences if the staff failed to come up to Petrov's exacting standards.

Finally, dessert was served.

"*Ptichye Moloko,*" Petrov announced, a Russian cake of some kind. Lifting his fork, he took a bite, groaned in ecstasy, and waved the fork to indicate they should try it. Light, soufflé-like layers of custard and sponge cake were covered with a creamy chocolate sauce and, like everything else, tasted delicious.

"This is amazing," Skye said, taking another bite.

Petrov seemed pleased. "It is a personal favorite."

Thick black coffee arrived in gold-rimmed, white porcelain cups. The waiter cleared the dessert plates, then disappeared.

Petrov sat forward in his chair, his onyx eyes fixed on Edge. "Now we get down to business." Dutch appeared in the shadows a few feet behind him, legs braced apart, hands crossed in front of him in bodyguard mode. "So you wish to go to work for me."

Time to play the game. A quick glance at Skye said she was equally prepared for whatever came next.

"We have skills to offer that would benefit your organization," Edge said.

"In return for substantial financial compensation," Petrov added.

"That's right. Unless you can't afford us. Your labs in Colorado and New Mexico both just took very big hits. Could be money's tight right now."

A muscle ticked in Petrov's cheek. "I came from nothing. Now I am worth millions. Do you think the mistakes of a fool like Henson could begin to destroy my empire?"

Edge's gaze remained on Petrov. "It occurred to me, but apparently not." He took a drink of the thick, black coffee. "So, to point out the obvious, at the moment, one of your top men is no longer available. You need to move things forward. We can help you fill the void."

Petrov toyed with the handle of his delicate cup. "*Da*, perhaps." He nodded. "You could be of great service to me, but first I must be sure I can trust you. For that to happen, you must complete the task I have set for you. If you do it with the skill and efficiency you promise, the two of you will have earned a place in my organization."

Adrenaline pumped through Edge's veins. "What is it you want us to do?"

"Not *us*, Mr. Logan. Not this time. You alone will go with Dutch to handle the pickup. Ms. Delaney will remain in Las Vegas as a guest in my home."

A chill went through him. He shook his head. "We work together. That's the deal."

Petrov tossed his napkin down on the table, an angry flush coloring the skin over his cheeks. "I give the orders here—not you. She stays. You go. Once you have proven yourself, we will do as you suggest and move forward. That is the deal."

"And if I refuse?"

"You no longer have that option." Petrov shoved back his chair and rose from the table. At the same time, Dutch stepped out of the shadows, putting a human wall between Edge and Petrov, the threat more than clear.

"Now if you will excuse me." The Russian turned to the platinum blonde. "Sasha and I are leaving. Ms. Delaney will be joining us. Dutch will explain your duties."

Edge's blood pounded. He didn't want Skye staying with Petrov. He didn't want her anywhere near the Russian. He forced himself to stay calm.

Petrov's gaze went to Skye. "I assure you, my dear, your accommodations will be as luxurious as your rooms at the Bellagio."

Skye flicked Edge a glance, then gave a nod of acceptance. She was ready for this. Edge knew how capable she was. He needed to trust her to handle the situation. They were in too deep to turn back now.

Still, everything inside urged him to protect her, to haul her out of the restaurant and as far from Petrov's slimy clutches as he could get.

He started to rise as Petrov led the women away, felt Dutch's big hand on his shoulder, warning him to sit back down. "Take it easy. We handle the job, then you come back and get your woman. Long as you don't fuck up, everything'll be okay."

Edge settled back in his chair, and Dutch sat down across from him.

"So what's the plan?" Edge prayed he sounded as confident as he was pretending to be. The DEA would be listening—he hoped. He needed Dutch to be clear about what was going down.

"There's a ship arriving tomorrow at the Long Beach harbor. The cargo we're interested in is scheduled to be offloaded onto a truck and hauled to a designated location. You, me, and a couple of the boys will be driving to the location to make the pickup."

"I assume this cargo is necessary for your meth operation."

"That's right."

"Same stuff you used to make the drugs produced in Blancha Springs?"

Dutch's gaze darted around, but there was no chance anyone could hear.

Except the DEA. With any luck, Edge fervently prayed.

"That's right," Dutch said. "Ephedrine. We used to buy it from China. For a while, it came up from Mexico. Our best source now is India. Over-the-counter retail sales are illegal there, but bulk manufacturing is still okay. Just a matter of finding the right supplier and getting the product over here and delivered to its destination."

"So we're driving where . . . ?"

Dutch shook his head. "That's information you don't need to know right now."

"Why not? Petrov has Skye. There's no way I'd do anything to put her in danger."

"Tomorrow," Dutch said, rising. "I'll pick you up at your hotel at eight p.m. tomorrow night."

Dutch handed him back his weapon and walked away. Edge holstered the pistol, took a deep breath, and leaned back in his chair. He needed more information. And he needed to talk to Special Agent Derrick Cross.

"I need a drink," he said aloud. It was the code they had agreed on. Cross would meet him at a place called the Cannery a mile off the strip. According to Cross, it was a bar that catered to vets and not a spot Petrov's goons would frequent.

Walking out of the restaurant into the night, Edge climbed into a cab and gave the driver the address. "Take your time. Let's have a little tour of the area first."

The cabbie just grunted and pulled away. Edge kept an eye out the back window to see if they were being followed. No sign of a tail.

But worry darkened his thoughts, and the back of his neck was tingling. Never a good sign.

CHAPTER THIRTY-THREE

Sasha led Skye across the two-story entry, up the curving staircase, down what seemed miles of wide, high-ceilinged corridor. Petrov had disappeared into his study moments after they'd arrived, leaving the blonde in charge, which seemed to please her greatly.

"Come." She opened the door to Skye's glamorous prison and stood back to let her into the room. "I will need your phone."

Skye had been expecting it. She handed over her cell as she glanced around her temporary quarters.

The bedroom was as sumptuous as the rest of Villa Milano, the Vegas version of the Doge's Palace meets the Taj Mahal. The huge white house was at least 15,000 square feet, with thirty-foot ceilings and gleaming white marble floors. Soaring columns, both inside and out, drew the eye upward to Romanesque arches protected by yards of red-tile roof.

"Fortunately, Ivan planned for your visit," Sasha said. "You will find clothes approximately your size in the closet. Makeup and toiletries in the bathroom." Hostile blue eyes ran over her. "Whatever happens, you will not be staying here long."

There was no missing the threat. Sasha considered Skye competition. Apparently, Petrov's interest had not gone unnoticed. If things went badly tomorrow night, she would be dead.

By now, Edge knew Petrov's plans. If the hidden microphone

was working, so did Agent Cross. With or without the DEA, Edge would be figuring how to get her away from Petrov. Edge was extremely protective. He would do whatever it took to get her to safety. If he was still alive.

Skye suppressed a shiver.

Sasha walked over to the big king-size bed covered in rich blue velvet. "If you want something, just press the first button on the wall." She pointed toward a panel above the nightstand. "Housekeeping will bring you whatever you need."

In a cloud of expensive perfume, the spangles on her ultra-short, fuchsia designer dress flashing, Sasha left the suite.

As soon as the door closed, Skye began a tour of the bedroom. None of the windows were locked, which didn't really surprise her. In Petrov's mind, she wasn't a prisoner. She was a bargaining chip. But his objectives and Edge's weren't the same.

She surveyed the furnishings in the suite. There were all sorts of glass perfume bottles and makeup mirrors in the bathroom that could serve as weapons. There were heavy crystal vases on the dresser and pottery jugs on the floor. As happened far too often, her host had underestimated her ability to defend herself.

Unconsciously, her hand went to the pistol strapped to the inside of her thigh. No one had searched her. Petrov wasn't afraid of being attacked. His power and authority kept people in line.

She went over to the window, spotted a guard roaming the manicured acres of grass, fountains, and beautifully lit blue pools. She was fairly certain she could escape, but if she left, she would be putting Edge in even more danger.

The leverage Petrov was using worked both ways.

She turned and walked back to the bedroom door, intending to turn the lock. A knock sounded just as she reached it, and her pulse kicked up.

The knob turned, the door swung open, and Petrov stood in the opening. The sight of him in a burgundy brocade dressing gown sent a slice of dread into her stomach.

"It's late for a social call," she said, refusing to show him any sign of fear. Petrov controlled everything and everyone in the house. If he was there to rape her, no one would stop him. No one but her.

"I wanted to be sure you had everything you needed," Petrov said. His black gaze slid over her like cold grease, returned to settle on her breasts.

Skye managed not to flinch. "I'm fine. I appreciate your concern, but it's late, and I'm tired."

He reached out and trailed a finger down her cheek. "You are alone tonight. Perhaps you desire a man to keep you company."

She thought of the gun she could reach through the pocket of her jumpsuit and found some comfort in that. "I don't think your friend Sasha would approve."

He shrugged his thick shoulders. "What I do is none of her business."

Skye smiled blandly. "I appreciate the offer, but not tonight." *Or any other night,* she thought.

"If our association works out, perhaps there will be another occasion."

Skye said nothing. She could feel every beat of her heart. "Good night," she said, and held her breath until Petrov walked away.

Closing the door behind him, she turned the lock and leaned against the smooth, white-painted wood. As she thought about what could have happened, her insides swirled with nausea.

What still might happen.

What did Petrov have in store for her tomorrow?

Worse yet, if the plan went wrong, what would she be facing tomorrow night?

The meeting place, the Cannery, was an unimpressive blue-collar joint crowded with locals. The ages varied, as to be expected in a spot that vets frequented. Their service to their country was their bond; the branch of the military or the war they'd fought in didn't matter. A few wives and girlfriends sat with their significant others at small round, Formica-topped tables scattered around the room.

Agent Cross was already there. Edge spotted him at a table in the back, away from the noise of the shuffleboard. Grateful for the dim lighting, Edge skirted the room and joined him.

"Looks like we've got a problem," Cross said. He was out of uniform tonight, wearing dark blue jeans and a navy blue T-shirt instead of a suit. He was trying to blend in, but with his creased jeans, short brown hair, and buffed nails, he still looked like a fed. With any luck, neither of them had been followed.

A bottle of beer sat in front of Cross, another in front of the empty chair on the opposite side of the table. Edge sat down, picked up the bottle, and took a long swallow. He set the beer back down on the table.

"Petrov has Skye." Which Cross would already know. "The question is, what do we do about it?"

"Figure a way to get her out."

Edge didn't bother to reply, since that was going to happen one way or another.

"Petrov is smuggling ephedrine from India into the country," Cross said, repeating the conversation the DEA had overheard. "We need the name of that ship and the location of the meet."

"Only one way to get it."

"You can't wear a wire. It's too risky."

"The DEA is high-tech enough to have a wireless device that won't be seen. I've got a mini recorder about the length of a paperclip and thinner than a dime. Surely you have something."

"We've got the best money can buy. I still don't like it."

"I don't see we have a choice." But if he got busted wearing the wire, Skye would be the one to suffer. Worry for her slid through him. He refused to call it fear.

Knowing Edge was right, Cross nodded. "I'll have housekeeping pick up your jacket first thing in the morning. It'll be one of our guys. We'll place the mic in the lining and return the coat to your suite."

"Voice activated?"

"That's right. With a GPS tracker, so we know where you are at all times. We'll be following you, but if we get separated, we'll still be able to find you."

"What about Skye? I want men posted around the house ready to go in if the bust goes south."

"Too risky," Cross said. "If one of our men is spotted, your cover is blown. That happens, Petrov will make Skye disappear."

It was true. And exactly the reason he had decided to talk to Conn and Trace, men he trusted to get Skye out before the DEA bust went down.

"Don't worry," Cross said. "We'll be in the area, ready to go in as soon as the drugs are secure and Petrov's men are in custody."

Not good enough, Edge thought. He'd handle it his way and make sure Skye got out safely.

Cross set his beer bottle down and rose from his chair. "Good luck tomorrow night." The agent made a deliberately unhurried exit and disappeared into the night.

Edge sipped his beer. He didn't leave until the bottle was empty. Then he walked to the nearest busy street corner and waved down a taxi. Instead of returning to the hotel, he instructed the cabbie to drive him out to Kingsbridge, the luxury gated community north of Vegas where, according to Zoe's information, Petrov's estate was located.

When they arrived, he tipped the cabbie a crisp hundred-dollar bill with the promise of another hundred if he waited twenty minutes. The cabbie snatched the bill out of his hand.

"You got fifteen. I'll wait twenty, but it'll cost you another hundred."

"Done," Edge said.

After Zoe had texted the address and a plat of Petrov's two-acre estate, he had studied a Google satellite map of the area. With the taxi parked down the road from the main gate, he made his way around the perimeter of a tall wrought-iron fence that surrounded the luxury development.

He had time for a quick recon of the property, made his way back to Petrov's mansion, but couldn't risk getting too close. As he stared up at the second-story windows of the house, his hands unconsciously fisted. It was all he could do not to storm the gates and haul Skye out of there. He had seen the way Petrov looked at her. The Russian wanted her, and now she was in his home, completely at his mercy.

Well, not completely, he reminded himself. Skye was armed, and there was no doubt the woman could be dangerous.

Edge relaxed a little and returned to the job at hand. Intriguingly, Petrov's estate and others in the area backed up to an unfinished golf course. The land under construction had been graded, the dirt leveled and smoothed into fairways, but the unfinished course was unpatrolled. Dirt and rocks didn't attract many thieves.

Staying out of sight, Edge circled Petrov's property again, surveilling the estate long enough to spot a guard making his rounds. Probably two men at least. He checked his watch. Time to go. Hurrying back to the taxi, he handed the driver the rest of the money he'd promised, and the cab headed back to the hotel.

Stepping out of the elevator, he made his way down the corridor to his suite. Before he'd left the hotel for the evening, he'd placed a long strand of Skye's dark hair across the door. The strand remained in place. No one had been in the room.

Petrov wasn't worried. At the moment, the Russian held all the cards.

Edge tossed his jacket over the back of a chair in the living room and phoned Conner Delaney. Conn was former marine spec ops. Skye's brother would do whatever it took to protect her.

Edge's second call went to Trace. It didn't take long to set up a three-way phone conversation.

"What's going on?" Conn asked.

"It's Skye. She's in trouble. We're in Vegas. I shouldn't have brought her with me in the first place, but—"

"But she didn't give you any choice," Conn said. "One thing I know about my sister, there's no stopping her once her mind's made up."

It was true, so Edge didn't argue.

"So what's the situation?" Trace asked, his voice a deep rumble roughened by sleep.

Edge spent the next half hour filling the men in on Petrov and his connection to Daniel Henson, the DEA's involvement, and the shipment of ephedrine coming into Long Beach from India.

"Petrov's using Skye as leverage to make sure I stay in line. He's taken her to his estate north of the city—which sits on two acres and is worth boo-coo millions."

"At least she'll have decent accommodations," Trace drawled, a touch of humor in his voice.

"I should have seen this coming," Edge said, in no mood for jokes. "I should have left her out of it."

"We all know that wasn't an option, so forget it," Trace said.

"What we need to do now," Conn added, "is focus on getting my sister out of the house before the DEA goes in after Petrov."

"I've got an idea how we can do that," Edge said. "How soon can you guys get here?"

CHAPTER THIRTY-FOUR

THE WHITE GMC PANEL VAN ROLLED DOWN INTERSTATE 15, HEADING south out of Las Vegas. A big guy named Riggins was driving, while the other man, Ketch, small, homely, with curly blond hair, rode shotgun. Edge and Dutch sat in the rear passenger seats.

"So where are we headed?" Edge asked. The mini voice-activated recorder was broadcasting from the bottom of the inside coat pocket of a lightweight black jacket. Dutch had taken Edge's Beretta with the promise to return it when the op was over.

Edge wasn't worried about the gun. He could disarm all three men and, should the need arise, permanently end the threat they posed. For now, he just needed information.

Turning a little in his seat, he spoke to Dutch, praying the hum of the engine wouldn't muffle the conversation being transmitted to the DEA.

"Okay, so we're on the road," he said. "Where are we headed, and how long until we get there?"

Dutch shrugged his shoulders. "I guess it doesn't matter if I tell you. We'll be there in less than half an hour."

Edge frowned. "Half an hour? You said the load was coming into Long Beach. I figured we were going somewhere in California."

"We are. Sort of. The meet is at a Flying J truck stop in Primm. You know, the state line? More than sixty thousand vehicles a day go through there. God knows how many are eighteen-wheelers."

"So we just blend in with everyone else passing through," Edge said. "Like hiding in plain sight."

"Yeah. Like that."

Edge knew the area, a truckers' paradise. Whiskey Pete's casino. Buffalo Bill's. The place was swarming with cars, big rigs, and tourists. Good for the bad guys. Not so good for the DEA. With that many folks around, people could get hurt.

He settled back in his seat. Less than an hour from now, the takedown would be over. He thought of Skye and knew she would be prepared for whatever went down tonight. She had her weapon. She had her smarts. And she had two good men set to go in after her.

But putting the operation together hadn't been easy. The drug bust at the truck stop was supposed to coincide with the raid on Petrov's house and the Russian's subsequent arrest. Getting Skye out before the DEA descended like a swarm of locusts was the problem.

A single phone call. That was the deal he and Cross had made. After arguing and threatening to back out altogether, Edge had brokered a deal. Cross would phone Conn five minutes before the raid.

Five minutes. Conn and Trace would have that small window of time to get past the guards, go in and bring Skye out before the DEA swooped in for the arrests. Which could turn the place into a shooting gallery if Petrov resisted.

He thought of Skye for the hundredth time since he had left her with the Russian. Was she all right? Had Petrov hurt her in any way? If the guy had touched her, he was a dead man.

As the van rolled along, Edge forced his mind back to business. If his thoughts strayed to Skye, the whole thing could blow, and he could get both of them killed.

"We're almost there," Dutch said.

The glow of gigantic neon signs lit the night sky in the distance. The van took the exit toward Whiskey Pete's and made a couple of turns as it wound across a sea of asphalt toward the area in the back where dozens of eighteen-wheelers were parked for the night.

If the plan was working, the GPS in the lining of his pocket would be leading Cross and his men to the exact spot where the exchange would be made. Riggins pulled the van up behind one of the big diesels along the row and turned off the engine.

Cold resolve slid through Edge's blood. He shoved open the van door and jumped to the pavement with single-minded purpose. Bring Ivan Petrov down, and bring Skye Delaney home.

"Over here," Dutch said, leading the way toward a big Peterbilt tractor-trailer with two men in the cab.

The driver's door swung open, and a heavyset man with dirty-brown hair jumped down. He and the African American guy in the passenger seat walked to the back of the truck and opened the double doors. The driver climbed in, shoved aside a stack of boxes, then shined his flashlight on the cargo they were delivering.

"One hundred ten bags, twenty pounds each," Dutch said, shining his own light into the back of the truck. *A metric ton, the measure that would have been used in India.* "Let's make sure it's all there." The bags were made of heavy brown paper, each with a printed label.

ACKERMAN'S NUTRITION FOR HORSES
40 ESSENTIAL AND NON-ESSENTIAL NUTRIENTS
RELY ON ACKERMAN'S TO GET THE MOST OUT OF YOUR
HORSES' TRAINING AND PERFORMANCE

Dutch climbed into the back of the truck, randomly selected one of the bags and jumped back down to the pavement. Pulling out his pocketknife, he sliced open the bag. Rough-textured white pills about half an inch long spilled through the opening. Dutch crumbled one of the pills in his palm, then licked his finger, stuck it into the lumpy powder, and tasted it.

He nodded. "All right, we're good to go." He tipped his head toward the little guy, Ketch, who handed a canvas satchel to the truck driver. The guy opened the satchel, looked at the money, and closed the bag.

Apparently satisfied, instead of returning to the truck, the two men disappeared into the shadows, while Riggins and Ketch headed for the truck and climbed into the cab.

Dutch turned to Edge. "You're driving the van back," Dutch said. The big rig engine fired up with Riggins behind the wheel and set up a steady rumble. Diesel smoke puffed out of the stacks, the gears ground, and the tires began to roll.

Edge glanced around. Nothing but rows of big rigs, one after another.

Where the hell were Cross and the DEA? A sick feeling settled in the pit of his stomach. What was happening in Vegas?

What the hell was happening to Skye?

Skye paced the luxurious bedroom, her nerves strung taut. What was happening to Edge? She prayed he was all right.

She walked over to the window and looked down on the magnificent grounds surrounding the mansion, her mind going backward over the hours she had spent waiting for nightfall.

Her day had started with a command performance on the terrace overlooking the pool, a gourmet breakfast that included everything from truffled eggs with hollandaise, baked sole, and filet mignon, to homemade granola, yogurt, and fresh fruit.

She managed to get down some yogurt and coffee, which wasn't that easy with Petrov's gaze filled with the same lust she had seen in his black eyes last night.

When Skye didn't respond to his silent invitation, Ivan excused himself for a day of meetings. Skye had inwardly rejoiced. The eighty-degree weather had encouraged Sasha to spend the day sipping umbrella drinks next to the pool. Skye had declined to join her.

After pleading a headache, she spent the day in her room until night had finally descended. With no way to communicate with Edge, she had no idea what could be happening to him or what might happen to her.

She returned to the window. The blue lights in the swimming pool reflected the cypress trees lining the concrete deck. The windows of the cabana were dark, but an hour ago, Skye had heard men's voices downstairs, and the guard patrolling the fence surrounding the estate had been joined by several other men.

Petrov was no fool. She and Edge had beaten him twice before. This time he was prepared. If anything went wrong with the transaction, Edge would pay the price. So would she.

She stared out the window, trying to see into the darkness beyond the fence. She was wearing a pair of designer jeans she had found in the closet, along with a short-sleeved peach knit sweater and a pair of sneakers. Not a bad fit, she admitted, and easier to move around in than the long white jumpsuit.

No way to hide the gun on her body. She had put it in the drawer of the nightstand.

Footsteps sounded outside her door, and her pulse kicked up. Petrov? She prayed it was the DEA or someone else who would help her. She pulled the gun out of the drawer and hurried across the room.

A light knock sounded. No peephole to see who it was. Taking a deep breath, she held the gun behind her back and opened the door. A sigh of relief whispered out when Conn slipped into the bedroom.

"You ready to get out of here, little sister?"

She smiled. "You have no idea."

"We've got five minutes. Let's go."

She stuck the little .380 in her front pocket, the telltale shape obvious but the feel of it comforting, and followed Conn out of the bedroom.

Gun in hand, Trace stood waiting at the bottom of the stairs. "You okay?"

"So far so good."

He gave her a crooked grin. "Let's go."

As they slipped quietly outside, she didn't ask either of them how they planned to get past Petrov's guards. They would have timed the patrols, but more men had arrived in the last few minutes, and now there was a swarm of them, all armed, walking along the paths and prowling the grounds around the house.

With Conn in front, Skye in the middle, and Trace behind, they moved silently through the shadows along the outside wall of the house toward the fence at the rear of the property. Trace broke away and veered out of sight off to the right.

"Back gate is unlocked," Conn said. "We meet up there." Conn veered off to the left.

Gripping the gun in her hand, Skye continued along the path, skirting the pool, slipping into the shadows of the cabana. As she eased back onto the path, a guard stepped out of the darkness in front of her, tall, muscular, wearing a camouflage tactical vest.

"What are you doing out here?" he asked.

She held the gun behind her back. "It's a beautiful night. I thought I'd take a walk." She smiled. "You want to join me?"

His jaw hardened. "Get back in the house. No one out here tonight. Mr. Petrov's orders."

She spotted movement behind the guard, a man rising up. Trace locked an arm around the guard's muscled neck, using a choke hold to cut off his air supply. In seconds, the man was unconscious. Trace eased him down to the ground.

"Go," Trace said as he dragged the guard out of sight.

Skye hurried along the path. From her bedroom, she had seen the wrought-iron fence along the back of the house. A lawn tractor had been brought in through the rear gate that afternoon.

Skye picked up her pace. No sign of Conn, but the gate was in sight ahead of her. Careful to stay in the shadows of a row of tall cypress, she hurried toward the gate. Behind her, gunfire erupted. Skye started running, nearly colliding with the looming figure that stepped in front of her.

"You are leaving so soon?" In the faint glow of a distant light, Petrov's hard features looked demonic. "I don't think so." He reached out to grab her, but Skye jerked up her pistol and shoved the barrel into his face.

"I wouldn't move if I were you."

Fury darkened the Russian's features as he stared down at the pistol. "You think you can stop me with that little toy?" Reaching behind him, he pulled out a big semiautomatic and aimed it at the center of her chest.

With no time for options, Skye leaped forward, knocking the barrel to the side. Petrov fired and so did Skye. She felt the sting of the bullet clipping her upper arm, saw Petrov go down, and started running. Bullets pinged off the stucco walls of the cabana. Gunfire echoed around her. She thought she heard Petrov firing but didn't slow to find out.

She made the gate just seconds after Trace arrived. He swung the gate open, and both of them bolted through and kept on running. More shots echoed behind them. *Conn.* He was giving them time to reach their destination—wherever that was.

The top of her arm was burning, blood trailing down to her elbow. She glanced around, trying to spot Conn, but saw only dirt fields and rolling hills.

She slowed. "Where are we going?"

"Helicopter," Trace said. "Should be here any minute. I'm going back to help your brother." Trace turned and started running. Skye raced up beside him.

"Dammit, Skye! Get over the first hill, and wait for the helo!"

"In your dreams," she said, and then both of them were firing as Conn raced toward them.

Skye glanced over her shoulder. *Where the hell was the chopper?*

"Keep going!" Conn shouted. "Get over that ridge out of sight!"

Skye and Trace both spun in unison and raced up the hill, leaving Conn to lay down cover fire behind them. They hit the ridge and flattened themselves on the ground just over the top of the rise. Petrov's men were firing from the bottom of the hill—what seemed an army of them.

"If they flank us," Skye said, "we won't be able to hold out long."

"Where the hell is that chopper?" Trace said, repeating her thoughts.

Skye watched Petrov's men spreading out, circling, making their way around their position on the hill. Her heart was hammering so hard she didn't hear the helicopter coming in until dirt started swirling around her.

The helo hovered. Trace raced for the cargo bay door and slid it open.

"Go!" Conn said. Skye took off at a crouching run, threw herself into the opening, and Trace followed her in. Then Conn was there, and the helo was lifting away.

She glanced toward the cockpit, glimpsed the profile of the pilot, recognized the shadow of beard that lined the hard jaw of Morgan Burke. So not only a marine but a marine helicopter pilot.

For the first time, it occurred to Skye that bullets were no longer flying in their direction. As Burke worked the controls and the helicopter gained altitude, she could see a wave of flashing, red-and-blue lights below. Law enforcement had arrived, and agents were swarming the house and grounds.

"Dammit, you're hit." Trace knelt beside her, eased her down on the floor of the chopper. Then Conn appeared at her side.

"It's only a crease," she told them. "It hurts like blazes, but it isn't serious."

Conn ignored her. He found the first-aid kit and went to work as the helicopter winged its way back toward Las Vegas. The sparkling array of lights continued to build below them as more law enforcement arrived, and Skye breathed a sigh of relief. Then she thought of Edge, and her relief disappeared.

"What about Edge?"

"No idea," Conn said, his features grim as he swabbed the gash in her upper arm. "None of us has heard a word from him."

CHAPTER THIRTY-FIVE

"LET'S HEAD BACK," DUTCH SAID, SATISFIED THAT THE TRUCK WAS on its way. They walked toward the van.

"Where are they taking the load?" Edge asked, his gaze following the big rig.

"The product's being dropped in two different locations." Dutch flashed him a warning glance. *No more questions.*

Edge watched the big diesel roll across the asphalt lot. Where the hell was the DEA? An instant later, the driver hit the brakes, and the taillights went on. The quiet erupted into the sound of sirens crackling through the air, and a tsunami of red-and-blue flashing lights descended on the eighteen-wheeler.

Cop cars were everywhere, at least half a dozen bearing down on him and Dutch. Dutch pulled his big semiauto and whirled toward him, pointed the gun barrel at his heart. "You bastard!"

Adrenaline and his training both hit him. Edge knocked the barrel of the gun away with his forearm, spun and kicked, sent Dutch's pistol flying, delivered a chop to the side of his neck, followed by an uppercut that launched him backward, into the side of the white panel van.

Dutch bounced off the side and charged forward. Edge's fist slammed into his stomach, doubling him over. Then a right to the jaw took him out. By the time Agent Cross arrived, it was over.

"Nice work," Cross said as two of his agents ran up, slapped handcuffs on Dutch's thick wrists, and placed him under arrest.

All Edge could think of was the woman he'd left in Las Vegas. "What about Skye? Is she all right? Did they get her out okay?"

"I assume she's all right. She wasn't on the premises when we arrived."

Which was DEA speak for *Whatever happened, we weren't involved. Nothing to see here.*

"During the raid, Ivan Petrov got into a firefight with a couple of our agents," Cross said. "Last I heard, it didn't look like he was going to make it."

"Now that's a real pity."

"Some of my men spotted a chopper in the area. Probably just a coincidence."

Relief filtered through him. Morgan Burke had surprised him by volunteering to help, and it appeared he had done the job.

"Yeah, probably."

Still, he couldn't be sure Skye was okay until he talked to her.

As DEA agents took Riggins and Ketch into custody and began going through the cargo in the back, Edge phoned Skye. When she didn't answer, his nerves ticked up. Edge phoned Conn.

"Did you get Skye out okay? Did everything go all right?"

"She's okay. Bullet creased her arm. We're heading to the emergency room."

His stomach burned. "How bad is it?"

"Hurts like hell, but she'll be fine. It shouldn't take too long. We'll meet you back at the hotel."

He'd rather go straight to the hospital, but it wasn't going to happen. The DEA would want to debrief him. He was still wearing the wireless recorder, and hell, he didn't even have a ride.

"All right, I'll see you there," he said. "Take care of her, Conn."

"Will do." The line went dead.

It was after three a.m. when one of Cross's men dropped Edge off at the Bellagio. He had talked to Trace, knew Skye had been released and that they were all back in the suite. But after the painkillers the doctors had given her, Conn had told him, Skye was already asleep.

Conn was sleeping on the sofa in the living room when Edge

walked in. "Take it easy," Edge said when Conn raised his head, alert in case of trouble. He closed his eyes and went back to sleep.

From his pallet on the floor, Trace mumbled something as Edge walked past. Sleeping in a chair, long legs stretched out in front of him, Morgan Burke lifted the camo fatigue hat over his face to confirm who it was, then resettled the hat and returned to sleep.

Edge walked past them into the bedroom and closed the door. Stripping off his jacket, he set his shoulder holster and Beretta on the dresser. His gaze went to the bed, and he realized Skye was awake and watching him.

The curtains were open, neon light from the casinos brightening the room through the windows. Long dark hair curled softly over Skye's pillow. The rounded tops of her breasts rose smooth and pale above the sheet, and emotion hit him like a fist. He'd been so worried. He had refused to recognize the fear he'd kept tamped down until now.

He moved to the side of the bed and crouched down beside her. "I hope I didn't wake you."

"I was awake. I'm glad you're here. Conn said you were okay, but I couldn't stop worrying about you."

He leaned forward and pressed a kiss on her forehead. "I've been worried about you since the night you left the Four Winds with Petrov." He reached for her hand, which felt warm and strong as it wrapped around his. "How are you feeling?"

"After the pills they gave me, I don't feel much of anything. I'm sure I won't be so lucky in the morning." She squeezed his hand. "Tell me what happened?"

Edge smiled and sat down on the side of the bed. "You first."

For the first time that night, Skye relaxed. Edge was here. He was safe, and so was she. Everything was going to be all right.

Skye told him about Conn and Trace showing up at Petrov's mansion and how just before they got there, Petrov had brought in more men.

"We bested him twice," she said. "This time he wasn't taking any chances."

Edge leaned over where she lay on the bed and lightly kissed her. "And yet here you are."

She swallowed, thinking of the firefight, remembering her fear. "Morgan Burke showed up with a helicopter. He did an amazing job of flying us out of there under a barrage of gunfire."

"I didn't know he was coming until the last minute. Conn wanted someone they could trust at the controls of the chopper. Trace and Conn both trust him. Now I do, too."

Burke was a good pilot. She could still recall the gunfire that pinged off the skids as Burke got the bird in the air.

Skye looked up. "I shot Petrov, Edge. He was waiting outside for me. I think he knew I would run. He didn't know I was armed. He pulled a gun, and I shot him, but I don't think I killed him."

"Petrov fired on a couple of DEA agents. Not a good move. Agent Cross got a call just before we wrapped up. Petrov didn't make it."

She closed her eyes for a moment. She wasn't sure what she felt beyond relief. "So it's over."

"Yeah. And I don't think the fact you put a bullet in the rotten prick will be a problem. Too much paperwork. As far as they're concerned, you weren't there. The feds like to keep things simple."

Skye looked up at him and drew back the covers. "Why don't you get undressed and climb in? You must be exhausted."

"I am, but . . ."

"But . . . ?"

"It's kind of like that fight we were in at the Buckhorn saloon. I'm exhausted, but I'm revved. You're alive, and so am I. We brought Petrov down, just like we set out to do. I want you, baby. So much I ache with it. But I don't want to hurt you. If I get in bed with you, I won't be able to sleep."

Desire curled through her. She wanted him, too, just as she had after the fight in the saloon.

"Maybe you could just be a little bit careful."

His blue eyes darkened. "You know your brother, Trace, and Burke are in the living room."

Reality dimmed her arousal. "True." An idea struck. "Why don't I make love to you this time?"

He closed his eyes as if he were in pain. "Jesus, baby."

"Take off your clothes."

Edge hesitated a moment, then stripped off his shirt and pants, and tossed them away. Skye's gaze ran over the beautiful, sculpted muscles on his chest, down his six-pack abs, and her body turned liquid and warm. They both needed this. Anything could have happened. Both of them could be dead. Instead, they were here, full of life and overflowing with passion.

She moved to make room for him on the mattress. As soon as he was settled, she leaned over and kissed him. She felt his hands sliding down her back, cupping her bottom, and hot need rose inside her. She made love to him slowly, trailing kisses over his spectacular body, down his flat belly, moving lower, giving him pleasure until he groaned low in his throat and lifted her astride him.

Moving quietly, she gave him what he needed and took what she wanted.

Afterward, she nestled against his side, Edge being careful not to hurt her bandaged arm. Her leg throbbed a little from all the exertion, but the pills worked their magic, and she fell deeply asleep.

When she awakened, Edge was gone.

Edge looked up as Skye walked into the living room. It was late in the morning, all of them recovering from a long, rough night. Skye's arm was bandaged, but there was color in her cheeks, and her smile looked soft and sexy. His body stirred, and he glanced away, afraid he'd get hard and embarrass himself.

"Morning." He walked over and pressed a kiss on her lips, lingered longer than he meant to.

"Good morning," she said cheerfully, but when she glanced at Trace and her brother and saw their serious expressions, her smile slipped away. "What's going on?"

Trace rose from the sofa. "Edge can explain. We've got a plane to catch."

Morgan Burke rose to join him. "Glad you're okay," he said.

"Thanks for the help," Skye said.

Burke just nodded. The two men grabbed their gear and disappeared out into the hall.

Conn walked over and bussed her cheek. "How are you feeling this morning?"

"My arm's sore, but other than that, I'm fine."

Her brother pulled his phone out and glanced at the time. "Like Trace said, we need to get going. We'll see you at the airport."

She waited for him to grab his gear and head out to join the other men, then turned to Edge. "What is everyone not telling me? Is it about last night?"

He took her hand, led her over to the sofa, and both of them sat down. "Last night is pretty much over. Petrov's dead. Riggins and Ketch gave up the other drivers' names and the location of the two meth labs, and you're in the clear."

"What is it, then?"

"I got a call from Grease this morning."

Her insides tightened. "And . . . ?"

"Rumor has it there's a big-time weapons deal going down, and Major Bradley Markham's smack in the middle of it."

"Gun smuggling?"

"That and more. Machine guns, grenade launchers. Might even include a helicopter."

"Unbelievable. So you're heading out?"

"The deal is set to close three days from now."

"In California?"

"In Mexico. Just across the Arizona border. Once I get down there, I'll make contact with Grease's source and find out more."

Skye fell silent.

"We've got to get back," Edge said, wishing they could stay in Vegas a couple more days and just enjoy themselves, but it wasn't going to happen. "The guys are meeting us at the airport. We need to pack up and get on the road."

"So . . . back to Denver, then off to Arizona?"

"That's about it."

His eyes widened as she propped a hand on her hip. "And you think you're just going to leave me back in Denver? Is that your plan? Because that isn't going to work, Edge. You and I were partners long before we were lovers. You helped me with Callie. We brought down Petrov together. I know how much returning to the Green Berets means to you. If you're going after Markham, I'm going with you."

He started shaking his head. "You've got a bullet wound in your arm right now. You could have been killed last night. There's no way I'm putting you in that kind of danger again."

"The bullet only grazed me, and it has nothing to do with what you're planning. I owe you. If things were the other way around, you'd feel the same. You'd want to repay your debt, and so do I. Take me with you. We work well together. We'll bring Markham down."

He felt her touch as she rested a hand on his cheek. "Let me help you get your dream back, Edge. Get back the life you deserve."

She wanted to go with him. And as he looked at her, he realized he wanted that, too. He respected her ability and her courage. She would be a tremendous asset. More than that, he wanted to be with her. For the first time in his life, he had let down his barriers and invited someone in. It felt good. Really good.

He refused to think of what would happen when it was over. Both of them had known from the beginning how this would end.

"All right, if you're sure that's what you want. We'll do it together."

Her features relaxed. She had made her case and prevailed. "Then it's settled. We go back to Denver and figure out what we need to do. Then we head south."

Edge just nodded. There was something in her voice, a note of resignation that hadn't been there before. It made his chest feel tight. Once he brought Markham to justice, he would go back into the army. It would be over between them. He could already feel the loss.

He would deal with his feelings for Skye once Bradley Markham was behind bars and his life back in order. That was all that mattered.

Or was it? Edge ignored the little voice he'd heard before.

"We'd better get packed," Skye said. "The longer they hold the plane, the more money it's going to cost." Skye disappeared into the bedroom, and Edge followed.

It wasn't the money Edge was worried about. Markham was a cunning, dangerous foe. Edge was worried about keeping both of them alive.

CHAPTER THIRTY-SIX

THE APARTMENT FELT EMPTY WITH LILA AND CALLIE BOTH GONE. Skye's bed felt empty with Edge back in his own apartment. She had surprised him with her decision.

"Now that you're going after Markham," she'd said, "we know this thing between us is coming to an end. Your life is aimed in one direction, mine in another. The weeks we've spent together have been great, but they've changed me, Edge. Being with you nearly every day, enjoying the closeness."

"I liked being with you, too," he said a little gruffly.

"And then there was Lila and the baby. I never suspected I'd want children, but I've found out I do. I want a husband and father who is there for me and our kids, not a guy I see a few months out of the year. Ending this now is better for both of us."

"There's no way to know what's going to happen. You can't predict the future, Skye. Why not enjoy the time we have left together?"

She just shook her head. "I can't sleep with you knowing there's a time limit on our relationship. I'm sorry, Edge, I just can't. I hope you understand."

He glanced away, walked over to the windows in her living room, and stared out at the city. Finally, he turned. "All right, if that's the way you want it."

It was the last thing she wanted. She loved him. She wanted the life she had described, and she wanted it with Edge. But that was impossible.

"That's the way I want it. In the meantime, we need to focus on the mission, get organized, and get down to Arizona." *The sooner the better.* Repaying her obligation to Edge and getting on with her life was the best thing for both of them.

They spent the next morning in the office, making a list of the weapons and gear they would need, strategizing, digging up info on the Internet, figuring out the best way to approach the problem.

Grease called with more information. The weapons were being smuggled out of Fort Huachuca Army Base in southern Arizona. Edge made arrangements with the jet charter company he had used before. They would be flying into the municipal airport in Sierra Vista, the town closest to the base, just twenty miles from the Mexican border.

While Edge worked on the flight and getting a rental car lined up, Skye checked out the local motel accommodations. She thought of the nights ahead—of sleeping in an empty bed in a lonely room when she could be lying next to Edge's warm hard body. When they could be making love, and afterward, she could fall asleep in his arms.

She gave herself a mental reality shake. What they had was over. It could never work. With a sigh of resignation and renewed determination, she booked two rooms with a connecting door.

Next, they cleaned and checked their weapons, gathered the rest of their gear and ammunition. From the office, they went back to their separate apartments to pack fresh clothes and collect whatever else they might need.

Skye was ready that afternoon when Edge picked her up for the drive to the private terminal at Centennial Airport. The three-hour flight was smooth until they crossed into Arizona. The hot, dry weather caused some turbulence as the jet descended to the airport in the small town of Sierra Vista.

A rented white Chevy Tahoe waited for them on the tarmac. Edge unloaded their gear and drove them to the motel. It definitely wasn't the suite they'd shared at the Bellagio, but the rooms were neat and clean, and the beds looked comfortable.

"At least there's a connecting door," Edge said darkly, tossing his gear bag on the mattress. "I don't like the idea of you being too far away. We have no idea what we could be facing. We need to stick together."

Skye nodded, knowing he was right. Making her way through the door into the adjoining room, she unpacked a few things and settled in. They were meeting Grease's contact, a longtime army friend, in a Mexican bar and restaurant called La Cantina at eleven o'clock that night.

As she closed the dresser drawer, she looked up to see Edge standing in the open doorway between the rooms.

"It's been a long day," he said. "We've got a little time until the meet. We should get some sleep before we leave." In a snug black T-shirt that outlined his amazing body, he looked good enough to eat.

There were shadows in his brilliant blue eyes, but they didn't disguise the heat. The invitation was clear. He wanted her. That hadn't changed. Since she wanted him, too, her decision to sleep alone suddenly seemed pointless.

And yet she knew she was doing the right thing. Every time they were together would make the pain greater when they parted.

"A nap sounds good," she said, refusing to acknowledge the turbulence in his eyes. She checked the time and set the alarm on her phone. "I'll see you in an hour."

Edge watched her a few seconds more, then quietly closed the door.

The bar at La Cantina was a lively, boisterous place, the interior painted bright orange, red, yellow, and green. Sombreros hung on the walls, piñatas from the ceiling. This late at night, the lights had been turned down, leaving the room softly illuminated.

Edge led Skye to a table in the corner, and they sat down. They both ordered Bud Lights.

"You think he's here?" Skye asked as they spotted their server, a buxom woman in her forties with black hair down to her waist.

"Enjoy," she said, setting a pair of ice-cold bottles on the table.

"Thanks." Edge took a second glance around. A couple of guys sat by themselves, each with the straight-shouldered posture of a military man. The base was less than ten miles away. Service members were a big part of the town's population.

"Could be he's here." But he didn't think so. None of the men in the room had shown the least bit of interest when they'd walked through the door. He amended that. None of the men had shown the least interest in *him.* Half a dozen men had cast long, appreciative glances at Skye.

She was always beautiful, with her mahogany curls and her sexy figure, but she looked tired tonight, as if the stress of the last few days weighed her down. If things were different, he'd make slow, languid love to her until that tired look faded, replaced by the glow of contentment.

He turned at the sound of footsteps.

"Mind if I join you?" The man was six foot and lanky, with threads of gray in his military short brown hair. "Logan, right?"

"That's right. And this is Skye Delaney."

"Colonel Sam Harding, US Army, retired." He pulled out a chair and took a seat across from them, a man in his early fifties with weathered, suntanned skin, and the eyes of a lion. Eyes that missed nothing.

The server returned, and Harding ordered a Tecate.

"Are you from around here?" Edge asked as they waited for the beer to arrive.

"Drove down from Tucson. It's only an hour and a half away." The buxom server returned with the Mexican beer, then headed out again.

Edge took a drink of his Bud, set it back down on the table. "I appreciate your coming. What have you got for us?"

Harding straightened. He was solid and broad-shouldered, a man who looked like he could handle himself. "The deal is going down tomorrow night. Armor-piercing .50 cals, grenade launchers, ammo. God knows what else. It's a big shipment, and it isn't the first."

"The weapons are coming from the base," Skye said. "How are they getting them?"

"They're stealing them through a crime syndicate that's operating on the base. Maybe as many as seven or eight men involved. The money's big enough to tempt a saint, and these guys are a far cry from it."

"How does Bradley Markham fit in?" Edge asked.

"Markham was a Ranger before he went Green Beret. He was a good soldier at first, but things went wrong at home, and he ended up divorced. He and a guy in his unit named Chico Orlando got to be friends. Chico had family in Mexico. Markham went down with him a couple of times for a visit. Apparently, family included some big cartel names."

"I'm beginning to get the picture," Edge said. "Markham gets handed a golden opportunity and can't resist."

The colonel nodded. "That's about it. Money was offered. *Big money.* Markham was pissed at the army for costing him his wife. Maybe he figured stealing the weapons was a way of getting back. Or maybe he just couldn't resist that much green."

"From the high life he's living, I'd say that's a distinct possibility."

"So how does it work?" Skye asked, gripping her beer bottle a little more tightly. Edge knew her well enough to see her nerves creeping up with every new piece of information.

"The cartels set up what's called an ant track. Vehicles loaded with weapons hidden in every conceivable location, from hubcaps to door panels, transport guns across the border. Some have special compartments built in. All Markham has to do is get the weapons off base, into the hands of the guys running them south into Mexico. A few of the Mexican drivers manage to screw up and get caught, but they know if they talk, the cartel will take out their families."

"Where does Markham find the men to help him?" Skye asked.

"He recruits other soldiers into his organization. Guys with money or personal problems. Like I said, the money is big."

"I started hearing rumors," Edge said. "That's how I got involved. I did some checking, found out he was talking to soldiers in the supply chain—specifically, men working in the armory. I went over his head, figuring the brass would start an investigation, but rumors aren't proof. When I pressed the issue, I ended up getting tossed out on my ass."

He felt Skye's hand on his thigh and realized the anger he was fighting had his leg shaking beneath the table. He covered her hand with his and took a deep breath.

"I was already out when I found out what was going on," Harding said. "Some of my men came to me with info, hoping I could help them do something about it, but they weren't willing to put their careers on the line without proof. I dug into Markham, used my connections in the spec ops community to find out everything I could. But until now I didn't have the kind of proof the army would accept."

"Which we're about to get," Edge said. "Assuming this actually goes down tomorrow night."

"Unless something changes between now and then, it's going to happen."

"How can you be sure?" Skye asked.

"Sergeant Gill Franklin—you call him Grease—has a lot of friends down here; some of them go all the way back to boot camp. A couple of his retired Green Beret buddies down in San Diego don't like what Markham's been doing any more than you do. They've been keeping an eye on the major's house in the city, collecting intel on his hideout in Cabo San Lucas. According to them, Markham's going to be at the meet tomorrow night."

Edge's whole body went tense.

"Markham's going to be in Arizona?" Skye asked.

"Mexico. He's flying in from Cabo to oversee delivery and payment of the weapons. Odds are he'll be landing at the Aeropuerto National de Cananea. It's only about thirty miles south of the border, not that far from Fort Huachuca. I should get confirmation tomorrow. More importantly, I'll know where the actual munitions transfer is going to take place."

"You know an awful lot about what's going on," Edge said. "What's your stake in this?"

In the dim light of the cantina, the colonel's features hardened. "My son Andrew served under Markham in Afghanistan. Andrew didn't make it home. What Markham's doing disrespects my son and every good soldier in the army."

The words tightened Edge's chest. He knew too many guys KIA in Afghanistan. "We're going to need some help. I'm hoping we can count you in."

"I'm in as deep as it gets," Harding said.

"We're all former army, but the three of us won't be enough," said Skye, always practical.

Harding's features turned feral, a man ready to go on the hunt. "I'm retired army, but I volunteer as a training officer with a militia group out of Tucson called the Desert Eagles. We stay in shape, train regularly. These guys are good, and they're in all the way."

"I want Markham alive," Edge said. "I want him to face charges for what he's done. I want him locked up in federal prison."

Harding leaned back in his chair. "I figured you'd say that. Here's the deal. Once we take these guys down, we can't just leave all that military equipment behind. We have to make sure it doesn't fall into enemy hands."

"So what do you suggest?" Edge asked.

"Grease isn't the only one with useful friends. I've got a contact at Fort Huachuca, a full bird colonel. There isn't time for a thorough investigation, which means he can't step in unless—"

"Unless the deal goes down. Millions in military equipment could fall into enemy hands, which means he's forced to call in spec ops to handle it."

"That's right. A Special Forces unit crosses the border, nice and quiet, handles the situation, brings home the stolen goods, and disappears. No international incident, no one the wiser. The army has the criminals in custody and all the evidence it needs to prosecute Major Bradley Markham and the rest of his band of traitors."

For the first time that night, Edge relaxed. He glanced over at Skye, and she smiled. "Looks like you're about to get your man."

Edge lifted his bottle of beer. "To Markham getting what he deserves."

"To justice," Harding said, and the three bottles clinked over the middle of the table.

CHAPTER THIRTY-SEVEN

Skye awoke cold and alone in the bed in her motel room. During the night, she had tossed and turned, reliving the horror of the IED explosion and the painful days of her recovery, the endless succession of surgeries.

Another explosion in her mind jolted her awake, her heart beating wildly, her body damp with perspiration. It didn't happen often, hadn't happened once during her nights with Edge. She shook the thought away and glanced toward the window.

It was still dark outside, but gray light seeped through the curtains. She got up and turned on the heater, then climbed back under the covers until the room warmed up.

She checked the clock on the bedside table. Six a.m. Now that it was morning, the mission they would be undertaking that night rode hard at the front of her mind. Like Edge, once she was committed, everything else took second place.

She mentally went over the meeting with Colonel Harding at La Cantina last night. They'd have what sounded like competent help to take on the cartel, as well as Markham's well-trained soldiers. How many would there be? Would she and Edge, Harding and his militia be enough to stop them and end the weapons-smuggling operation?

She tried not to think of what would happen once the mission was over and she and Edge returned to Denver. She had already ended things between them. She wouldn't reverse her decision. It hurt too much to be with him, to love him more every day, and then watch him leave.

Once the room had warmed up, she went into the bathroom, showered, and dressed for the day in stretch jeans and a navy blue T-shirt. They were meeting Harding and some of his men that morning to lay out the plan for tonight. Harding would have the details of the exchange—where, when, and what weapons were being smuggled across the border into cartel hands.

Edge hadn't pressed the colonel for details of how he was getting the information. Sam Harding wore authority and competence like a comfortable shirt. The man inspired trust. It was as simple as that. Tonight, she and Edge would be following his plan. His information, his men—he carried the greater risk.

Her stomach was growling when she heard a knock on the connecting door, walked over, and pulled it open.

"Good morning." She managed to smile, then paused at the odd look on Edge's face, a cross between amusement and relief. "What's up?"

"We've got company." He stepped back to invite her into his room, and she recognized the handsome, brown-haired man with the smiling blue eyes.

"I figured you could use a little help," Trace said.

Warmth slid through her, along with the same hint of relief Edge was feeling. The three of them worked well together. The odds of success had just crept higher in their favor.

"How did you know where to find us?" Skye asked.

Trace grinned. "I asked Zoe to ping Edge's cell phone."

Skye's eyebrows went up. "Wow, that must have taken an extra dose of charm. Tracking down a coworker wouldn't be high on her list."

"I told her you two were heading into trouble and I wanted to help. That was enough to convince her."

Edge closed the door between their two rooms—sleeping arrangements Trace clearly hadn't missed.

"We're damned glad you're here," Edge said, speaking Skye's

thoughts aloud. "The three of us make a good team, and tonight could be rough. We've got a meeting at ten a.m. with the guy I was telling you about."

"Colonel Sam Harding," Trace said.

Edge nodded. "We're meeting Harding and his men to go over some fresh intel—a place called the Lady Bug, a local café. We'll have time for breakfast before they get there."

"Sounds good to me," Trace said.

"Me, too, I'm starving." Skye returned to her room to grab her leather bag; then they all climbed into Edge's rented white Tahoe.

It was an hour later that Colonel Harding walked into the little café, followed by three other men, all of them moving with the confident, square-shouldered bearing of soldiers.

"There's a room in the back Sadie lets us use for our meetings," the colonel said.

Skye rose from the booth where they had just finished eating and followed Harding and his men into a private dining room with two long tables in the middle that ran the length of the room. Edge and Trace walked in behind her.

"They use it for Rotary groups, Chamber of Commerce meetings, stuff like that," Harding explained. "The Desert Eagles meet here once a month, but we do training exercises at least every two weeks."

"Sounds like your men will be ready," Edge said.

"More than ready. They'll do their jobs out there tonight. You can count on it." He turned to them. "Pete, Clint, and Randy, meet Edge, Skye, and . . . ?"

"I'm Trace. Good to meet you all."

The men mumbled a greeting. Pete was short and stout, with biceps like cannons. Clint had a shaved head and a sleeve of tats on his right arm. Randy had neatly trimmed blond hair and looked like a university professor or maybe a surfer, until you noticed the danger lurking in his dark blue eyes.

At the moment, first names were enough, so they all sat down across from each other at one of the tables. Skye noticed Edge sat down beside her, though he had to change places with Trace to do it. Two thermal pots of coffee sat in the middle, along with a stack of heavy white china mugs. They each took a mug and passed the coffeepots around.

"So what have you got?" Edge asked, filling a cup for Skye, then one for himself.

Harding's strong, weathered features turned grim. "Deal's even bigger than we thought. Besides the .50-cal rifles, machine guns, and grenade launchers, these guys are selling state-of-the-art night-vision equipment."

Clint whistled. "Man, those babies are hard to come by."

The colonel nodded. "The army's got millions invested in the technology. Worse yet, Markham's peddling Stinger missiles."

Skye felt a shock of adrenaline. A Stinger could blow an airliner out of the sky. That a soldier would sell them to the enemies of his country was unthinkable.

Harding must have read the look on her face. "If you think that's bad—they're using a helo to transport some of the weapons. The chopper is part of the deal."

"Jeezus," Trace said.

Skye's gaze locked with Edge's. She knew he'd been afraid that might happen.

"How the hell can they steal a helicopter?" Trace asked.

For answer, Harding turned to the guy named Pete, who was clearly in charge of computer data. It took more than a few people to put an operation of this size together.

"It's actually pretty simple," Pete said. "According to army records, the helicopter doesn't exist. If it doesn't show up in the inventory, it isn't there. Computers are man's best friend and also his worst enemy."

Silence fell as they pondered the ramifications of what could be done with the right people in control. Skye couldn't imagine the millions of dollars that must be involved.

"How many men will be delivering the shipment?" Edge asked.

Harding took a sip of his coffee. "Can't say for sure. Enough to keep the cartel soldiers from just overrunning Markham and his men and taking the shipment."

Edge shifted forward in his chair, his blue eyes fierce as he took the measure of the guys at the table. His attention returned to Harding. "How many of your men can we count on?"

"Including me, Pete, Clint, and Randy, ten Desert Eagles will be geared up and ready to go in."

Skye could feel her heart thumping against her ribs. "Into Mexico, you mean."

"That's right."

"Where's the exchange taking place?" Edge asked.

Harding passed the baton to Clint. "The outskirts of a town called José Marie Morales. Guy was a famous Mexican revolutionary. Town named after him is about halfway between the airport and the base. There's an old cabin on a ranch north of town, about ten miles south of the border."

Harding picked up the conversation. "Along with the helo, they'll be using four-wheel ATVs to get the weapons to the location."

"There's a spider web of trails in those mountains," Clint added. "But once they get down into the valley, it's wide open. Easy place to land the chopper."

Edge's features darkened. "Yeah, and close enough to the airport for Markham to make an easy escape."

"Which isn't going to happen," the colonel said. He unrolled a set of topo maps on top of the table and used the thermal coffeepots to hold them down.

"This is what it looks like." Harding's lion eyes demanded the attention of every man in the room. "The exchange goes down at midnight. We'll rendezvous here at twenty-two hundred." He pointed to a spot on the map. "That gives us plenty of time to reach the location of the exchange and get in place. We've already reconned the area, but we'll have time to look around, make sure we don't run into unexpected trouble."

Clint grinned. "What would be the fun in that, Colonel?"

Though he ignored the remark, the edges of Harding's mouth faintly curved. "Any other questions?"

No one replied.

"All right. See you all tonight."

Chairs scraped as men rose from the table and headed out the door. Skye, Edge, and Trace were the last ones to leave. Edge left a sizable tip for Sadie, they climbed into the Tahoe, and he drove back to the motel. No one said a word along the way.

When they reached the motel, Trace pulled Skye aside as Edge continued down the corridor and disappeared into his room.

A good nine inches taller than she, Trace peered down at her. "What the hell is going on with you two?" He was the same height as Edge but brawnier, his chest and shoulders heavier, yet she never felt overwhelmed by him. He was a good man, strong, capable, and caring. She wished he could have been the man she had fallen in love with.

Trace huffed out a breath. "It's like he's put up some kind of wall around him."

The words dredged up the pain she was trying so hard to ignore, making her heart ache.

"We talked things over. Edge and I will always be friends, but this thing between us isn't going to work. Edge knows that. He's dealing with it, that's all."

"I don't get it. He's crazy about you. You're crazy about him. I thought that was the whole reason two people got together."

Her heart ached. She didn't want to think about what it would be like when Edge was gone. She wished she could tell Trace it was none of his business, but they were too close for that.

"He's leaving, Trace. The army means everything to him. After tonight, he'll be able to prove his innocence and go back to the life he loves."

Trace fell silent. "Maybe he'll change his mind."

She smiled at him sadly. "You don't believe that, and neither do I. His mind is made up. He knows what he wants, and he's going after it. I can't fault him for that. Can you?"

Trace glanced away. "No."

"I appreciate your concern. You've always been a good friend. Now we need to focus our attention on the mission. We both love Edge. Let's bring Markham down and give him back his dream."

Trace leaned over and kissed her cheek. "If you were my woman, there wouldn't be any dream better than spending a lifetime with you."

Skye's eyes filled as Trace walked to the door, used the extra key, and disappeared into Edge's room. Steeling herself against the emotions squeezing her insides, she focused on the job that needed to be done that night.

With a sigh of resignation, Skye went into her room and quietly closed the door.

CHAPTER THIRTY-EIGHT

THE NIGHT WAS CLEAR, THE STARS CRYSTALLINE IN A BLACK VELVET sky. Only a fragment of moon lit the harsh desert landscape. Cactus and boulders, low hills, and ravines spread out through the mountains and the valley below.

They had traveled, two men each on four-wheel ATVs, spreading out in different directions, driving along narrow dirt trails through the barren peaks south of the base, into the flat land on the other side of the Mexican border.

Colonel Harding and his men led the way, having been in the area before to recon the site of the weapons exchange, assuming their intel proved correct.

Edge, Skye, and Trace were in the last group to arrive, Skye on the back of Edge's ATV, while Trace rode behind Clint. They were early. Plenty of time for the sound of the machines to die away and the group to take positions out of sight in the rocks and gullies.

The landing zone had conveniently been marked by a circle of floodlights that could be turned on to indicate the flat ground and open space necessary to accommodate the approaching chopper and its rotor blades.

Edge smiled at that. They had caught a break there. The lights were a fairly good indicator that their intel was correct. It was a makeshift landing pad. Only one use for that.

He glanced at Skye, who had settled behind a cluster of granite boulders not far away, the barrel of her M4 carbine stabilized between two rocks. She also carried her Glock and probably an ankle gun.

The hours slipped past. The eighty-degree daytime temperature had fallen only as far as the low sixties, which meant their black tactical vests, weapons, and gear were enough to keep them warm.

Edge heard a voice in his earbuds. "The first ATVs have been spotted coming over the ridge," Harding said. "They'll be dropping into the valley in the next ten minutes."

"Roger that." Edge glanced over at Skye, who touched her earbud and nodded that she had heard the call.

"Copy," Trace added from his sniper hide sixty yards out. By now his MK22 would be set up on its tripod, ready to fire.

Edge shifted the M16 slung across his chest. His M9 Beretta rode in a holster at his waist, his Ka-Bar knife strapped to his thigh. He was ready. So was Skye. Still, his worried glance swung in her direction.

He had let her come, and now he regretted it. He didn't want her near this kind of danger, the kind that could wind up getting her killed.

But he had accepted long ago that Skye Delaney was her own person. She had a mind of her own, and she made her own decisions. He respected her for it and for being the strong woman she was. He loved her for it.

The words hit him hard, though it wasn't the first time they had slipped into his head. He was in love with her.

And yet, as Skye had said, they were headed in different directions. She didn't fit into his life, and he couldn't fit into hers. Another truth he accepted.

"The chopper is in the air." Harding's voice came through crystal clear. "Visual contact with the first ATVs."

Edge took out his night-vision binoculars and focused on the trail leading into the valley. A line of six ATVs, each pulling a two-wheeled trailer loaded with boxes of munitions, rolled toward the landing zone. Six well-trained members of the United States Army, equipped with the finest weapons and gear in the world, drove the machines.

Taking them down wouldn't be easy.

He swung the binoculars in the opposite direction, saw vehicle headlamps bumping over a dirt track he had noticed when they'd first arrived. Five SUVs. As they passed the abandoned cabin and neared the landing zone, he could make out the profiles of three men in the first vehicle, two or three in each of the others.

Best guess—Markham, his top lieutenant, and a driver in the first car; at least eight cartel soldiers in the other four SUVs. Plus six US Army soldiers. As many as seventeen men, and the helo hadn't yet arrived.

The good news was, he and the others were positioned on the high ground. Always better in a firefight. And they had one of the best Ranger snipers in the army ready to help take the bastards down.

All but Markham. Edge had shown Trace his photo. Markham would stay alive—for now.

One of the men turned on the floodlights in the circle around the landing zone, and Edge switched back to his regular binocs. The thump, thump, thump of a chopper grew louder as the helicopter approached. It hovered above the circle of lights, stirring up clouds of sand and small rocks, then swayed side-to-side as it settled onto its skids.

The rotors slowed to a soft spin but didn't stop. The doors slid open, and two men jumped down. SUV car doors popped open, and cartel men poured out. As one of the men in the first car stepped out and walked into the light, Edge recognized Major Bradley Markham, and fury burned through every cell in his body.

"Hold your positions," Colonel Harding commanded through the earbuds.

"Roger that," one of the militia men replied.

"Copy," Edge said, clamping down on his control. He wanted to grab Markham by the throat and drag him all the way back to Fort Campbell.

Nobody moved.

Edge glanced at Skye, could barely make out her slender figure in the darkness. Worry for her settled in his chest. He vowed, as he had a dozen times, that he'd do whatever it took to protect her. Even bagging Markham wasn't worth getting Skye wounded or killed.

They were minutes from the takedown. Tension filled the air. Anything could happen. He flicked a glance toward Skye's position, worry for her filling him with dread.

He shook his head to clear it. Too late to change things now. He focused on the action happening near the circle of lights, watched Markham pace over to the helo, then motion for his lieutenant to join him. The guy was a big, muscular man with close-cropped, reddish-brown hair and a tat on his neck behind his ear. He was carrying what looked like a black vinyl laptop case.

Another man approached, this one with coarse black hair and a thick mustache, wearing a dark sport coat over a white shirt, and a pair of tan slacks. The fit of the clothes and the way he moved said he was the man in charge.

The ATVs rolled up to the chopper, engines went off, and men began unloading the two-wheeled trailers stacked with wooden boxes. Through the open bay doors of the chopper, he could see the ends of a pile of narrow boxes. The Stinger missiles must already be on board the helo; they would have come from a different location on the base.

The militia men were in position around the helicopter and the men working to load it, all but a pair of cartel soldiers who'd been left to guard the dirt road leading in from José Marie Morelos.

Harding's deep voice came through the earbuds. "Get ready." While the rest of the militia held their positions, the colonel rose in the shadows just out of sight.

"You're completely surrounded!" Harding shouted toward the men in the valley. "Stay right where you are!"

Heads jerked up. Men reached for their weapons. From their location among the rocks, militia men fired into the dirt at their feet.

"No more warning shots!" Harding called out. "Throw down your weapons! Do it now!" With no idea how many men were ready to blow them to pieces, no one moved.

Then two cartel men fired wildly, spun, and started running. A barrage of gunfire from the rocks took them down. Three army soldiers turned and raced back toward the trail leading over the mountains to the base. A single sniper shot hit the first man, and he went down. Edge's bullet took out the second soldier, while Trace was busy firing into the helicopter to disable it before it could lift off with the Stinger missiles on board.

The third soldier made it to the rocks and disappeared not far from Edge's position. With a glance at Skye to be sure she was safe, he slipped into the shadows and went on the hunt.

More cartel men bolted. The echo of gunshots drowned out the sound of the damaged chopper struggling to get into the air. Car engines roared to life, and cartel SUVs shot backward into the darkness, bullets pinging against their front grills. Since it wasn't the Mexicans they were after, the militia ignored the men who reached the cars, and the fighting turned back to the men who remained.

"Toss your weapons!" Harding demanded as armed Desert Eagles, dressed head to foot in camouflage, stepped out of the shadows, their rifles pointed at the enemy in the circle of light. "On your knees! Hands in the air!" Men dropped to the ground and raised their hands.

Behind them, the helicopter wobbled and lifted thirty feet off the ground before the blades quit spinning. The chopper came down hard, jolting into the ground and flipping onto its side. Spinning rotors dug into the dirt, some of them breaking up, whining and slicing like knives through the air.

Men on both sides hit the ground and covered their heads until the blades stopped spinning and the danger passed. Then Harding's guys took over again, holding cartel men and soldiers at gunpoint.

Counting on Harding to keep things under control, Edge continued his hunt for the soldier who had managed to slip away. Spotting a hint of movement ahead of him in the darkness, he circled around, crept up on a rock, and pointed his rifle down at the top of the man's head.

"One move and you're a dead man." The soldier froze. "Step out in the open, and toss your weapon. Do it nice and slow."

The man eased up from his crouched position. He tossed his pistol into the air, and it disappeared into the darkness.

"Turn around and put your hands behind your back." Edge caught a glimpse of his face as he complied. The guy was young, no more than mid-twenties, tall and well-built. Sad way to end up at such a young age. Edge moved up behind him, pulled a zip tie out of his pocket and tightened the cuff around the kid's wrists.

"Time to join the others. Head on down the hill." The soldier started walking, his boots thudding on the trail as he marched along. The noise muffled the sound of the man coming up fast behind him.

"Edge!" Skye stepped out of the shadows between him and another army soldier. She fired as the man brought up his pistol. The soldier squeezed off a round as he hit the dirt, the bullet missing Skye's head by inches, pinging against the rock next to where Edge was standing.

He looked at Skye, her legs braced apart, the rifle steady in her hands.

"You okay?" she asked, swinging the rifle toward the soldier Edge had captured.

He managed to nod. "Thanks to you." He had never seen anything so magnificent as this woman he loved. He would be dead if it hadn't been for her. "You kill him?"

He caught Skye's glance in the faint light from the sliver of moon. "He's hit pretty bad. Looks like he's still alive."

"If you'd hesitated, I'd be dead."

Their eyes met and held an instant before Skye turned back to the man on the ground. Edge thought of how close she had come to dying, and his mouth dried up.

They got the wounded man on his feet and marched both of them back to the circle of light. Edge spotted Markham's lieutenant, the muscular man with the reddish-brown hair who'd been carrying the laptop case, presumably to make the funds transfer.

But where the hell was Markham? The last Edge had seen, his driver had made a run for the car and sped back down the dirt road, leaving his boss to fend for himself. Harding had Markham's lieutenant in custody, but the major was nowhere in sight.

Then he spotted Markham's familiar figure propped against the busted-up chopper, blood trickling down the side of his head—a victim of the crash. Definitely poetic justice.

Edge walked toward him. "Looks like we meet again, Major."

Markham's eyes widened. He wiped a trickle of blood off the corner of his mouth. "Logan. After all this time. I should have known you wouldn't give up."

"Not even close. I'm sure you'll recognize a lot more old friends when you get back to Fort Campbell."

Markham shook his head. He was a good-looking guy, with an athletic build and neatly trimmed light brown hair. His wholesome appearance had always worked in his favor—until now. "No way I'm going back. I'd rather be dead."

"I'd be more than happy to make that happen, but I'd rather see you behind bars for the next fifty years. You would have been happy to see me in Leavenworth. Looks like you'll be taking my place."

Edge glanced up at the rumble of voices, saw Harding and his militia men looking toward the trail coming out of the mountains. A line of soldiers fanned out, making their way silently into the valley.

Edge couldn't stop a grin. The Green Berets were here.

CHAPTER THIRTY-NINE

Skye was back in Denver. Edge and Colonel Harding had gone to Fort Huachuca to be debriefed, but Harding's militia had made their way back to Sierra Vista. She and Trace had accompanied them and prepared to return to Denver the next day. The militia had just disappeared.

As the originator of the initial complaint against Markham, Edge had been flown to Fort Campbell, Kentucky, to answer more questions. He had phoned a couple of times to make sure she was okay, told her things were progressing even better than he'd hoped, but their conversations had been brief.

Edge was exactly where he wanted to be, and Skye was happy for him.

She took a deep breath. Edge was clearly satisfied with the way things had turned out, but Skye was depressed and surprisingly lonely. She had never been one of those women desperate to have a man in her life. She had ended her engagement to Brian and never looked back.

What she was feeling now was different. As if she had lost a part of herself. Like the missing pieces of her leg, it was a loss she would learn to live with, but it wouldn't be easy.

As she rambled around her empty apartment, she realized how painful it was to lose the man you loved. What she felt for Edge was the deep, unshakable kind of love that never went away.

As time went on, she might meet some nice eligible man, marry him, and have a family. But he would always be a substitute for the man she wanted but couldn't have. It wouldn't be fair, but life rarely was, a lesson she had learned long ago.

With a sigh, Skye slung the strap of her purse over her shoulder, grabbed the big cardboard box on her coffee table, and headed downstairs to her red Subaru Forester. Storing the box in the back, she took Lincoln Street out to Curtis Park, one of the oldest neighborhoods in Denver.

The beige duplex on West 23rd was older, with a pointed roof, dark brown shutters, and a covered front porch. The property, which appeared to be in very nice condition, was enclosed by a wrought-iron fence, the yard well-maintained.

Callie and Lila had just moved in. Lila had gotten a job with an accountant, while Callie had registered for the spring semester at the local community college to finish the courses she needed to graduate. In the meantime, she was working as an assistant to an older woman who wrote children's books.

Skye unloaded the box from the car and carried it onto the porch. Since the duplex wasn't furnished, the women had been taking donations from family members, everything from a sofa and chairs to mattresses. Conn had an attic full of old furniture he had gladly volunteered, including some very pretty antiques.

Skye was contributing household items—pots, pans, towels, things she had picked up at the local Target. She balanced the box on her knee and knocked on the door. Callie pulled it open and grabbed the box.

"Come on in." Callie grinned, clearly happy with her new accommodations.

"How's it going?" Skye asked, following her into the living room. Skye could see the work the women had done. The sofa and chair, covered with a pale green flowered throw, sat in front of a faux-brick fireplace that held a pretty potted plant. A patterned foam-green rug sprawled under a walnut coffee table. Several framed posters of flowers hung on the walls.

"We're almost settled." Callie carried the box into the kitchen and set it down on a round oak table with four matching chairs. Skye recognized the table from when she and her family had occupied Conn's old Victorian.

"It looks great, Callie. I'm so happy for you." Skye leaned over and hugged her.

Her sister's blue eyes welled with tears. "If it hadn't been for you and Edge—"

"Hey. All of that's behind you. Nothing but sunny days ahead."

Callie smiled. "A little rain is just part of life, but moving in here with Lila has really been fun. Oh, and I heard from Molly. She still won't tell me where she is, but for now, she seems okay." Callie opened the box and started putting the pots and pans away. "These are great, thanks."

When she finished, she turned and looked at Skye. "So what about Edge? Is he still in Kentucky? Is he going to come back or stay there?"

Skye managed not to glance away. "He's back where he belongs, Callie. At least that's what I tell myself."

This time the hug came from her sister. "You deserve to be happy, Skye. You'll find someone else. Edge isn't the only man in the world."

Skye smiled sadly. "Maybe someday." She looked up to see Lila walking into the kitchen, her thick, dark hair a curtain of silky black around her shoulders. The long-sleeved, pale blue T-shirt she wore with a pair of stretch jeans curved over her full breasts and outlined her rounded belly.

Skye walked over and pressed her palm on the swell of Lila's child, feeling the baby inside. "She's growing." Lila now knew the baby was a little girl. Everyone was already in love with the unborn child. "How are you feeling?"

"Much better. No morning sickness, and the baby feels stable, like she's making herself at home."

"What's the doctor say about your due date?"

"I'm further along than I thought. Almost four months, he says."

"You look beautiful. Pregnancy agrees with you."

Lila smiled and started to reply when the sound of the front door opening had them turning in that direction. All three of them filed back into the living room, where a black-haired man stood in the middle of the room.

He was six feet tall, in his early thirties, smooth shaven, black eyed, and incredibly handsome.

"Lila. *Mi amor.*"

Raul Ramirez. The tortured look on Lila's face left no doubt.

The handsome Latino took two long strides and dropped to his knees in front her. "*Mi querida.*" He reached up and caught Lila's hand, pressed his lips against the back. "I never thought to see you again."

Lila jerked her hand away. "How did you find me, Raul? What are you doing here? You're supposed to be dead. I never want to see you again. Get out and leave me alone!"

Raul rose, his features stricken. "Do not say that. I love you. I came as soon as I could. Please listen to what I have to say."

"I told you to get out!" Her eyes welled, but her spine remained ramrod straight. "I don't know you. I never did. Get away from me."

"What are you talking about? I am your husband, the man you married."

"The man I married would never have gone away and left me with a monster like Daniel Henson."

Raul's black eyes glistened with unshed tears. "That is not what happened. I would die before I would do that to you. I almost did." His gaze ran over her rounded belly. "*Mi querida* . . . you carry my child?"

Lila stiffened. "You abandoned your child when you left me in that terrible place. The child I carry is mine alone."

Raul reached out to touch her cheek, but Lila turned her face away. Raul brushed a tear from her cheek. "The night I left, I went to work, as I had been doing since we arrived. I had already made up my mind to find a way for the two of us to leave. I never should have brought you there. I was a fool to take the job in the first place."

Lila's features didn't soften.

"Daniel must have suspected," Raul continued. "That night, two of his men forced me to go with them at gunpoint. Cisco Vasquez and Klaus Mahler drove me into the desert. They beat me, then they shot me and left me for dead."

He pulled up his T-shirt. There was a healed bullet wound on his side and a web of scars covering a portion of his chest and shoulder.

Lila's hand flew up to stifle a gasp.

"It was God's miracle I survived. Thinking of you is all that kept me going. I dragged myself to the highway—I don't know how far it was. Twice I thought I would not make it, but there you were—in my mind and in my heart—telling me to come home to you. Telling me how much you needed me. Telling me I could not let you down."

Lila made a sound in her throat but didn't move.

"Finally, I reached the highway. A family stopped when they saw a man lying on the side of the road."

Lila began to tremble. "Raul . . ."

"I was unconscious for three weeks. When I finally woke up, I began to remember what happened. I told the police about Daniel Henson and what he was doing at Blancha Springs. I begged them to let me go so that I could return and get you out of there."

He sank back down on his knees, his black eyes filled with tears. "I love you so much, *querida*. You and our baby. Please forgive me."

Tears washed down Lila's cheeks. Her throat worked, but no words came out. More tears fell. Reaching for Raul's hand, she drew him to his feet.

"I've missed you so much, Raul. I love you so much." Raul pulled her into his arms, and Lila clung to him, sobbing against his shoulder.

Skye realized her own eyes were filled. Skye looked at Callie, who was also crying, and both of them slipped quietly back into the kitchen.

She could hear Raul telling Lila the rest of what had happened, how the police had turned him over to the DEA and he had agreed to help them. Then both of them were crying.

It was going to work out. Skye was happy for the woman who had become her friend, but seeing Lila with her husband made Skye think of Edge, and her heartache deepened. She had known the risks, but the pain of losing him was so much worse than she had imagined.

She prayed he was happy enough for both of them.

CHAPTER FORTY

THREE WEEKS PASSED BEFORE ALL THE QUESTIONS ABOUT MAJOR Bradley Markham had been asked and answered. Edge's good name had been restored, along with his rank and his position in his old Green Beret unit.

Three weeks to think about his life, his priorities, and the kind of future he really wanted.

Three weeks to get his fucking head on straight and go after Skye.

He prayed it wasn't already too late. She worked in an office full of good-looking, capable men. Edge hadn't phoned her in the last two weeks. He couldn't handle it. Just the sound of her voice sent him into a downward spiral.

He missed her, ached for her. Wanted her endlessly. She was his. They belonged together. He knew that now, without the slightest doubt.

But how did she feel about him? He had never told Skye he loved her. The way he'd seen his life at the time, it wouldn't have been fair. He was going back into Special Forces. He'd be gone a good part of the year. Skye deserved better than a part-time husband. She wanted a family; she deserved a man who would be there for her and the children they would raise.

It had taken him all this time to realize he wanted that, too, wanted a home, a wife and a family. But only if the woman by his side was Skye Delaney.

He prayed he could make her understand, convince her this wasn't just some whim because he was lonely. This was real. Skye was what he wanted. The life she wanted was the life he wanted, too. He loved her with everything inside him.

He flew back to Denver the week before he'd planned to reenlist. Everything was set. He'd be deploying shortly after his return to Fort Campbell.

If Skye didn't want him.

His stomach knotted at the thought.

It had taken him weeks to realize how much he had changed in the last few years. He'd made a life for himself in Denver. He had friends at Nighthawk, men as close as his brothers in the army, women friends he admired and respected. And he was proud of the good he had done as a detective, the lives his work had helped or saved.

As soon as he had arrived in the city, he headed straight for his apartment. He didn't call Skye. He wasn't sure what to say. Wasn't sure how she would react. Wasn't sure if her feelings for him were as deep as his feelings for her.

He'd been in Denver three days when Trace called.

"I heard you were back," his best friend said. "Conn and I are going down to the Goat for a couple of beers. Can you make it?"

He didn't want to go. He wanted to talk to Skye, get things straight between them, but he wasn't quite ready.

"Yeah, okay. What time?"

"After work. Six o'clock. You sure you'll be there?"

"I'll be there." Edge hung up the phone. Maybe he should just call Skye, tell her he wanted to see her, get it over with. If she rejected him, at least he would know how she felt.

He was staring at his cell phone, trying to figure out what to say, when a knock came at the door. Edge walked over, checked the peephole, and smiled as he pulled it open.

His brother Gage stood in the doorway. "Welcome back."

Edge's smile widened. "Hey, bro. Good to see you. Come on in."

Gage walked into the living room. They were brothers, but they didn't look much alike. Gage was tall, with the same blue eyes as Edge, but his hair was brown, not black, and he was more muscular through the chest and shoulders. They were both extremely fit, Edge from his military training, while Gage stayed in shape to tackle the conditions he came up against as an explorer.

"You want a Coke or something?" Edge asked. "I'm meeting Trace and Conn down at the Goat. Why don't you come with me?"

Gage nodded. "Sounds good. I'll take a Coke in the meantime."

They walked over to the bar, and Edge pulled a couple of Diet Cokes out of the fridge. He popped the tops and handed one of the cans to Gage. Edge sat down on the black leather stool behind the bar, and Gage sat down on the other side.

"So . . . I heard you were back in town," Gage said, tipping up the icy can and taking a long swallow. "I wasn't really sure."

"Everybody seems to have heard."

"Abby sends a hug. How's Skye?"

"I don't know, I haven't talked to her yet."

Gage frowned. "So everyone knows but Skye."

Edge just shrugged. He didn't tell his brother he was trying to work up the courage to face her.

Gage set his Coke can down on the bar. "You remember when you came to see me about my feelings for Abby?"

"I remember."

"You told me Abby and I were perfect for each other. You said God doesn't give us those kinds of gifts very often."

Edge nodded, smiled. "Yeah, and I was right."

"Yes, you were. Marrying Abby was the best decision of my life."

Edge set his Coke on the bar. It wasn't like Gage to show up at his door for no reason. "What are you trying to tell me, bro?"

Gage's blue eyes met his. "The way I see it, you and Skye are perfect for each other. If you go back in the army instead of staying here and building a life with her, I'm worried you're going to regret it."

Edge felt the beat of his heart picking up, pounding a painful rhythm inside his chest. "You're right. It took me a while to figure things out. I'm in love with her. After we came back from your expedition in Mexico, the attraction I felt for her just kept getting stronger. I told myself to leave her alone, but it was impossible to do."

"I could see how much she meant to you whenever the two of you were together."

"I was just beginning to figure things out when I found out about Bradley Markham. It seemed like the time had finally come to clear my name, go back in the army, and get on with my life. But once I was back at Fort Campbell, I began to realize it wasn't the army I wanted. It was Skye."

Gage smiled. "I thought you'd figure it out—eventually. I'm a little surprised it took you so long."

"I'm going to ask her to marry me, Gage. If she says yes, I won't re-up. I'll stay in Denver with Skye."

A broad grin stretched over his brother's face. "I should have known you'd come to your senses." Gage stuck out a big, suntanned hand. "Congratulations."

Edge ignored the handshake. "Not yet. I have no idea how Skye feels about me. I'm not sure she'll say yes."

"She loves you. She'll say yes."

But Edge wasn't completely sure. Skye had a mind of her own. He might not fit into her plans for the future.

Gage checked the time on his phone. "Let's go get that beer. A couple of drinks might help you get your courage up to propose to the lady you love."

Edge nodded, hoping his brother was right.

It was dark by the time they reached the Fainting Goat. Trace was waiting near the front door with Conn.

"I got us a table in the backroom," Conn said.

Edge followed him, less enthusiastic by the minute. He didn't want a beer with his friends. He wanted to talk to Skye. He shouldn't have waited.

He started to say he had changed his mind, when Conn opened the door to the backroom and stepped aside so he could look inside.

A cheer went up that echoed against the walls of the room. "Surprise!"

Jesus. Edge flashed a phony smile. A surprise farewell party. Just what he didn't need.

He glanced around, saw that everyone he knew was there. Besides Trace and Conn, Morgan Burke and a couple of part-timers were there; Zoey Rosen and her boyfriend, Chad; Kade and his wife, Ellie; and Gage's wife, Abby. Callie and her mom were there; Lila and her husband, Raul—a story he had heard from Trace over the phone.

He had to admit it made him feel good to know he had so many friends who cared about him. He glanced at Gage. "You knew about this?"

"I was sent to make sure you got here."

Edge looked around the crowded room. "Where's Skye?"

Gage followed his gaze and frowned. "She was supposed to be here." He made another survey of the room. "I don't see her."

Edge turned to Conn. "Where's your sister?"

"I don't know. She said she was coming."

Standing behind him, Trace tapped him on the shoulder. "You talked to her, right? You called her when you got to town?"

"No. I should have. I had things I wanted to say. I just wanted to get it right. But—" He pulled out his cell and hit her number. It rang straight through to voice mail. "She's not picking up."

"You screwed up, dude," Trace said. "She knew you were in town. I figured you'd call. You owed her that much."

Edge's chest clamped down. He raked a hand through his thick black hair. "Dammit." The last thing he wanted to do was to hurt Skye. He gave the room a final glance, and his stomach balled into a fist. "I've got to go. I've got to find her. Call my cell if she shows up."

"Will do," Trace said. "Good luck."

Edge hustled out of the backroom, down the hall, and out the front door. He had no real idea where to look. He'd start with her apartment, but she could be anywhere. What was she thinking right now? That he didn't even care enough to call her when he got back to the city?

His heart hurt. He knew how he would feel if Skye had done that to him.

The Goat was a neighborhood bar only a few blocks from the office, which was only a few blocks from Skye's apartment. He tried her cell again, got voice mail, started jogging, then broke into a run. What if something had happened?

Or maybe she'd decided he wasn't worth the trouble and was out with someone else.

He burst into the lobby of her apartment building, waved to the guard, who knew him by now, hurried into the elevator, and hit the button for the eighth floor.

Please be home, he thought. *Please forgive me for screwing up. Please love me.*

The elevator doors parted. Edge hurried down the hall and started pounding on Skye's door. When she didn't answer, he really started to worry. She was an investigator. She had enemies.

"Skye! It's Edge! Are you in there?" And some of Daniel Henson's goons were still on the loose. "Skye!" He hurried back down the corridor, dialing her cell again, getting no answer, cursing the elevator when it stopped on the sixth floor to pick up a passenger.

Finally, he reached the lobby and hurried over to the guard at the front desk. "I need to check on Skye Delaney. Apartment 815. I need to get in, make sure she's okay. She's had trouble before."

The guard rose from behind his desk, a gray-haired guy with a paunch over his belt. "Yeah, I heard." He ambled toward the elevator, punched the button, and whisked them back upstairs.

The guard let him into the apartment, but a hurried search told Edge she wasn't there, and there was no sign of trouble.

Where the hell was she?

The Nighthawk office was his next stop. It wouldn't be unusual for her to work late. Anxiety welled in his chest. Or maybe she just didn't want to see him. Going to the party would force them together. Maybe she had decided he wasn't worth the trouble.

Either way, he had to know. Edge picked up his pace.

CHAPTER FORTY-ONE

Skye sat on the floor of the office, her back braced against her oak desk, her legs curled beneath her, her bad leg aching. Duct tape cut into her wrists, which were bound behind her back. Her lip was cut and bleeding, a painful bruise forming on her cheek.

Klaus Mahler loomed over her, his arms and shoulders bulging with muscle. The Viking. The guy Daniel Henson had picked for Callie to marry.

Klaus's big hand flew out and slapped her hard enough to make her ears ring. "I'm not going to ask you again. Where is she?"

Skye didn't answer. She glanced at the other man in the office. Klaus called him Webb. Webb Rankin hadn't been found after he'd fled the Children of the Sun compound, but there was an arrest warrant out on him for armed robbery. He was also a person of interest in the death of Sarah Simmons.

But Klaus had been arrested. How had he gotten out of jail?

Seconds ticked past. So far, Skye had refused to answer. No way was she letting this animal get his hands on her sister again.

Klaus's wide palm connected with her cheek, knocking her into the side of the desk, and pain shot into her shoulder. "You're pushing your luck, lady."

"Go to hell, Klaus."

The two men had broken into the office through a window in

the employee lounge. Skye had been distracted, thinking of Edge, sick at the thought he had been in town for days and hadn't bothered to call her.

By the time she'd realized she was no longer alone in the building, they had been on top of her. She had tried to fight them, but it was too late.

Webb moved closer. He was dark and menacing, with tats over every inch of his thick neck. "Let me have her, Klaus." He grabbed his crotch. "I know how to handle a woman like her. Give me five minutes, I'll have her begging to tell you anything you want to know."

An icy chill raced along her spine. Webb had been one of the men who had beaten Sarah to death. He was a stone-cold killer. Klaus was just as bad.

The blond giant shook his head. "No way. You aren't getting laid before I do." Klaus wrapped a big hand around Skye's throat and started to squeeze. "Where's my woman?"

Skye couldn't breathe. The last breath she'd taken was wedged in her throat. She gagged, fought to suck in air. Her chest constricted. She tried to break free of Klaus's crushing grip, but he was too strong, and blackness hovered at the edges of her mind.

Klaus was going to kill her. She struggled to twist away, but his hold only tightened. Her lungs were starving for air. If she passed out, it was all over.

She started nodding, a last-ditch effort to stay alive. "All . . . right," she managed to croak out.

Klaus loosened his hold. "Tell me!"

Air rushed into her lungs, and the mind fog slowly faded. She reached for the idea that she had been mulling over for the past ten minutes. She prayed she was doing the right thing.

"I'm waiting," Klaus warned, looming over her.

"Callie's . . . at a . . . party."

"A party? What the fuck? Where?"

"Over at the . . . Fainting Goat." She could imagine what was going to happen to these men when they went up against a roomful of former military elite. It was her best chance of staying alive, and with luck, Edge, Conn, Trace, and the rest of the Nighthawk crew would be able to handle the situation, protect Callie, and put an end to the threat these men posed.

Unless something went wrong.

Skye didn't want to think about that.

Finally, Klaus let her go and backed away. He looked over at Webb. "I changed my mind. Go ahead. You can have her. Just make it quick."

Oh, dear God! Skye summoned the last of her strength, preparing to fight as Webb jerked her up from the floor and started dragging her over to the leather sofa in the entry.

The only light in the office was the brass lamp on her desk. Webb hauled her into the shadows and shoved her down on the sofa, roughly groped her breasts though her cashmere sweater, started dragging up her long, dark green wool skirt, clothes she had chosen for Edge's party, before she decided she couldn't handle seeing him again.

Skye waited till the skirt was above her knees, then lashed out with her good leg, managing to kick Webb in the groin with her leather ankle boot.

"You bitch!" Hissing a curse, Webb's hand went to his crotch, and he bent over in pain. Furious, he grabbed her ankle and jerked her off the sofa onto the floor, then drew back his boot to kick her in the ribs.

The blow never landed. Instead, Webb's powerful leg went flying upward, knocking him off balance, his body landing hard on the floor.

Edge!

Klaus's fist doubled up as he raced across the room to aid his friend. Swinging a hard punch Edge ducked, the Viking recovered and swung again, but Edge was ready. Whirling, he jumped and high-kicked Klaus in the face, sending him spinning backward to land hard against the wall.

Webb was back on his feet, gun in hand. Edge knocked the gun aside and punched Webb in the stomach hard enough to double him over; then Edge slammed the ridge of his hand against the side of Webb's neck, hitting his carotid artery. Webb went down as if his legs had been cut off at the knees.

Klaus charged like a bull. Skye stuck her good leg out and tripped him as he ran past, and Klaus went flying. Edge grabbed his head as he staggered past and slammed it into the wall. Klaus and Webb were both down and out.

Skye looked up as Edge ran toward her. Crouching on the floor at her side, he pulled her into his arms.

"I've got you. Everything's okay. They won't hurt you again." Dragging out his pocketknife, he cut the duct tape binding her wrists, eased her up from the floor and back into his arms. Skye could feel him trembling.

"Everything's going to be okay," he repeated, then drew in a steadying breath. "I'm calling an ambulance. How bad are you hurt?"

Skye shook her head. "No ambulance. No way. I don't need an ambulance—I'm okay." She hurt all over, but it wasn't pain that made tears well in her eyes. It was the way Edge was holding her, as if she were something precious, as if she was the most important person in the world.

He kissed the top of her head, eased her up to her feet, swept her up, and carried her over to the sofa.

"Don't move. I'll be right back." Hurrying to his desk, he opened a drawer and pulled out a handful of zip ties. In minutes, Klaus and Webb were cuffed, hand and foot, completely immobilized, and gagged with the same duct tape they had used to bind Skye. Edge called the police, told them the nature of their emergency, and gave them the names of the men who had broken into the office.

Edge returned to the sofa, sat down beside her, and eased her into his arms. "Looks like they roughed you up pretty good. We need to get you checked out."

Skye shook her head. "I've got cuts and bruises, but my head's okay, so no concussion. I'd rather just go home."

He smoothed the back of his hand down her cheek. "Are you sure?"

"I'm all right." She managed to smile. "I would have been in serious trouble if you hadn't shown up when you did. How did you know I was here?"

"I didn't. I looked for you at the party. When I saw you weren't there and you didn't answer your phone, I went to find you. You weren't at your apartment, so I came here."

He leaned down and pressed a very gentle kiss on her puffy lips, using extra care not to hurt her. "I've missed you."

Blinking back tears, Skye glanced away. "Why didn't you call?"

Edge caught her chin and gently turned her to face him. "I screwed up. I wanted to call. I wanted to see you more than anything in the world. But so much has happened since I left. I had so much to tell you, so much I wanted to say. But I . . ."

The tender look in his eyes sent hope into her heart. "But you . . . what . . . ?" Uncertainty rose. What was he going to say? What if he asked her to go back with him to Fort Campbell? She loved him so much she was afraid she would say yes.

"I wanted to get everything just right," Edge said. "I was afraid I would only get one chance to convince you. I didn't want anything to go wrong." He took her hand, lifted it, and kissed her fingers. "But I waited too long and screwed everything up."

There was something in his eyes she had never seen before. Something that made her heart squeeze painfully inside her. She thought that it might be fear, but there was nothing Edge Logan was afraid of.

She had to know—one way or another. "Maybe you didn't screw anything up. Maybe you can say what you wanted to say, and everything will be all right."

He tipped her chin up. "I want to kiss you so bad right now, but I don't want to hurt you."

Skye leaned into him, pressed her mouth over his, and just tasted. The little zip of pain was worth it.

When the gentle kiss ended, Edge looked at the two men tied and gagged on the floor. "I wish we were someplace else, anyplace but here."

Skye started to tell him it didn't matter where they were, only that he was there and they were together, but a hard knock sounded, rattling the glass in the front door.

Edge kissed her softly one last time and went over to let the police into the office.

Along with the cops, an ambulance arrived. EMTs pronounced Mahler and Rankin well enough to be taken into custody. They checked Skye out, cleaned and treated the cut on her lip and the tape burns from the bindings on her wrists. Nothing they could do about her bruised ribs and miscellaneous aches and pains from fighting off her attackers.

Two Denver PD detectives arrived to take their statements, one of them Zach Powers, the guy who had been with Callie on her twenty-first birthday. He wasn't happy to find out Klaus was still stalking her.

"How did the bastard get out of jail?" Edge asked.

"Mahler posted bond," Powers said darkly. "Unfortunately, the judge set some minor amount Mahler could easily afford to pay with the money he made from Henson's drug operation."

"Klaus was determined to find Callie," Edge said. "I guess he figured Skye was his best chance of doing that. He got lucky and tracked her to the office."

"Yeah, well, Mahler's not getting out again. Callie's safe. I give you my word on that."

Interesting, Edge thought, catching the protective glint in the detective's blue eyes.

Edge said little as he walked Skye back to her apartment. He still felt guilty for not calling her. None of this would have happened if he had. Or maybe it would have. He had yet to find out where he stood.

He took her key and opened her apartment door, waited till she walked inside, then closed and locked the door.

"How are you feeling?" he asked, still pissed every time he noticed the bruises on her face.

"Other than a few aches and pains, I feel okay."

His stomach knotted at what could have happened if he hadn't gotten there in time.

"I know you must be hurting. We don't have to talk tonight," he forced himself to say. "We can talk in the morning."

"You're leaving?"

"No! I mean, no." No way was he leaving after what had happened. "I'll sleep on the sofa," he said, instead of finding out if Skye still wanted him, if there was a chance she loved him.

"You said there were things you wanted to say."

A thousand things. He had no idea where to begin. "It can wait until you're feeling better."

"Can it?"

Edge looked at Skye's beautiful face. To hell with it. He'd just tell her and be done with it.

"I love you. That's what I wanted to say. None of the rest of it matters if you don't feel the same way."

Skye's pretty green eyes welled. He could read the sadness there, and his chest clamped down.

"I love you, too," she said. "You have no idea how much."

Edge moved toward her, but Skye held up a hand. "I love you, Edge. But sometimes love isn't enough. What I want out of life, and what you want—"

"I want exactly what you want. I want to stay in Denver and make a family with you. I want you to marry me, baby. Will you?"

The tears in her eyes spilled onto her cheeks, and Edge's insides splintered. "Don't say no. Please. At least hear me out."

Skye's voice trembled. "You have a chance to get your old life back, Edge. It's what you've always wanted. Right now, you think you want to give that up, but what if you regret it later?"

Edge reached out and took hold of Skye's hand, led her over to the sofa, and both of them sat down. He'd been hoping it wouldn't come to this, but it was time for him to let her in, tell her what had made him the man he was.

"I lost my mom when I was a kid," he said. "Kade loved the ranch, and that gave him a bond with my dad. Gage was obsessed with seeing the world. I don't think he needed anyone until he met Abby. I was the youngest. I was the lonely one. I just accepted that I would always be alone and made the best of it. That's the way it was until I joined the army. In the Green Berets I found a family again. I wasn't alone anymore."

He brought Skye's hand to his lips and kissed her fingers. "I'm a different man now. I realized that when I went back to Fort Campbell. I have friends here. I've made a life here. I like the life I've made. I don't need the army anymore. This is where I belong. Here in Denver, with you, honey."

"Edge . . ."

"Say you'll marry me, Skye. I'll always be lonely without you."

More tears washed down her cheeks. "Edge . . ." She went into his arms, and Edge held her, feeling the soft beat of her heart against the nervous beat of his own.

"I need you, baby. I love you so much."

"Oh, Edge—I've loved you for so long."

Everything inside him seemed to settle and return to the way it should be. Edge eased back to look at her. "Is that a yes?"

Skye gave him a teary smile. "It's definitely a yes." She kissed him, then stood and drew him to his feet. "I don't want you to sleep on the sofa."

"Are you sure? After fighting those two big goons, you have to be hurting."

Her pretty eyes sparkled. "I trust you to be careful."

Edge couldn't stop a smile. He kissed her softly, then followed her into the bedroom.

Half his life, he had been searching for a home.

With Skye, he had finally found one.

EPILOGUE

Six months later

SPRING HAD ARRIVED IN THE ROCKIES. MOUNTAIN SNOWS STILL COVered the peaks in the distance, but a warm sun encouraged the grass to break through the soil, and the trees had begun to bud out.

After a productive day of working with Edge on a burglary case that involved the recovery of a woman's valuable jewelry, Skye sat next to her husband at a table in the Fainting Goat. Around them at nearby tables, the after-five crowd laughed noisily, the sound echoing off the exposed brick walls, but Skye's attention remained on the man she had married.

Her husband. The words made her smile.

She glanced down at the beautiful diamond wedding band on her left hand, wiggling her fingers to make the diamonds sparkle, then looked over at the gold band Edge was wearing.

Just weeks after Klaus Mahler and Webb Rankin had been arrested, they'd been married in an intimate ceremony with family and friends in a small, white-steepled chapel. Afterward, Conn had arranged a reception in his lovely old Victorian, the house Skye had grown up in. She and Edge had honeymooned in Aspen, in a suite at the five-star St. Regis Resort.

Now they were back in Denver, living in Edge's apartment,

which was larger than hers, with more closet space and even better views. Skye had changed a few things to make the place feel more homey, and they had settled in. They were comfortable and enjoying married life, but it hadn't taken long before they were ready to get back to work.

Though Daniel Henson was in jail, serving eight to ten years in prison after cutting a deal with the DEA, law enforcement was still hunting the rest of Henson's crew, names Daniel had traded for a lesser sentence. Skye and Edge were particularly on the lookout for Harley Purcell.

Skye took a sip of the ice-cold Coors the bearded server had brought and looked up to see Trace approaching them. Tall, handsome, and usually smiling, he strode toward them with a frown on his face.

"What's up?" Edge asked as Trace pulled out a chair and took a seat across from them.

"I just got a call. I'm headed out to Boulder. Could be trouble."

Skye and Edge exchanged glances. "If there's trouble, you might need backup. You leaving right now?"

Trace nodded. "Yeah."

Edge looked at Skye, interest and anticipation in his sexy blue eyes.

Skye drained the last of her beer and set the mug down on the table. "Then let's get the check and get out of here."

Edge grinned, leaned over and kissed her. He was happy, and so was she. They were just as good a team as they had been before, only now they got to go home together every night, got to spend time talking about their day and making plans for the future.

"My Yukon's parked out front," Trace said.

Edge tossed some bills on the table. "We're right behind you." He turned to Skye. "You ready?"

She smiled. "I'm always ready."

Edge gave her a long, hot glance. "That's one of the things I love about you."

Skye laughed. "Later," she promised, trying not to think how good it would be when they got home and ended the day in bed. "In the meantime, we have work to do."

Edge just nodded, his mood turning serious. He took her hand, and Skye followed him out the door of the Goat. They made a stop at the office to collect a few more weapons, then climbed into Trace's big black SUV.

Whatever the situation, one thing was clear. Their relationship would never be boring.

Skye exchanged a look with Edge that said he knew exactly what she was thinking. Then they both settled back in their seats, turned their attention to the road ahead, and focused on their upcoming mission.